MW01166994

JUMPED

Book One of the Dimension Series

D.C. Reed

Print:
ISBN-13: 978-0692375259

Digital:
ISBN-13: 978-1-7372419-9-7

Cover design by: DC Reed
Library of Congress registraion number: TXu2-214-504
Printed in the United States of America

This book is dedicated to any and all who have ever had a dream and a vision, and to the people who have supported them every step of the way.

ACKNOWLEDGMENTS

First I would like to thank everyone who has read or listened to me prattle on about this book. To the people who have edited it and to all the people who have supported me through it. Thank you to all of my teachers whose tough love shaped my thinking and writing style.

To all the people above and those I have forgotten:

Thank you

D.C.
Reed

CONTENTS

CHAPTER ONE

Without a Paddle

disappearing summer day shadows over a small school. A testament to stone masonry, the school's intricate towers and detailed stone work create an enchanting, ancient look. A deceptive appearance contrary to the knowledge and modern ideas held inside.

On three sides the school sits, nestled in a valley, between rolling hills that cover the surrounding countryside. Lush gardens of roses and violets interrupt hill's soft grass and wild flowers, filling the air with fragrances of joy. Elaborate terraced decks and walkways snake their way up the hill side disappearing into the setting sun. Decorated with magnificent marble fountains, intricate benches, delicate railings and ornate lamps make the decks a labyrinth of art on the picturesque hill side.

A ringing bell signals the end of the day as students, ages 12 to 23, disperse from the castle-esque structure ready to enjoy the fading sunlight. Some students find their way to the lush decks. Others plop down on a grassy knoll relaxing after the long day. A few students retreat to the river that flows behind the school, between the school and mountains that stand watch as silent sentinels. Wading in the shallow water students avoid the large boulders which create treacherous rapids that disappear into the omnipresent and mysterious mountain range.

Sitting at the top of a hill, that isolates the school from the valleys beyond, three kids have separated themselves from the rest of the world. They sit at the end of the last wooden path that connects to an abandoned dirt road. These kids don't dream of escape. This spot is simply their sacred retreat. A sanctuary they like to keep to themselves.

"Scoot. Come on. We've got to get back at some point," Mikey encouraged his friend.

"Yeah Scoot. Come on. We don't have all day," Michelle, a girl who stands five six with hazel eyes and wavy black hair, adds to Mikey's plea.

As if hit by a rock Scoot, a boy around Mikey's age, turns and stumbles. Falling onto his belly Scoot glows red, before standing to catch up to his friends.

"I'm coming,' Scoot stammered to his friends. 'Sorry, I was a little distracted."

"Really? We never noticed," Mikey replied with a chuckle as Scoot catches up.

"We thought you were here with us the entire time," Michelle sarcastically points out as the sun sets and they venture back to the school together.

After dinner and some studies, Michelle bids her friends farewell and says goodnight, going to the school's West Wing. The boys go to the East.

Laying awake Michelle listens to her roommate's sleep. A few toss and turn mirroring her thoughts.

"Why can't you fall asleep?" Michelle asked herself as something weighs on her chest. "Classes started back last week. It's really not that bad yet…." She tries to talk the feeling out of her chest. "I guess I'm just being dumb. There is no place safer," Michelle finally tells herself. Identifying the feeling in her chest as fear.

With a heavy sigh Michele turns over and cuddles her pillow. Tossing and turning Michelle is unable to shake her feeling of dread. Even though she knows, like everyone else, that this place, this school, is the safest place in The Dimension.

◆ ◆ ◆

Seventy-three degrees and a partly cloudy sky created the perfect weather for lunch the next day. Frolicking, laughing, playing, and flirting fill the crisp air as students enjoy their fortune and settle in after the morning's classes.

"Where's Scoot?" Michelle asked Mikey, with the lunch line already starting to form.

"Not sure, but I'm hungry."

Searching the grounds Michelle and Mikey cannot find a single person who has seen Scoot. Fifteen minutes into their lunch they are about to give up when they spot Scoot on the main deck enjoying the flowers.

"Scoot, get down here." Michelle yelled to him.

Alarmed and a little scared Scoot turns to realize that his friends had been waiting for him yet again.

"Sorry guys, I was at the road and…" Scoot started to explain when a flash of light and a strange twitch change everything.

"Scoot. Come on man. Get down here," Mikey, shielding his face from the glare, yelled to Scoot after he stopped walking towards them.

Staggering like a drunk Scoot attempts to take a few more steps when he freezes again.

"Scoot, stop messing around or we will miss lunch," Michelle jokingly yelled up to her friend as the light clears from her eyes. "What's wrong?" Michelle asked herself as Scoot fell to the ground.

Michelle initially thought Scoot's new gait was the latest in a long line of daily pranks. However, that thought was a distant memory as she and Mikey race up to their friend.

"What's wrong?" Michelle asked as she and Mikey breached a group that had formed around Scoot.

No one would answer, some kids shook their

heads, others were taking defensive postures, while a few looked on with intrigue. Michelle could hardly imagine what would make her classmates think Scoot's fall was so funny so she asked again.

"Is Scoot okay?"

"Sorry to ask, but who is Scoot?" a voice at the center of the circle inquired.

Reaching the circles inner group Michelle found someone sitting in front of her that she did not recognize. He was older than Scoot, his hair was different, and most importantly he was not her friend.

"Who are you?" Michelle accused the person who had replaced Scoot.

"My name is Ian and who is Scoot?"

"So, you are: 'Ian.' And who exactly is Ian?" Michelle continued.

Her thoughts were racing, trying to understand what had happened here and to her friend. Michelle was pretty sure someone would have gone for help by now. It was a waiting game and she just had to keep him talking. "And who exactly are you?"

What does she mean who am I? I am Ian. Who is she? More importantly, where am I and how did I get here? Ian thought to himself as he took stock of his surroundings.

Alone in a crowd Ian was lost in a new land. A minute ago Ian had been in his dorm room doing yoga and now, he was outside on a wooden deck being interrogated by a teenage girl.

Ian searched the crowd for a friendly face, however, most people appeared suspicious. Like the girl interrogating him they all seemed to be at different stages of panic about Ian's arrival. Some had crossed arms, posturing strength. Others loudly whispered about him. On a deck above, Ian spotted a group of five giggling girls who looked closer to his age. Fearlessly Ian got up and moved towards them. The sea of people parted letting him pass up the stairs.

"Do you know where I am?" Ian asked the first girl he reached.

The girls stopped giggling as four of them stepped back defensively. The fifth girl, the one Ian asked, did not retreat, however, but averted her gaze with a mischievous grin. Her hands nervously held a book over her hips as she ground her toe into the deck. Bewildered, Ian could swear she was flirting with him as she reached her hand forward with an answer.

"I do."

Finding a little comfort in this strange land Ian took a step closer and reached for her hand. Brushing her fingers tips Ian felt a slight spark between them, one he wanted to explore, when a hand on his shoulder turned him around and pulled Ian back to reality.

"Ian Alcock. I'm glad to see you. And you made it here all right," a man introduced himself without telling Ian his name.

"Hi...But... where... how..." Ian was trying to explain himself as the crowd around him dissipated. Apparently the appearance of this man had calmed any fears, spinning his head Ian found himself alone, everyone else was gone, with this new man.

"Ian, my name is..."

BOOM

The beautiful day was gone with the crack of thunder louder than any Ian had ever heard. Dark purples, blacks, and blues ripped across the blue sky, spreading in uneven jagged places like a freshly torn canvas. A giant vortex swirled above them in the darkened sky. Looking into its origin an emerald dot appeared and began to grow, snaking out from the center. Before long an emerald dragon took shape. Glass like scales, ruby red eyes, and an echoing roar filled the valley and paralyzed Ian.

"This is not good..." Ian heard the man next to him say, bringing his attention away from the dragon. "Ian follow me."

"What is-"

"-Not now," the man cut Ian off as he began dragging him down the decks towards the school. Constantly looking back Ian was trying to gauge what was happening as chaos began breaking out around him.

As they ran Ian got a clearer view of where they were going. Ian, the man, the students, were all running not towards the castle, but towards a small concrete shed. Around them, teachers and staff rushed out to engage the dragon.

"What are those?" Ian asked pointing over his shoulder where another swirling portal, on ground level, was opening up about thirty feet away.

"Trouble…" the man said as he turned to Ian. "Take this,' the man said as he placed an orange poker chip in Ian's hand. 'Don't lose it and show it to anyone who questions you. Get to that shed and follow the group. Get in a boat and wait for me at your destination."

Before Ian could ask anything the man was gone. Alone Ian wanted answers, but after seeing the dragon Ian did not want to wait to see what would emerge from the portals sprouting up around him. Alone and without hesitation Ian rejoined the race towards the shed.

Despite the chaos Ian had one comfort, except for the students, running in terror, the staff was prepared for something like this. They had weapons and were taking up defensive positions. They were ready and if you saw through the bedlam you could see everyone had a job, a role, and was doing one thing: protecting the students.

"What are you doing?" Ian was stopped by a woman running to join the fight.

"I was going towards that room," Ian said holding up the orange disk hoping to get by.

"No you're not… Follow everyone else… Go to the

river. That way is not safe."

Ian wanted to argue, but couldn't. Over her shoulder three portals had opened near that shed and the staff was doing their very best to subdue an invading army trying to come through. Turning away from the woman Ian nodded and followed the rest of the students towards the river.

Another roar cracked like thunder as millions of darts started raining down from the sky. Running as fast as he could Ian tried to avoid other students as the hail storm of darts began reaching the earth around them. Darts that did not find a human host went through wood, concrete, or stone as if they were butter. Anyone struck simply fell, never to rise again.

"Oww, that stings," Ian thought after a dart nicked his wrist ten feet from the river.

What started as a stinging sensation grew worse as pain ascended through Ian's arm. Five feet away from the water Ian knew if the sensation reached his chest he would be gone. Despite this knowledge his steps became heavy and Ian was about to fall when he felt two people grab him.

"Get in the water. It will be better," one of them said as they unceremoniously threw Ian into the river.

Cold as ice Ian felt his body flail trying to regain some sense of equilibrium. Gasping for air, Ian quickly realized he was not actually out of breath, but was simply in shock from the sudden temperature change. Around him students struggled, like Ian, to keep afloat as the river pulled them along like driftwood. Distracted by the grasping current Ian did not notice the pain dissipate from his arm after he hit the water.

The fight for survival became reality as some of the students began losing the fight and disappeared under the choppy waters. Rapids that some of these students had avoided the night before now showed their teeth. As a last ditch effort panicked students tried grabbing onto rocks and boulders that breached the river's surface. Doing everything they could to avoid a watery tomb.

Grabbing an exposed boulder Ian tried to catch his breath as the water battered him. On the boulder with him, a scared girl, no older than 13, held on for dear life. Looking into her eyes Ian saw something he had never known before: true fear. Ian wanted to, but knew he had no way to help her. Ian also knew they could not hold on forever and if they tried they were sure to die. With no real way to help her Ian found her eyes and tried to reassure her that everything would be okay. Offering his hand Ian was about to take her's when the current pulled him away. Certain he was going to die Ian fought the rapids around one more bend when the water unexpectedly calmed.

"This could not be the plan," Ian said after getting to shore doubled over as he tried to catch his breath. Behind him, the thirteen-year old had made it as well. Not doubled over she simply walked towards a small metal hanger on the bank of another river.

"Ian, are you okay?" a new nameless man welcomed Ian before he could follow the girl.

"Yeah... I guess....Tell me this was not the plan..." Ian blurted out, overwhelmed with what was going on.

"Ian we do not have time for that," the unknown man said. "Go to that building, put on a suit, and get in a boat. Do you still have the chip?"

Shocked the man would ask, Ian looked down and was surprised to find his hand clutched around the orange chip.

"Good now go..."

Before Ian could ask a question the ground shook with a violent tremor. A bolt of lightning and clap of thunder gave Ian all the motivation he needed to rush into the building.

Inside Ian was singled out and greeted by one of the school's staff. They looked him over, checked out his arm, and his chip. After deciding he was fine they put him in a wetsuit and directed him towards a line. Uncomfortable and self-conscious, in the skintight suit Ian waited and watched the scene unfold.

Everyone was scared. Some of the staff were treating people's wounds while others kept the circus going. The students waited in line, like him, to get in a boat that Ian assumed would bring them to safety.

Every few minutes non-responsive students and staff were rushed to the front of the line and immediately loaded onto boats. Despite the chaos there was a method to this madness which brought three comforting thoughts to mind:

First: some of the same faces he saw disappear in the rapids were here in this room.

Second: the sounds of battle had faded and

the general commotion of the room was now the backdrop for his thoughts.

Third: the people around him, staff and students, though concerned, were relaxing and calming with every minute that passed.

"Ian you're here. Good," a different staff member commented as Ian reached the front of the line. "This boat will bring you to safety. Get in."

"How?" Ian asked. The man didn't have a map and the boat didn't have a motor or an oar.

"Ian get in... The boat will do everything."

Again Ian did not know how this man knew who he was or why this would work. But before he could ask the man placed Ian into the boat and launched him out of the building and towards safety. Like an amusement park ride as soon as Ian was gone another boat rushed in to take his boats place.

In a line the boats guided themselves down a river and into a lake that disappeared into the mountainous tree canopy beyond. It took a few minutes for Ian to get comfortable, but the small, mahogany, boat clearly knew where they were going. Floating down their own unseen path.

As the journey continued Ian watched the line of boats brake off from one another taking their own paths down the different streams and tributaries. Before long Ian was alone twisting and turning down different waterways. After each turn Ian felt safer. Without one of these boats no one would be able to navigate this labyrinth of waterways.

After hours of gliding through lakes, rivers, and small tributaries, the boats entered one final lake and picked up speed. The peaceful sounds of nature replaced by the murmur of controlled chaos.

Rushing across the final lake, Ian, was one of a dozen boats, racing towards a series of troughs and docks on the sandy shore. Each trough wide enough for a single boat and its occupant. Racing into a trough Ian's boat came to rest at the end of a dock.

As Ian stepped out of his boat three people rushed towards him. Two gathered the boat, placing it on a rack; the other ushered him off the dock to prepare for the next boat's arrival.

The shore was a mess of energy as boats kept coming in. Ian, ready to relax, found a seat on the bank to watch the docks. Boats continued to glide through the troughs and to the docks. Like clock work, one person got people off the docks as two more prepared the dock for the next boat.

Every once in a while a boat came in requiring more help. Sometimes the person was injured and rushed away. Other times it was simply a mishap by the boat's occupant. Watching the dance Ian did not see people though ,only the beauty of the dance.

At one point Michelle reached the dock and Ian missed her. Once she reached shore her mind wandered back to that feeling she had the night before and wondered: **Are we safe?**

CHAPTER TWO

A Campfire Story

Still mesmerized with the precision of the docks Ian was greeted by a petite woman.

"You must be Ian."

"And you are?" Ian irritably snapped when a loud rumble interrupted him.

On the docks a boat was coming in too fast. A boy no older than 14 thought it would be a fun idea to rock the boat as it raced towards the docks. His boat dangerously swinging from side to side and was moments away from being thrown from the trough.

"Use your body to steer it in. Lean with the turn." Ian's new friend yelled to the boy. "Calm the boat down and you will be fine."

The boy did his best to take her advice and with a little work and luck the boat raced around the track and into the same dock Ian's boat had landed in.

"There you go." the woman yelled as four people rushed towards the boat. "God, I hate the young ones, they come in too fast, think this is some sort of game, and almost kill themselves in excitement. I'm Laura." The woman finally introduced herself after turning back to Ian.

Shaking her hand the woman was young, like everyone else here, but older than him. Probably 25, slight, maybe 5'2", and petite. She had black hair and was lightly tanned. If he had been home Ian would have guessed she was hispanic, but here he had no idea how to place her heritage. Ian only knew that her skin tone was that of a light caramel.

"Follow this path to the tent at the top of the hill. Jerry is waiting for you," Laura said as she pointed up the hill behind him.

Knowing better than to ask a question Ian nodded and started up the forested hillside hoping to get some answers. All around him Ian was more and more impressed with this group's efficiency. Tents were being put up by a mixed group of students and staff, others were creating paths and clearing brush, and the smells of dinner were wafting through the air. Close to the summit Ian was just starting to relax when a loud explosion flooded the air.

Startled, Ian looked over his shoulder to see the river engulfed in flames. Tense and ready to flee Ian wondered if the enemy had followed them here when a familiar hand on his shoulder caused him to flinch.

"Don't fret about the fire. It is no threat or enemy. It is only the path clearing itself."

It was the voice of the man who had first greeted Ian. Without the chaos of battle distracting him, Ian finally got a good look at the man. The slender man was older, 42 or 43, fit, with years of stress showing in his greying hair and tired brow. Beyond the stress though Ian saw a man who exuded strength, confidence, and compassion-all traits which helped Ian relax.

Together they watched the fire sprint away from the bank. Without knowing that path there was no way to find them here. Considering how prepared everyone seemed Ian had no doubt that they were safe. After the flames had disappeared the man invited Ian into a large canvas tent at the top of the hill.

"Before we begin I would like to properly introduce myself and our gathered company: my name is Jerry..."

The rest of Jerry's greeting was lost on Ian as his

eyes darted around the tent searching for a reflective surface. In the corner Ian found a slick black kettle and saw his five o' clock shadow begging to be shaved, short hair waiting to grow long, and light green eyes full of worry. Pinching himself Ian confirmed that this was not a dream and he certainly was not on Earth anymore.

"Ian are you okay?" Jerry asked bringing him back to reality.

Ian's focus jumped back to the tents other occupants. Jerry was the oldest of this small gathering. The two others did not look a day over thirty, but their eyes showed the stress and torment from a lifetime of war. Everyone in the tent was clearly shaken and exhausted from today's events.

"Jerry what is going on? How did I get here? Where is Scoot? What happened back there? When can I go home? How-"

After being bottled up all day Ian had millions of questions fighting to get out at an uncontrolled pace.

"-Ian, you are on world 184 known as Esmerelda," Jerry interrupted Ian to stop the flow of questions. "You came through a portal on your home world, world 256, Earth, to get here."

Letting his words linger Jerry knew that what

he just said would be hard for anyone to hear or comprehend. The look on Ian's face told Jerry what question to answer before Ian could ask.

"This world is connected to 364 other worlds through a place known as The Dimension. Today The Dimension is an expansive, desolate place filled with rolling dunes that appear in a state of constant twilight. However, history tells us that it used to be a lush paradise filled with life. Thousands of years ago our ancestors lived in The Dimension when they came across the first world connected to it. Some emigrated there to a place we now call "World One." As time passed more worlds were discovered and settled. Each and every planet was unique and different from the others. Some were like Earth, diverse and teeming with life. Others were full of glaciers and snow. Some were nothing more than perfect weather and sandy beaches, while others were small deserts that are hard to survive in. Every world was and is connected to The Dimension through portals that opened and closed periodically. By the end of their expansion our ancestors had discovered 364 worlds leaving The Dimension mostly abandoned."

"It sounds wonderful…" Ian said, thinking about having over 300 worlds to visit.

"For a long time it was," Jerry continued with a polite smile. "For a long time people still ventured into The Dimension. Some out of curiosity, for exploration and discovery, but most for trade and communication. Surprising as it may be our ancestor's language, known as English on your world, is the common tongue of The Dimension"

This surprised Ian. Ian knew that English was not the dominant tongue on his planet and was relatively young. Ian wondered how this was possible and if his own history was in fact different than he thought, however that was a question for another day.

"What happened?" Ian asked wondering why Jerry spoke so sentimentally about The Dimension.

"We did not understand our role in The Dimension's ecosystem and when we started settling other worlds we left a hole that was not filled. For hundreds, maybe even thousands, of years we watched The Dimension die. Records tell us once green forests, scurrying with life, turned into grey sands, deplete of life. What once was habitable became something else and slowly The Dimension died and so did people's need to explore it. With limited knowledge on how to save it or how the portals worked people's curiosity turned into fear and left The Dimension mostly abandoned. Except for a little trade."

"But why did they let this happen?"

"Ignorance. We did not understand the connection between the planets and The Dimension or how the portals worked. We did not understand our role in The Dimension's ecosystem. All of this contributed to what happened."

"But how?" Ian asked unable to grasp how something so profound could happen.

"Ian, think about your own world and what is going on. How even though people can see things getting hotter, that the weather is changing, they still deny it.

As time passed so did people's ability to survive inside The Dimension and trade that was already treacherous became suicide. When no one knew how or why some people could survive inside The Dimension it became a death trap for anyone who got stuck there. Maps became irrelevant and with people no longer exploring new ones were never created. As an emergency measure knowledge of The Dimension, communication between worlds, and control of the portals became the full time job of a few families on each world. However, as civilizations grew and time passed governments were busy with their own problems and took a hands off approach to The Dimension. Worlds secured their borders and left the portals under the protection of these families. On most worlds The Dimension was either forgotten entirely or became stories used in folk lore, myths, legends, and religion. Forgetting about The Dimension worked for many planets until war began."

Palpable tension rose with the mention of war. Jerry didn't move, but Jerry's colleagues shifted uncomfortably as the talk of war began. Sitting at attention Ian waited for Jerry to continue.

"Surprising as it may sound, before this war conflict between worlds was almost nonexistent. Some people chalk this up to limited contact. Others think it was because no one had the technology to bring war into The Dimension. Personally I like to think that human nature is one of peace. Regardless, over a century ago, the existence of The Dimension was forcibly reintroduced when World One made their first attack."

"Why did they attack?" Ian asked before Jerry could continue.

"The people of World One claim a birthright to The Dimension. They feel that they have the right to rule The Dimension and every world attached to it. They claim that The Dimension's death was the fault of other planets and that it had to be saved. For the good of every person and planet within The Dimension, along with The Dimension itself, they had to rule it all. They told us we had had our chance and failed. However, I think the war is about what every war is about: power and resources."

The other two in the tent simply nodded in agreement with Jerry, Ian thought back to his history classes and saw the truth in what Jerry was saying. It made sense, most of the conflicts on his own world had been about those two things.

"How long did the war last?"

"The war has lasted over a hundred years."

"Has lasted? A hundred years? Wait, how is that even possible?" Ian asked skeptically.

"War is not as easy in The Dimension. Think about the technology available on your planet a hundred years ago. No computers, no advanced science, no understanding of worm holes or particle physics, both of which are needed to control and manipulate the portals. Even with the knowledge we have gained this past century war is still hard. Controlling portals is difficult and only a handful of people can survive inside The Dimension, meaning that your army is even smaller and more selective than it would be in a normal population. In many ways warring across The Dimension is like warring with a country separated by a sea and only having row boats to get there."

A hundred years earlier Ian's world had been on the cusp of its first World War. Ian thought of how primitive that war was compared to all those that have come since and could hardly imagine what a war between planets would be like.

"If that is the case what has been going on for the past hundred years?"

"The beginning has been lost to time. Our records are at best incomplete, however we do know that when the war started World One understood The Dimension better than the rest of us. When we left it to die they studied it and that gave them the upper hand. They used centuries of knowledge to their advantage to gain an upper hand. At first some worlds, I would say most, tried to resist but that was easier said than done. World One, or as we call them now The Evil, invaded and pushed themselves into worlds that were sill figuring out how to get along with themselves let alone an invading force from another world. When The Evil would invade it was not delicate and their brute force was simply too much to overcome. Overtime some worlds joined World One willingly, I believe out of fear for their own safety. Others were taken by force. Some planets, like Earth and Esmerelda, successfully resisted invasions and learned how to truly control our portals. Regardless of your side all worlds know about the war, however most choose to keep it secret if they can. What started as a fast and furious battle for planets and control has turned into a chess match between our two sides in a strategic war that continues to this day."

The tent's small fire flickered as Jerry's abrupt stop took Ian off guard. From what he could tell the war sounded like the war on terror that had a momentous start but no clear end.

How bad was the war? How did they control the portals? Who knows about the war? Were all questions Ian wanted to ask, but seemed inconsequential to the question that had burdened him ever since he had arrived on Esmerelda.

"Who is Scoot?"

"Scoot was your Double. Everyone who can enter The Dimension or jump between worlds has one. Much of the process is still a mystery, however we do know the ability to jump is genetic and was carried by our ancestors in Akhona.-"

"-Akhona?" Ian asked.

"Is the ancient name for The Dimension," the young woman next to Jerry answered Ian's question.

"Doubles are normally born within five years of each other and we loosely believe that Doubles are assigned by some familial association," the

28

man next to Jerry picked up the discussion on Doubles where the young woman had left off. "Our working theory is that after people began colonizing planets and trading between worlds they would marry, spreading their genes. We think that descendants are drawn to their parent's home world. While we don't know how we do know people are always drawn to their Double's home world."

"Unfortunately all of this is weak speculation," Jerry sourly and defeatedly scolded himself and his assistants.

"Regardless, having a Double allows you to enter The Dimension in the first place. Scoot was your Double and once we discovered this connection you both were trained on how to jump," the woman sprung back into the conversation to cover Jerry's pessimism.

Ian's head finally settled after feeling like a pinball for that last exchange. Focusing on the other two Ian felt like the smiles of the two assistants were very forced and instead looked at Jerry who was clearly frustrated and a million miles away.

"What's wrong?" Ian asked Jerry.

"Days like today bring up bad memories and remind me of how little we know. They remind me that I need to work harder."

Ian could see the pain in Jerry's eyes. Something ran deep there and unwilling to make the day worse Ian asked about something else.

"What is jumping? You said I was trained, but I don't remember that."

"Jumping is simply what we call it when a person enters or exits The Dimension. And you wouldn't remember being trained, it is done covertly." The woman answered Ian.

"But why does it have to be such a secret?" Ian asked.

"For many centuries jumping was messy and indeterminate. On many planets random disappearances or spontaneous combustion were explanations for failed first jumps. Fortunately through failure we learn. We now know that every being, every person, plant, and animal, on every world has a presence felt within The Dimension. We have an arbitrary raking system, 30-1, to measure each being's presence within The Dimension. Most beings within this interconnected web of worlds sit at level 30 and will never grow beyond that point. To progress one must enter and subsequently leave The Dimension in increasing nano-second increments. And to do that you must have the right genes and be performing a special jump position. This position channels you through a small portal and over time you level up. At level three you physically and cognizantly enter The Dimension and exit in your Doubles world."

"That's great, but why does it have to be a secret? How long does it take to get to level three?"

"We don't know how long it takes. Each person is different. We can roughly measure level through the number of nano-seconds you are in The Dimension, that time is constant and how we determine the levels. In a perfect world you and Scoot would have made this jump at the same time, unfortunately this did not happen," the woman answered Ian.

"But-"

"-Ian we keep it secret normally until someone reaches level four or five because of what it means," Jerry interrupted. "This ability is enough to scare anyone. Many times when it is not a secret people try to avoid their jump position, but if we have learned anything it is that The Dimension craves balance and will get it one way or the other. You can not run from this ability, delay it maybe, but you have to be ready in case your Double is. Not telling people is our way to avoid this conflict; the war along with this ability is enough to scare anyone into hiding. Normally we catch people at level four or five to avoid situations like today. Unfortunately we did not do our job well enough this time leading to today's events."

"What happened to Scoot?" Ian asked flatly needing a straight answer to what he had done.

"Ian, it is not that you took Scoot's body, but his matter, his body's place on this world. Unfortunately Scoot was only level 26 and when you jumped..." Jerry stopped mid-sentence to carefully pick his words. "He would not have made it to Earth in one piece."

"So we could maybe gather him. Put him back together?" Ian vainly tried infuse some perverted hope of Humpty Dumpty into the situation as the weight of Scoot's death fell on his shoulders.

A kind face did not meet Ian as the woman shook her head "no". The other man looked away form Ian's gaze.

"The laws of nature and conservation of mass apply not only on your world, but on every world and within The Dimension as a whole. During your first jump you are re-introducing your being to The Dimension and your new world. To balance the scales you replace matter already present in the world you are entering, thus your Double."

"But he. His being is still there, his molecules-"

"-Are scattered across your planet. Ian it would

be like trying to put a log back together after burning it in a fire. After the first jump your matter has been completely re-introduced to The Dimension your existence becomes a part of The Dimension's complex system. What happens to your body during a jump is unknown. We do know you only have one chance at a first jump though."

"Is there any chance we can save him?" Ian tried to grasp at any hope as tears fell.

"The system is imperfect and at times we lose people because of it. We lost more than Scoot today and will be doing damage control for weeks."

"I'm… sorry," remorse leaked out as Ian broke eye contact. Unable to cope with what he had done. Not only had Ian killed Scoot, but from what Jerry just said he had thrown Esmerelda into chaos as well.

"Ian, I misspoke." Jerry quickly tried to catch himself."You did nothing wrong today and you can not dwell on what happened. This tragedy was well out of your control and is the product of an imperfect system. We knew you were close to level three, however, about a year ago you stopped progressing and we thought we had more time to prepare Scoot. This loss is an unfortunate mishap that is no one's fault, except my own."

A natural moment of silence fell upon the tent. Ian heard Jerry's words, but struggled to accept them. No matter how Jerry said it Ian was responsible for Scoot and all the other disasters that had happened today.

"Before, you said that once you have jumped you can jump at any time. Does that mean I can go home?"

"In theory. Yes. In reality, no," Jerry flatly replied. "We are in the middle of a war and most of the time when students are ready to make their first jump it takes months to set up. We do whatever we can to mislead and distract our enemy. We know that there are spies everywhere, so we spread as much false information as we can to keep everyone safe. During a first jump everything is calculated, because even in a perfect world first jumps can be disastrous."

"But if people enter The Dimension all the time, if people are entering in nano-second increments then surely something like this could have happened at any time?" Ian pushed trying to find any opening to get home.

"When people are progressing the portals do not open long enough for anyone to enter a world, let alone invade. A rip like yours has not happened in a long time and took everyone by surprise. By the time our enemy, '*The Evil*', as we call them, realized what had happened the portal on Earth had closed because Scoot was not ready. The portal here, on Esmerelda, did not because you came through. The dragon, the portals on the ground, the enemies you saw were part of The Evil's forces following you. It took a lot to secure this world again and, truth be told, it is not safe to travel through The Dimension right now. If you tried to leave you would never make it home and Esmerelda and Earth would probably perish as well."

Without intending it Jerry's explanation had drained all hope from the tent. It also simultaneously placed more blame on Ian cementing his guilt.

"Who are The Evil? Why would they call themselves that?" Ian asked trying to change the topic and not think about his future or what he had done.

"That is what we call them. They call themselves '*The Unifying League,*'. You will find here in the resistance, *Akhona's Guardian*, we simply call them what they are '*The Evil*'."

"I see... and..."

Ian trailed off as the conversation slowed. The tent was tense as Ian dealt with guilt and his new reality. *I'm never going home...* Ian thought to himself, his face projecting his thoughts.

"Do not despair Ian. Our world is not an awful place to be. We are the safe haven where all the special jumpers train."

"Special Jumpers?" Ian asked. The question slipping out before he could stop it.

"There are two classes of jumpers. The majority of jumpers can only safely jump between their home planet and their Double's home planet, what we call their sister planet. We call these people non-special jumpers because while they can jump between worlds they cannot survive inside The Dimension itself. Special jumpers can survive inside The Dimension. This ability allows them to personally open portals inside The Dimension and jump to any planet they want."

"How do you know who are special jumpers?"

"People born here or whose Double reside here are special jumpers. We classify them S3, S2, or S1 based on how many planets they have jumped to. We don't know why, but for some reason people born here and their Doubles are able to survive within The Dimension like our ancestors could."

Ian was still learning to read Jerry, but felt a twinge of misdirection. He had felt it a few times during the conversation and was certain Jerry knew more and was trying to obfuscate certain things.

"Ian, you are a special jumper and we have over 300 students here training to join the fight. Even after today we have 500 special jumpers waiting to become a part of Akhona's Guardians. We have an additional 20,000 regular jumpers ready to make their first jump.

"Beyond the students, we have around 10,000 jumpers, special and not, fighting the enemy right now. Our numbers are not huge, however, remember that on the resistance controlled planets we have armies of millions ready to defend their planet from an invading force."

Ian saw through Jerry's smile. He didn't know how many people it took to fight in The Dimension, but the math didn't add up unless almost everyone here and their Doubles were ready to jump. Even if the math was right they lost at least a hundred students today. A hundred more deaths that could be placed on him. That hardly seemed like enough people to defend against an invading force. *20,000 soldiers maybe? That can't be enough to win.* Ian thought to himself thinking that the planets that had already been invaded surely had that many soldiers ready to defend them.

"Jerry, this doesn't seem right. I mean there are

billions of people across The Dimension correct?"

"Yes?"

"And say half of those are under the control of the UL?"

"We can use that number."

"Then how is it possible that 20,000 people are enough?"

"Ian," the man next to Jerry spoke up. "I know that number seems small and believe me it is not ideal, however you have to remember that we are fighting between planets and this war isn't like it used to be and isn't like any other war. Many planets that were conquered or taken by force was done in the first few years. During the last few decades only a handful of planets have changed sides. The Evil while having more resources does not have unlimited resources, and while 20,000 may not seem like enough it is more than enough to turn the tide. Know that now, more than ever, because of our resistance free planets are better prepared and ready to fight."

The tent nodded in agreement with this man and while Ian wanted to press the subject Jerry interjected before Ian could.

"Ian I know this is a lot to find out. I know you must be tired and need time to think, but before you go I have two things I must say. First, I want to apologize about everything that happened today. It was not your fault. It was not anyone's fault and if you want to place blame place it on me or The Evil."

Ian felt the tone of the tent shift. While Jerry's aplogy was nice Ian could feel him pulling this gathering to a close faster than he wanted to. Ian was not tired, but caught off guard. Taking Ian's silence as forgiveness Jerry continued.

"Secondly, now that you have been thrust into this war, I must ask you to become a part of Akhona's Guard. We will train you and with hard work you will become a great warrior and an even greater leader for us. Do you accept?"

The choice shook Ian as he weighed his options. *I assumed I would be in the fight... I just thought at a desk job or as a cook or something. I mean do they really think that I can be a soldier?* Ian thought to himself as he grappled with the new reality of a choice he thought he would never have to make.

"No matter what you choose we will protect you, your family, and friends," Jerry added to his offer.

Just tell him no, you are not a soldier. You can't kill. I mean I can see that he needs help, but you are not a killer. You are barely in good shape.

Despite his better judgment and objections deep

down Ian knew that he didn't have a choice. Becoming a soldier and ending this war was the only way he could ever restore peace to his life. It was the only way he could get back to his friends and family. Everything had changed today and Ian had to do all that he could to bring this horrible war to an end. Ian could not turn his back on it now.

"Do you accept?" Jerry pressed Ian for an answer.

"Jerry, I accept, but have one request," Ian responded after a few tense moments of silence and a deep breath. "Can you let my friends and family on Earth know that I am safe?"

"We are taking care of that as we speak. You will not be able to talk to them now, but hopefully, in time, you will be able to," Jerry answered joyously. "Ian I cannot tell you how excited we are to have you join us, but after today everything else can wait. Go eat and get settled in. We will continue tomorrow."

CHAPTER THREE

Falling Awake

"Heads up!!!"

Was the only warning Ian heard as he emerged from his tent the following morning. Wiping sleep from his eyes Ian opened them to see an arrow coming straight for him out of the rising sun. Diving, tripping, and flinching, all at once, left Ian with a face full of leaves and earth at the entrance of his tent. The arrow bisecting his pillow a few feet behind him.

"Sam!!!" Ian heard a familiar voice yelling from the river valley. "How many times do I have to tell you: Do not do clout shots in camp!!!!"

Coming back to his senses Ian watched Laura reprimand a group of young boys responsible for his near death experience. Reaching into the tent Ian retrieved the arrow and began chuckling to himself. Part of him wondering if this place was always this dangerous, part of him reminiscing about his own rouge clout shots.

Turning out of the tent Ian fell onto his back again. This time because an angel burst through the morning sunrise.

"You okay?" Marissa asked as she sat down next to Ian.

"I'm..." Ian said, sitting up as straight as possible as he turned towards Marissa.

Marissa's strawberry blonde hair flowed delicately, and fell perfectly to frame her flawless complexion. Rosy cheeks and mysterious chestnut eyes greeted Ian as he lost himself in Marissa's beauty. Completely forgetting about the arrow, that had almost killed him, Ian felt another spark run up his arm as Marissa took his wrist.

"You seem to be fine, but your pulse is up,' Marissa commented as she checked her watch against his pulse. 'Do you think it is from the arrow or do you like what you see?" Marissa asked with a mischievous grin. Her fingers tracing his wrist before she released it.

She's funny and flirting, Ian thought as he fought for something to say.

"Do you want an arrow?" Ian mumbled as he

offered Marissa the arrow.

"How romantic," Marissa giggled as she took the arrow.

Ian felt foolish. Last night, on Jerry's suggestion, Ian had vainly searched every camp fire for Marissa. As Ian left the tent Jerry told him Marissa's name and that she had asked about him. Smugly, Ian had thought *I should apologize to her for all the commotion* and use it as a pretext to see if there was something to that spark. In the morning sun, Ian immediately lost any smug cockiness and wondered why she had asked about him.

Sitting in silence Ian could not take his eyes off Marissa as she waited for him to speak.

"Let me give you a hand," a deep voice behind Ian finally broke the silence for him.

Before Ian could stand, respond, or even turn his head he was lifted from his dirt throne.

"You gotta love waking up that way," the strong voice said as he patted Ian on the back.

Dusting himself off Ian was about to turn around when several people walked around him to meet him. Silhouetted against the rising sun Ian immediately recognized Michelle and Michael, a boy a few inches shorter than him, probably 5'4-5'5" with short buzzed hair. Michael and Michelle were both young no older than 15.

"I'm John," the strong voice that had lifted Ian introduced himself as he reached out his dark, muscular hand in welcome. "These two are Rich and Evan," John continued, introducing the two boys over his shoulders.

John's handshake confirmed what Ian initially thought was a trick of the eye: Evan, Rich, and John were, in fact, Greek Gods.

John stood about 6' feet tall with broad shoulders and a shaved head. Deep ocean blue eyes exuded confidence and even in baggy pajamas there was no doubt that John was stronger than anyone Ian had ever met.

Rich was a hair taller than John, probably 6'2 or 3". Also chiseled out of stone Rich's strong shoulders, sky blue eyes, blonde hair, and perfect smile made him look like the stereotypical Southern gentleman. He was every mother's dream, the pride of every father, and would be the star athlete for any team back on Earth.

Evan, 5'10", stood a few inches taller then Ian. And while Rich struck Ian as the perfect child, Evan was the nerd who had grown up into a strong man. Lankier than the other two Evan was still sculpture like. Rounded glasses, brown eyes, and disheveled brown hair complemented Evan's smile that told everyone he was ready to hack your computer or be your best friend.

Sucking in his gut, Ian tried to stand as tall as possible in front of his new group of friends, painfully aware of how he did not measure up. Ian had some work to do.

"If you are done with introductions we should give Ian the tour before his first day of training," Marissa piped up, after Ian shook everyones hands, hoping it would make Ian feel less self conscious.

Walking towards the river valley below Ian was overwhelmed with the growing city of tents and supplies lining the hills that rimmed the river valley. Various sized tents created an intricate tapestry on the dense tree laden landscape. Century old hardwoods provided shade to the camp. The warm glow of the sun poking through holes in their ancient canopy.

The large lake shore, which had been home to kick ball the night before, was now a makeshift archery range. The docks stood still. The boats that had transported everyone had already been moved and looking across from the shore, towards the East, Ian saw a large cleared field at the crux of the hills' western and southern faces.

"Pretty amazing, isn't it?" Marissa said softly as they traveled down the hill. "I never thought we would need it, but I'm happy we have it. Jerry brought me here a few times while they were doing preliminary preparation: Clearing the field, creating the docks. The tents are temporary; soon Jerry and his staff will build a whole city in the trees," Marissa explained pointing out the plans as she spoke. "There will be…"

Following her hand and Ian began visualizing what would come when he inadvertently blurted out:

"It will be like the Endor."

"Endor," Marissa stammered. Trying to recover from her broken train of thought.

"It is… It is a … A fictional place where everyone lives in trees," Ian answered. Frozen, in awe, by the camp as it was and what it would become.

Sounds of a waking camp filled the lull in their conversation. Chirping birds mixed with the sounds of breakfast and play. Ian's migrating gaze soon brought him back to Marissa's chestnut eyes.

"Earlier you asked me why my heart rate was up. I think I know why," Ian started to speak as he turned towards Marissa. A spark rushing though him as he took Marissa's hand.

"Really? Why is that?" Marissa asked in a playful, shy, and flirtatious tone as she leaned closer to Ian.

"Well-"

"-Hey, hurry up," John interrupted their moment as he yelled up the hill.

True to form Ian found and slipped on a log after John startled them, falling onto the hard forest floor again.

"Let me give you a hand."

Once again Ian felt the strong connection between Marissa and himself as she helped him up. Ian knew she felt it too and just as a moment began again John interrupted.

"We're waiting for you two."

As Ian followed Marissa down the hill to his new friends a painful thought intruded his mind.

What about Nicole?

Yesterday had been so hectic Ian had not really thought about his girlfriend. A world apart Ian did not know what they were anymore. Could a relationship survive this distance? And what did he feel with Marissa? Sighing, Ian had another complication to add to his ever-growing list.

Breakfast was a blur. Arriving at the mess tent Ian was overwhelmed as people continually introduced themselves. In the commotion Ian got separated from his new friends and spent much of his breakfast trying to grab bites to eat in-between shaking hands and greeting people. Before long John was tapping Ian on the shoulder with a question.

"Ready for your fist day of training?"

"Yah, I guess…" Ian said relived to get out of the tent.

Leaving the mess tent John and Ian trekked up the hill towards the field. Searching ahead of them Ian was trying to locate Marissa when he asked John a question to fill the silence.

"Where are we going?" Ian asked as he located Marissa.

"If you looked further up the hill, instead of at one thing on the hill, you would see where we are going," John replied.

"Oh."

"It's fine man," John laughed as he patted Ian on the back. "Follow me and you'll be fine."

"*Maybe they are dating?*" Ian thought, seeing past John's friendly smile and kind words.

Ian quickly dismissed the thought though. Unless he had misread Marissa, John and Marissa's relationship was platonic; however, Ian could not help but wonder why he was on John's radar.

John had interrupted their moment twice this morning and with every comment John steered himself between them.

"You coming?" John asked pointing to a small brick building adjacent to the field.

Lost in thought Ian had not noticed they reached the top of the hill and before he could reply John spoke again.

"I mean you can do what you want, but training in pj's doesn't sound like much fun."

"Just show me my locker," Ian punched John's arm as he ran towards the changing room, not prepared to let John run everything.

...

"Took you long enough," Rich joked as John and Ian came onto the field.

"First day, had to get this one some clothes," John answered Rich.

"We all had to do that..." Rich joked. "But I guess he didn't have anything."

The communication between Rich and John was hard for Ian to read. They were clearly sizing Ian up, there was clearly something going unsaid, but before he could worry about that Evan spoke up.

"We need to stretch and get warmed up guys."

Watching Rich, John, and Evan for guidance it only took Ian a second to recognize their warmup as a variation on his own yoga regime. Relaxed that he finally knew something Ian fell into rhythm with his new friends.

Focussing on his routine Ian never saw Jerry racing across the field and without warning Ian was on the cold hard earth for a fourth time this morning.

"Jerry?" Ian blinked a few times, trying to verify that Jerry had just tackled him.

"Sorry about that but we couldn't risk it," Jerry panted. "We had to get this to you before you could start training."

Jerry handed Ian a heart-rate monitor and its partner watch as he got off of Ian and stood up.

"Uh, thanks," Ian awkwardly accepted the gift. "I know a heart rate monitor is important to a proper workout, but I didn't realize you guys took it that seriously. If I had know I would have grabbed mine before I jumped." Ian tried to joke as he sat up.

"It's not about a workout," Jerry responded unfazed by the joke. "You need to wear these to stop you from jumping again. This watch is much more than a heart rate monitor Ian. This watch will guide your jumps, track your vitals, and do so much more."

"This watch will do all that?"

"In time. Right now, it will just monitor your vitals, tell time, and keep you here." Jerry answered as Ian looked over the watch.

On the fence about the device Ian was beginning to see a pattern emerge: all of his questions were going to be answered later. Giving the watch and monitor another once over Ian was not convinced that he should put them on.

The bands were as soft as silk, but seemed stronger than leather. They also matched the flat black marble that made up the watch face and body of the monitor. They were clearly technological marvels, but Ian was unsure they would come off once they were on.

"Ian we all have them," John broke the stalemate Jerry couldn't.

Looking around the field Ian noticed that everyone had a watch on. Evan and Rich had even pulled up their shirts showing off the monitor.

"You will forget it is on," Evan endorsed the device.

"Yah, they're great," Rich nodded in agreement.

"You wear them all the time?" Ian asked after spotting a matching watch on Jerry and Marissa's wrists.

"We do. But again you will forget it's even on." John echoed Evan's comment.

Taking a deep breath Ian looked at the device once more before giving Jerry a nod.

"Let me help you," John said, taking the heart monitor and strapping it to Ian.

"Thank you John," Jerry said as Ian put on the watch. "Ian, even though unlikely, we were worried you might accidentally jump again. Late last night we discovered that a certain yoga pose was your jump position. We had to get the watch on as an extra precaution to avoid repeating yesterday."

Finished Jerry turned and walked away without another word. Jerry's abrupt departure startled Ian who could not start stretching without asking the question lingering at the tip of his tongue.

"Jerry how did you find out?" Ian asked as he raced after Jerry.

"Well... Last night we were able to make contact with a jump coordinator on Earth. He found your jump history, which allowed us to figure out what happened yesterday to trigger your first jump. Your position is a yoga stretch, one you do every day and one that you practiced in Aikido when you were younger. Once we lined it up it all made sense."

"That sounds good. You made a connection. Found out a lot of information. Will I be able to talk my family and friends soon? My girlfriend?" Ian asked with eyes full of hope. Excited to hear that Jerry had made contact with Earth.

"Well, that's the bad news," Jerry answered dejectedly. "The Dimension is more hostile than we thought and we had no choice but to collapse the channel we used last night. As it stands you will not be able speak to anyone on Earth."

The hope drained from Ian's face.

"Do not worry Ian. Your friends, family, and girlfriend have notified of what happened to you and are getting a protective detail as an extra precaution. We explained the reality of the situation and told them to move on with their lives without you."

"You did what?!?" Ian screamed. "What do you mean you told them to move on?!?!"

"Ian… Ian you have to understand that you won't be able to talk to any of them for a long time. We did not want to interfere with your personal life, but had to for everyone's safety," Jerry started to explain hoping to quench Ian's anger. "The Evil only knows that someone jumped through The Dimension. They do not know where, why, how, or who. Only when. Ian, we work under the assumption that The Evil has forces on every planet and if we risk further contact with Earth we put everyone at risk. Even with how disastrous yesterday was we caught a break."

"But-"

"-The Evil will find your family and friends and will torture them for information they don't have or know. If we are not careful they will die protecting information they do not know."

Frustrated, Ian knew that Jerry was right. The last thing he wanted was to put his loved ones in danger; however, considering everything else going on, this brought little relief.

"I know it sucks, I know this is all new, but you have to stay focussed. Your family, friends, and former girlfriend are all safe. Considering the circumstances that is all you can wish for. We need you to move on from your old life whether you want to or not."

Ian could not help but notice a shift in Jerry's tone from the night before. Last night Jerry was selling Ian on the resistance, this morning he was giving him instructions on how to live and adjust.

"What exactly did you tell my family Jerry?"

"Ian… We did what we had to. I know it is not easy, but you have to break yourself from your former life."

"You didn't answer my question. What did you tell them? And who gave you the right to tell my family, my girlfriend, that I am gone? Who are you to tell me how to live my life?" Ian's hands curled into fists as his anger simmered. Ian had agreed to help Jerry, not to become a slave to the Guardians.

"Ian we did what we had to and I know you agree with what we did. You want everyone on Earth to be happy and safe. I know you don't want them waiting their entire lives for you to come home."

"That is not what I asked," Ian pushed through gritted teeth.

"And I do not divulge communications to student soldiers," Jerry answered bluntly. "They still love you Ian, but you are gone. Use them as inspiration. Love them from a far, but do not lose sight of the larger picture. We are in a war and you have to move on if you are going to survive.

You are in a new place filled with new people and new opportunities. Yesterday sucked for them too, but they understand. Ian I implore you to let your new family in. Take chances. And move on."

Ian wanted to follow Jerry as he walked away, to keep this going, but couldn't. At some point John had joined them and now had stepped in-between them. John was holding Ian back, standing as a rock in his way. Ian wanted to tell John to go to hell but that was not an option. Ian did not have the emotional or physical strength to fight either one of them.

How did they possibly think it was okay to break apart my already shattered life? Who does he think he is? Ian thought as he cried to himself.

"Come on man, it's okay. We can talk about it on our run," John said trying to offer some comfort.

Giving up Ian followed John to the track. Moving at a slow to moderate pace Ian, John, Rich, and Evan ran around the two mile track in silence, everyone waiting for Ian to say something.

The beauty around them helped relax Ian as they ran. Snowcapped mountains secured their little haven. The grand river that brought them here snaked through the mountains and into the horizon. Flowering plants and the sounds of life rushed past him as Ian tried to sort out his own thoughts.

Lunch came and went in silence. After another round of yoga, strength and conditioning workouts, and another run, all passed in silence, night settled in.

Bonfires, ruckus, and general buffoonery filled the night and Ian took Jerry's advice and enjoyed the activities. He met some new students, but again found himself searching for Marissa, Evan, John, Rich, Michelle, or Mikey.

That night Ian found out that school was run almost year round and even though classes had just started back, free nights, like this one, were rare. Most of the students came here when they were twelve and stayed until they joined the war in some way. They all knew of the war, but Ian quickly discovered that the war was not their primary concern.

Dating, breaking up, having fun, and getting into trouble were a larger part of their life than the war. Almost by design this place avoided the war at all turns. Talking to different students Ian quickly discovered that until you were 17 or 18 the war was not touched upon in any class. You studied strategy, trained in martial arts, but it was intentionally not connected. Jerry tried very hard to keep the war on the back burner.

Jerry didn't burden anyone who he didn't need to. Even after what had happened the day before the camp had fallen into an uneasy understanding as everyone tried to treat this new "normal" as exactly that.

However Ian felt it. He was sure everyone did too, that despite the happy veneer everyone felt the pains of the war just from being at this school. Ian was not sure if it was amplified because of what had happened the day before, but he was sure of one thing: the war never slept.

Every time he looked at his watch Ian was reminded that this war wouldn't sleep until someone won.

CHAPTER FOUR
A Dash of Understanding

After another night of nightmares Ian found himself running silently with Rich, Evan, and John. It was their final run after another long day of training.

What is Jerry not telling me? Should I really move on? Who is Jerry to tell me to move on? Does the camp blame me? How did they overcome the loss so easily? Who does Jerry....

Ian had been on Esmerelda for a month and his first day had become his routine. The days were jam packed with workouts. Nights full of fun and relaxation.

Outside of these daily runs the only other time Ian had to think was at night, after the parties were done. Nightmares haunted Ian every time he laid his head on his pillow. His family's death, The Evil taking over, were just a few of the images that filled his nights of horror. On Earth Ian would have shared these things with Nicole or his mother. On Esmerelda Ian had no desire to burden his new friends with these thoughts.

Despite Jerry's upbeat attitude the shadow of the war hung over the camp and what Ian had brought to them. It was clear Jerry tried to keep the war at arms length, however, Ian's arrival broke that delicate veneer. Ian could not pinpoint it, but he heard it in the back of his peer's voices, the forced happiness when they spoke to him, and in the glances when he ran around the track. Even if they would not say it Ian knew some of the camp held him responsible for what had happened. Ian did not blame them. He felt responsible.

The second week he had been here they had a group funeral for anyone who had passed. It was a day full of tears and closure. After that, life went on. People spoke of their lost friends, counselorswere available, but loss wasn't the primary focus. Most of the camp had moved on and that only confused Ian more.

How do they do it? Ian thought to himself every time he saw someone talk to another as if nothing had changed. Over the past month he had watched people rebuild their entire social circle around campfires and a training field. *If a thirteen year old can be that strong why can't I be stronger?*

And that was the problem for Ian. This place, Esmerelda, was a land of contradictions. The war was kept at arms length and yet shadowed over everything they did. His fellow students were able to mourn the lives they had lost while not missing a beat. Inside Ian was a wreck and yet somehow everyone around him seemed to push on.

"Ian, we are all here for you," Evan broke the silence.

Everyday someone said this to him during the run. For Ian the runs were his time to think. Meals and other training were not done in silence, however the runs were his time to be away.

"I know, but I don't think you guys would understand," Ian responded as Marissa passed them. Smiling at Ian as she ran by with two of the girls Ian had first seen her with.

"Probably not everything man," Evan acknowledged Ian and Marissa's situation with a nod. "But, we understand more than you would think. We all understand missing loved ones and being separated from your home."

Despite everything that had happened Ian was still distant and guarded, justifying it with two contradicting thoughts: *How could they possibly understand what I'm going through?* and *who am I to burden them with my problems?*

Running around the track's eastern bend Ian took a second to think about Evan's comment. Everyday he had an exchange with one of them like this. And every day, when he had a chance to respond he stayed silent. Ian didn't want to burden his new friends, but more importantly, Ian had realized a few nights earlier, he did not want to let them in. If he kept them at a distance then there was always a chance one morning he would wake up back in his bed on Earth. If he didn't give in then maybe this wasn't real.

"We really do Ian," Rich spoke up not letting today's run settle back into silence. "I'm from Vekelva, world 213, and can only easily jump between 213 and 211. Unlike you; Evan, John, and I are not special jumpers. We all came here to train after The Evil decimated our worlds."

The words hit Ian hard as John and Evan nodded. They had been together for weeks and this had never come up. Ian had always assumed that everyone here was a special jumper.

"You're not special jumpers? Are more people-"

"-Just us," Rich cut Ian off a little prematurely. "Sorry bout that, we're the three outliers; every other student is a special."

This revelation made Ian realize how distant he

had been. Sure it had been hard getting used to this place; however, now Ian felt bad. He had been hanging out with these three guys, training with them, eating with them, and this had never come up. It had never come up because Ian never asked them for their stories.

"What happened?" Ian asked.

Knowing they had made a break through Rich started to tell his tale as they ran around the track's next large curve.

"My parents are Jerry's friends and through him they knew something big was coming. When I came here Jerry was in the middle of a hundred things it seemed, I think I was supposed to be a part of a project, but for whatever reason, plans changed and I was brought here to train".

"When was that?"

"A few years back."

"Oh..."

"It was not smooth sailing though," Rich resumed his story. "To get here took take two jumps and while my first jump went perfectly, the second jump did not. After my first jump, I waited on my sister planet for a few days for my second jump. Now I know that I was waiting for Evan to get there."

"You and Evan are from the same world then?" Ian asked.

"No we have the same sister world. Before the day we jumped here Evan and I had never met."

"Oh...I never would have thought, I just assumed-"

"-No biggie. I was waiting on world 211 when Jerry came running into the jump vault with Evan. Evan was dead silent, I had no idea what was going on, and Jerry was frantic. Before I could say a word Jerry set up a bridge portal and the three of us had jumped here safely."

"A bridge portal?" Ian asked skeptically.

"It's what Jerry calls the pathways that allow non special jumpers to travel through The Dimension to planets other than their home or sister planet."

"Oh, Cool."

With the picture of jumping becoming a little clearer Ian was waiting for Rich to continue but instead he simply kept running around the track. Ian wondered if Evan had more details. From what Rich said the jump didn't sound too awful, nothing like killing hundreds and destroying a school. Turning to Evan Ian spotted a few tears running down his face as the memories of that day rushed back.

"You okay?" Ian asked.

"Yeah," Evan replied wiping away tears. "Ian I didn't want to make my first jump. They had to force me because I wanted to stay and protect my family and friends from The Evil. The day I made my first jumped The Evil attacked both our home planets."

Ian looked to Rich who confirmed Evan's story with a nod. Somehow Rich had forgotten to mention that his world had been lost.

"Horrible, faceless enemies rushed through portals all around my planet. My people tried to resist, but we were no match for them. My people are not fighters, were relatively new to The Dimension, and knew little about it. We had no idea how to react," Evan said.

"That's awful," Ian muttered, taking a little comfort in the fact that his world was safe.

"I would have stayed, but Jerry would not let me. It took them over an hour to secure the portal, but apparently we got out in the commotion. When I got to my sister planet we rushed to the jump vault and came here. I lost everyone that day and have not heard from them since."

Ian struggled to grapple with Evan's story. How could he, Ian, have been so selfish? How could he have been so naive? Earth was fine. His family was fine. Rich and Evan's planets were gone and *"Sorry,"* didn't seem like enough. Not wanting to press Evan Ian asked Rich a question.

"Rich did your family escape?"

"Yeah," Rich responded dismissively. "I hear from them every six months, but haven't seen then since that day."

Ian hit a sore spot without trying: Rich was dismissive of his own fortune. He had not seen his family, but he knew they were alive. Ian wanted to know why when Evan filled in the blank.

"Rich there is no reason to feel guilty. I'm happy you still hear from your family. I know someday you will see them again."

"It's just not fair. I get to speak with them and you never hear from yours. Your world was completely taken, while mine, well, while mine was able to protect itself and well... You don't even know whether your family is safe."

Ian was now very confused. He assumed Evan had lost his family in the attack.

"Ian, about three months after our jump an

emergency message was sent from my home world. Many people survived, but are in dire need of help. Rich's world survived and *"serve"* The Evil, more as equals than slaves," Evan clarified Rich's statement.

"Oh… my… I am so…" Ian stuttered as words escaped him.

"We received two more messages, like the first, before they stopped about a year ago. There is nothing we can do from here and everyone here has told me to move on. In my bones though I know that someone is waiting for me to save them."

Ian felt that he had failed to put his own situation in perspective. Rich and Evan were offering empathy and comfort to him for a situation much better than their own. The Evil had destroyed their lives, taken their homes, and Evan and Rich were here for him. They were here for someone whose planet was not only safe, but under the best protection possible.

"Don't feel sorry for us," Rich broke the silence. "Everyone has a war story and it takes all of us time to cope. We deal with it every day and use it as inspiration and motivation. You can't let it overcome you. Work through your grief at your own pace, but don't let it consume you."

Finished with their last lap the run came to an

end. Rich and John both ran off to the locker rooms, while Evan grabbed Ian to keep him behind.

"Ian, I know our stories are sad, but they in no way overshadow your own. I want you to know that we are all here for you. Everyone's situation is different and we are all working through something at our own pace."

"But... how-"

"-Ian everyone has something. Don't overplay our grief and don't downplay your own. We are here for you," Evan said not letting Ian demote his own struggles. "Don't ever think that you are being strong by holding it in. I did for a long time and it is not worth it man. This was not your fault and you are only weaker if you lock us out."

The field had mostly emptied out and every rejection that came to mind Evan had seemingly just solved with his last few words.

"Evan I do have a question?"

"What is it?"

"What's up with John and Marissa?"

"Marissa and John have never been and will never be together. So if you're worried about stepping on anyone's toes don't."

"You sure?"

"Yeah. John's been here a little longer than us, but he's her protector and she is smitten with you. If that is what you are really asking."

Smiling Ian felt a little embarrassed but had another question.

"What happened to John?"

"That is John's story and I'm sure he will share it with you in time. Is that all?" Evan asked him, not wanting to leave before Ian was ready.

"Yeah, I should probably get showered. Marissa wanted to show me something tonight."

"Well then we should get moving. You don't want to keep her waiting," Evan answered with a slap on the back as they left the field.

...

Ian stopped at every tent and campfire trying to find Marissa. After hearing Evan and Rich's stories he eagerly awaited Marissa's welcomed distraction. Unfortunately for Ian everyone had seen her, but no one knew where she was.

Reaching the river bank Ian spotted Laura. Ian had not had a chance to talk to her much since that first day but knew she kept camp running while Jerry built the permanent settlement. If anyone had seen Marissa it was probably Laura.

"Hey," Ian yelled as he approached Laura.

Laura turned towards Ian for a second before turning away.

"You okay?"

"Hey... Ian," Laura welcomed him. "Sorry about the tears, something got in my eye."

Laura's body betrayed her words. Her soft skin had goosebumps and she would not make eye contact. Looking out over the fading horizon Laura bit her lip as she waited for someone. From a distance she could fool you into thinking that she was taking in the breathtaking sunset, however, standing next to her, you could see Laura searching for something beyond the horizon.

"Who are you waiting for?" Ian asked searching the horizon with her.

"Am I that obvious?" Laura chuckled with a tear, as she looked away from the setting sun.

"You were staring a hole in the sunset," Ian responded trying to lighten the mood.

"I know he's not coming, but I can't lose hope..."

Without warning Laura's brown eyes welled up with tears as she tore away from Ian's gaze and back towards the sunset. Before Ian could respond Laura snapped her head and hair back breaking through her sorrow. Through forced composure, she met Ian's eyes and started to speak.

"The man who put ya'll in the boats was my fiancé Tommy." Tears battled their way back as Laura fought to continue. "We finally got done going through the ruins today and...well..." Laura could not finish as grief overtook her.

Putting an arm around Laura Ian tried to console her as they sat down on the shore.

"I'm sorry Lau-"

"-It's fine...It's fine Ian," Laura cut Ian off in a cold, despondent tone as she broke away from his grasp. "It's a miracle that you made it through and I'm just happy we all made it here."

Laura's tears had stopped and she tried to force a smile but it fell flat.

Tommy is another life lost because of me. Another life lost, family destroyed, all because I jumped early.

Ian had known that they were searching the ruins, but it appeared that after a month the search was over. Trying to break out of his own self pity Ian was going to ask Laura a question when she made an off hand comment.

"I sometimes think that if we had lost you, a special jumper, or another world to The Evil Jerry may have finally given up."

"What??! What do you m-"

"-We are losing this war Ian. I'm sure that Jerry told you about our grand numbers and painted an upbeat picture, but, the truth is, this war is all but over. We are sitting in a castle under siege while The Evil squeezes the life from us. This can't be that much of a surprise though. Despite their happy demeanor and devotion I'm sure you have noticed the camps melancholy undertone."

It was the first time someone else had acknowledged the grief and dread Ian had noticed since he got here. Laura was right, but Ian had simply thought that people were still mourning.

"We are lucky you survived. You are a special jumper, because your double was born here. Scoot allows you to fight, survive, and adapt inside The Dimension."

"Jerry told me all of this Laura. But, and I mean no offense, but why would Jerry be giving up?"

Puzzled by her pessimism and troubled with the thought of his own death, Ian could not think of a better way to ask. He understood that she had just lost her loved one, but Ian knew that the people of Earth would mobilize against an invading threat and could not understand her position.

"We have lost over 140 worlds, which mean any jumpers, special or not, are pretty much useless until we regain control of those worlds. Jumps between "free" worlds are very unsafe, especially the first jump. We are losing soldiers faster than we can replace them. All while our enemy grows exponentially stronger."

"I still don't under-"

"-Ian, after your jump we have roughly 200 or so healthy students left. Maybe, another 50 or so may rejoin training eventually, but we lost 26 to injury and another 30 to death who will never fight. If you include their doubles and are generous we have roughly four or five hundred new special jumpers ready to join the force in the next ten years. Out of those over half of their doubles are on worlds The Evil occupies taking away half of our new force, reducing our new specials to well under 300. A jump into an evil infested world is difficult, a first jump is suicide. That will leave most of your classmates stuck at level four or five."

Ian did the math and by his estimates her facts lined up. It would mean that they lost around 50 of his peers the day he jumped and that was not counting the staff they lost.

"At least we are all a little older?" Ian thought out loud. Considering most of the people he met were older teenagers. At least they were at an age where they could join the fight.

"If they were ready to join the fight or if it was possible that would be a good thing, but most of the students here either do not know the extent of the war or know that the greatest contribution they can make is to raise a child in the hopes that this world lasts long enough for their kid to join the fight."

"They want us to have children?" Ian asked completely surprised by this revelation.

"Of course, but do not think you're livestock. It all has to do with genetics you know that," Laura responded with a genuine chuckle at Ian's question.

"Ian you will fight and lead in this war, but because you carry the right genes and are from Earth you are expected to become a father, sooner and more so than other kids here. Having a child with the right person guarantees us two more special jumpers."

"How? Jerry told me that they do not know how doubles are assigned?" Ian responded a little uneasy now with how actively interested Jerry had been in Ian's romantic pursuits.

"Your home planet is Earth and it is likely, almost guaranteed, your kid's doubles will be on Earth. Ian don't you see that you have two abilities most people around here would give their right arm to have."

"But-"

"-Ian," Laura pressed, a fire raising in her eyes that could set the forest ablaze. "People who have children together here may have special kids, but their double will be randomly assigned. Every child has an even shot of giving The Evil another soldier. Your kid would give us two."

Tears welled up in Laura's eyes as the tolls of the war manifested themselves. Ian felt numb from Laura's honesty.

"Don't you see? Most students are caught in a catch 22 here: if they choose to have kids then they may be supplying The Evil with more forces to use against us; but, if they do not have kids we have no way to replenish our forces to turn the tide of the battle.

"We are missing a major piece we don't have the full genetic picture. So even though there are probably hundreds, maybe even thousands of special jumpers living in the cities across Esmerelda we will never know who they are or how to train them. At best they are lost to us at worst they are a liability.

"Ian don't you see? We are losing ground every day. We have lost more worlds and soldiers than we choose to admit. We can't replenish our forces fast enough and fear has paralyzed us. Fear is taking hold and it is slowly eroding confidence and peoples ability to fight."

Following Laura's gaze, across the river, the sun had almost set. The mountains stood aglow in the fires of a dying day as Ian searched for something to say.

"There must be a way to recapture a world; we have more than special ju-" Ian started before Laura cut him off.

"-Ian, there isn't. We have a limited number of special jumpers now. The ones we have are spread thin and dying faster than we can replace them. To retake a world we need an invasion force that is not coming. We are fighting at a constant handicap. We are fighting a cunning foe who captures planets with collusion and friendship as much as force. Ian you can't ever underestimate The Unifying League or think of them like some sort of playground bully. The UL have might and force, but only use that when necessary. They have the upper hand Ian. They are smart and cunning and, Ian, they don't make mistakes, however;" Laura paused as if something joyful had suddenly hit her. "I guess we did win something that they cannot take away."

"And what is that?" Ian said dejectedly unable to believe that there was anything good coming out of all of this.

"We won hope. You showed that even with how knowledgeable and powerful The Evil is they can make mistakes too. When you got here we were reminded that they do not know everything and that... if we try... there may just be a chance. Ian, we got you."

Laura and Ian watched the golden glow disappear after which Ian rose and left with a heavy heart. Laura's complete one eighty had left Ian more worried, troubled, and confused. Ian knew Laura was in mourning, but she had also revealed more to him than Jerry had wanted him to know.

Walking away Ian had not forgotten about Marissa's plans, but needed some time to sort all this out. Evan, Rich, and Laura had all revealed new creases in this war and what Jerry had told him, what Jerry was hiding, and what his endgame really was.

CHAPTER FIVE
Sunset Despair

Marissa's silhouette filled Ian's vision against the overcast skies. Extending her hand she gave Ian a quick hand up and they were soon back in starting positions. A soft thud was all Ian heard. He was on his back again.

Ian knew he had moved toward her, he knew he had done something, and yet he was on his back. The soft grass falling in-between his fingers, Marissa giggling as she approached.

"I have to give you credit Ian. You may not remember much, but you know how to fall," Marissa joked as she pulled Ian back to his feet.

"Yah..." Ian replied for once wishing Marissa wasn't with him.

It had been a long day so far, two weeks after his talk with Laura Ian woke this morning earlier than normal, realizing for the first time that he was on Esmerelda not Earth. Marissa had joined him with a cup of coffee and they had discussed all the changes that had been happening around camp.

The dirt path that used to go to the field had been replaced by a beautiful wooden staircase, that stood as the foundation to a series of decks and walkways that snaked their way around the trees connecting a series of buildings that would create their new home. One building, the new mess hall, was a focus of their conversation because it was closest to being completed leaving Marissa and Ian to wonder what was hidden inside.

They had become lost in conversation as they looked at the paths, discussed what had been done, and what was left.

"Okay Ian, you ready?" Marissa asked Ian as he took his stance once again.

"I think so?"

Becoming more unsure Marissa came at Ian with a strike that he tried to block that she immediately turned on him, throwing Ian through the air and onto his butt over five feet away. Landing on the soft grass Ian could not help but think of how different this was than the aikido at home.

At home things were practiced static so you could perfect form and precision before turning it live. On Esmerelda everything was live. If you did not have your opponent's balance they would take yours in a moment. Everything was about real world application and this adjustment was, and had been, difficult for Ian.

"You okay?" Marissa asked after Ian had not immediately popped up.

"Yah, just thinking about how different this all is and how much Jerry pushes us."

Marissa nodded as she took a seat next to Ian.

Earlier that morning they had spent a lot of time discussing Jerry. And despite Ian's misgivings, despite everything that Laura had told him Ian only had one thought about Jerry:

He's amazing. Somehow Jerry does everything while keeping us safe.

Jerry was always working and was also always there for all of them. He worked late into the night counseling students and staff, contacting worlds, and as far as Ian knew leading the war. Today he found out, from Marissa, that Jerry was also the first one up every morning ready to direct everything from construction to training schedules. Even with how busy he was no one was undeserving of his time and Ian had seen time and time again. If you needed him, Jerry was always there.

"Did you ever really practice aikido or were you just trying to impress me?" Marissa poked at Ian, waiting for him to move.

"If I hadn't you would have broken me in two by now," Ian batted back.

"True. Although if I broke you I would put you back together," Marissa quipped with a smile and a wink.

That smile caught Ian off guard again. That smile was trouble and he knew he was falling for her. That mischievous grin made him feel powerless. However right now her eyes were not right. They were longing for something.

"What's on your mind?"

"What is Nicole like?"

"What?" Ian asked, caught off guard. Reminded of when he spilled coffee on himself earlier that morning.

"What is Nicole like? I mean we know a lot about you, but I want to know more about her?"

The wind swept Marissa's hair across her face; obscuring eyes filled with wonder and concern. Ian could not help but appreciate Marissa's empathy. It was the first time anyone asked him who Nicole IS. Marissa understood Ian's struggle and wanted to listen.

"Well,' Ian started still shaken by the question.

'She was amazing. She's very short and tiny, but it makes her more adorable. She was smart and lovely, but most of all she let me be a kid. We were so comfortable around each other; it was simply ama.."

Ian stopped himself when he noticed it. Without thinking, he was describing what their relationship had been. Looking inside himself Ian knew that no matter how hard he tried Nicole was slipping away. Even if he didn't want it, Ian knew he was fighting a losing battle.

"Nicole is great. She is caring, compassionate, and her ability to love is simply amazing. I have never been with anyone like her and miss her greatly. What we had, was great...."

Training fell on the back burner as Ian and Marissa sat there. Marissa was quiet, only asking a question here and there, as she let Ian speak. Ian's directed use of had, was, and is was not lost on Marissa as she watched him fight to move on.

"Thank you." Marissa said to Ian, a tear rushing down her face as they came to a natural stopping point.

"No thank you, but I think we should probably-"

"-Get back to training."

Awkwardly the two of them got back into sparring positions. The fragrances of lunch were starting to fill the air, accompanied by the smell Ian had come to associate with Marissa.

"Is that Lilac?" Ian asked as they circled each other.

"Do you like it?"

"I do. Although it isn't fair. It's distracting."

"All's fair in love and war," Marissa winked. "On the other hand I'm only using Aikido, so I think we are fair..."

Before she had finished Ian launched himself towards Marissa right as a sudden breeze had blown hair into her eyes obscuring her vision. Marissa slipped as she tried to react which was all the opening Ian needed. Changing his stride and stepping in with a double-tencon Ian caught Marissa and used his hip to throw her to the ground. With a firm hold, on her arm, Ian pinned Marissa for the first time that day.

"I guess I have not totally lost it," Ian chuckled as he offered her a hand up.

Marissa took his hand and used it to take his balance and throw him past her.

"That's for cheating," Marissa informed Ian as she stepped over him.

"I thought all was fair."

"You still don't cheat."

Her smile deceived her and fortunately for both of them a whistle blew signaling the end of their training. Both Marissa and Ian aware that the balance of flirting to sparring had been breached. A little sore Ian followed Marissa back to their team who was listening to Rich's pre-competition speech.

"We have fourteen point matches after lunch: seven against yellow and seven against red. Point wise all we need to do is win one match outright and put up an effort in two. These points are important, but can be made up this afternoon. As a bonus, John is not participating in a sparring match."

Earlier that morning all of the students had been divided into three teams for a friendly competition. Ian quickly found out that these tournaments had happened at least two to there times a week and were a real point of pride in the camp. Dinner line, showers and bragging rights were all determined by it. Rich, Evan, Marissa, and Ian had all ended up on the green team. John was on the yellow, and Mikey and Michelle were on the red team.

The competition itself consisted of sparring, sword/weapon work, and archery. Archery was their ace in the hole, and according to Rich and

Evan Ian was their secret weapon. The green team was clearly the underdog team, being made up of many kids under 16, however John sitting out sparring certainly improved their chances.

"Why isn't John participating?" Marissa approached Rich as their team dispersed to prepare for their matches.

"We accepted his challenge under the condition he not compete," Rich answered simply.

"And what was his challenge?"

"That he gets to have an unofficial match with Ian before lunch," Rich answered as nonchalantly as possible.

"You can't be serious Rich," Marissa asked flushed with anger as Ian's life flashed before his eyes.

"It is just a fun little spar before lunch. He won't hurt Ian and we are removing John from official competition. It is a win-win for all involved."

Rich's second rate answer did not fool Marissa.

"And why did John accept this Rich? Why did he ask for it in the first place?" Marissa archly continued the interrogation. "If you watched us at all you would have seen that Ian can barely do Aikido right now, let alone something more advanced. What were you thinking?!?!?"

Ian agreed with Marissa and did not share Rich's optimism. Ian had sparred with Marissa, but he knew that in the "real matches" the goal was to win at all costs, using whatever technique you could to achieve that goal.

"And why did John accept this Rich? Why did he ask for it in the first place?" Marissa asked again.

"He saw you sparring and asked for a match. And, well, we saw an opening... and..."

Reality hit Ian and Marissa: John had seen Marissa cry, he thought Ian had hurt her, and wanted to teach him a lesson.

"Rich you know how John feels about me. You're setting Ian up for slaughter based on a misunderstanding!!!"

"Marissa all John wants is a quick, *friendly*, spar with his friend," Rich said as he patted Ian on the shoulder. "Everyone knows we are training and there's no way he thought Ian was trying to hurt you."

His answer only confirmed what Ian and Marissa had deduced and did little to quell Marissa's anger or relieve Ian's fear. Walking away from the group Ian needed a minute to think. To plan.

If John thought Ian had hurt Marissa then he was a dead man walking. On the bright side, Marissa seemed to understand and acknowledge John's guarded ways around her. At least Ian was going to his death bed knowing he was not crazy. One other positive was despite how sore he was Ian was reminded of how to fall this morning and maybe that would be enough to save him. If not how much more pain could John cause that Marissa hadn't, that was two positives, Ian thought to himself.

Taking a deep breath Ian hoped the smells of lunch preparation would take him away. Instead his senses were greeted by the delicate smells of lilac as Marissa approached.

"I'm sorry about John. He has a soft spot for me," Marissa apologized.

"Never noticed," Ian answered with a shaky voice. "I just wish I knew why I was going to be slaughtered."

Marissa took a seat beside Ian. Looking into his green eyes Marissa broke a silence filled with fear and sadness.

"John's just a little protective of me."

"But why?" Ian pressed.

"I want to tell you, but I can't. This is as much his story as it is mine and… and…" Marissa tried to answer as she welled up in tears.

Ian had been trying to figure out John's story for weeks and now Marissa echoed Rich and Evan. Ian had hit another dead end and managed to upset Marissa.

"I did not mean to upset you. I'm just scared and worried that you will run away while I piece everything together," Ian said as he put his arm around Marissa.

"I'm not going anywhere. Whenever you catch up with your feelings I'll be waiting to give them back ten fold."

Marissa broke their embrace. Smiling at each other, tears that had once been for fear and pain now trickled down in a mix of joy. An understanding had formed between them: Ian had time to figure things out and Marissa wanted this as much as he did.

"Thank you," was all Ian managed in a barely audible whisper before the moment was cut short. They didn't hear the footsteps, they didn't see his anger, and they didn't notice the group of people coming towards them. Before Ian could explain the fight was on.

CHAPTER SIX
Pulling the Right String

Without warning John started the match and luckily for John, Ian knew how to fall. For a few minutes John threw Ian around like a rag doll. People yelled, screamed, and cheered although no one was quite sure what John was doing or what was actually going on.

Quickly the spar turned into a beating and Ian spent more time on the ground, each time getting up slower and slower. Upset with his lack of speed John was getting more aggressive as the bout went on. Throws were quickly turning into punches and kicks; Ian was not going to last long.

"Get up man... Come on..." John yelled at Ian, as he goaded him to get up, trying to pump up the crowd.

The crowd, once rowdy to see the spar, was souring on John as this was turning into a street brawl. Feeling the energy shift John raised his fists and faced Ian.

"If you won't get up then I guess I'll come to you," John announced and was about to go after Ian when Evan and Rich finally stepped in, grabbing him just in time. Ian, who had braced himself on one arm while shielding his face with the other, collapsed onto the ground.

Mike, Michelle, and Marissa went to Ian's side and the sound of the lunch bell cleared the crowd. The match was over.

As the crowd left so did the red in John's eyes. Coming back to his senses John was horrified to see what he had done. He strained against Rich and Evan, not wanting to attack, but to check on Ian.

"I didn't... I'm so sorry." John started as Evan and Rich held him back.

"Calm down man, We... got you...." Evan and Rich said to John as they held him back.

Caught up in the struggle none of the three were listening to each other and none of them had noticed that Marissa had gotten up from Ian's side and was walking towards them.

The crisp autumn air was broken by the crack of Marissa slapping John. The three of them stopped struggling as John's hand rose to soothe his face. Fire burning in Marissa's eyes, anger exuded from a quick wave of her hand that sent Rich and Evan scurrying away.

Huddled around Ian the group of five waited for Marissa to explode and after a few tense moments Marissa gathered herself and in a stern, unwavering voice she began quietly berating and relaying a message to John.

Three minutes later Marissa turned away from John and walked back to Ian. Arriving, Rich and Evan had stood up to apologize when Marissa found Rich and slapped him. No words were exchanged this time but everyone knew that the incident was over. And they all knew it would never happen again.

Lunch while friendly was tense. John spent much of it apologizing and making sure Ian was okay. Marissa brooded and Rich didn't say a word as he ate quickly and then escaped to help scheme for the afternoon events.

Even without John the sparring competition went exactly as expected; the yellow team cleaned up. Sword and other close combat training commenced next. The training itself was uneventful; however, the competition was not. The yellow team lost most of their matches and most of their large lead. Their poor performance meant places in the kickball game would come down to archery.

Unlike the other events about half of each team participated in the archery tournament, giving each team a good chance to make up points and avoid laps. To Ian's surprise archery was not the camps strong suit. As good as everyone was at sparring, sword work, and running, they were awful with the bow. All the teams performed poorly, however, while there were a few decent shots on the green team, they struggled most. Their performance as a whole was abysmal.

John performed better than Ian had expected and put the yellow team in second place. John's performance, while one of the best, was far from perfect and placed Ian in an interesting position: He didn't have to be perfect, but close to perfect for the green team to sneak into the kickball game over the yellow team.

The course started rough for Ian. Getting the feel for his new bow Ian used all his allotted misses on his first few shots. With the groans of his team mates behind him Ian had make every shot matter and, under pressure, that is exactly what he started to do.

Clout and lob shots, hitting turkeys, and hay barrels alike, every shot raised the tension in the air. What started as exasperated disappointment grew into excited whispers and then exploding cheers as Ian executed the course flawlessly. Going into the final shot the green team trailed the yellow team by a single point and if Ian made the final shot his team would win. Normally each shot was worth a single point, but because no one had made this shot, splitting a bamboo wand from 45 yards away, its value had risen to three.

With an orange knock resting on the corner of his mouth Ian lined up the decisive blow. Silence fell over the field and only the low murmur of the workers building the permanent settlement could be heard. Ready to fire, Ian held steady as he waited for the wind to die down.

Ian's wrist went limp, as his bow arm moved forward with the shot. His solid base accepted the force and his bow swung loosely in his grip as Ian admired his shot flying straight and true across the field. Ian smiled and waited for the inevitable crack of the cane.

Thwak

The sound of splitting confirmed what Ian already knew: the green team had won.

"Really?" John muttered in disbelief as the green team began celebrating all around him.

"Impressive shot Ian and considering the reactions I think we all know the scores. Yellow start jogging. Red and green get your lineups set so we can start the game," Jerry's voice barely rose above the euphoric cheering of the winning teams after joining the spectators during Ian's impressive run.

Ian was mobbed as he reached his team. Hands slapped his back as a roar of excitement and jubilation filled the air. Trying to break through this mayhem Rich spoke up.

"Okay, okay. I know we are all happy about Ian's performance, but if you don't calm down you are going to kill him."

"I doubt that. John tried earlier and couldn't manage it," a student, Vernon Lewis, joked.

Laughter erupted as a few more people slapped Ian on the back for good measure.

"All the same let's give him a break. Ian what position would you like to play?" Rich directed the choice to the team hero.

Ian had no idea what to say. He never expected to win, let alone be allowed to pick his spot. Looking at Rich and Evan he saw their smiles, not sure if they had really believed in him this much, even if they had told him that earlier this morning. Now though his teammate's eyes waited excitedly for a response. The few seconds of silence turned into an eternity, broken by a voice no one expected.

"Nice shot. I mean really nice shot."

Ian turned to see John at the edge of the group offering his congratulations. His face full of honesty, respect, and camaraderie. Taking his chance Ian escaped the team huddle to shake John's hand.

"Again man, great shot," John's eyes apologized once more for everything that had happened as they finished their handshake.

"Rich, Evan, do whatever you want with the line up. Just make sure we win. I'll be watching from the track."

The group went quiet and surprised as their hero ran off to join the losing team.

"You heard him. Rich what's the line up? Because I don't want to disappoint Ian." Evan brought the team back to the task at hand, proud of what his friend was doing.

The rushed gait of Ian's footsteps alerted John to Ian's approach. Turning around he saw Ian running up to meet him.

"Thank God you stopped. I would have never caught up," Ian spat out, doubling over to catch his breath as he reached John.

"You know that you won? And that I am about

to run laps with my team?" John said as he stood Ian up and placed his hands on his head for him.

"I know I won and may be a little tired, but I want to come on this little jog with you."

"Fair enough."

And with that Ian and John joined the rest of the yellow team on the track. The autumn breeze cooled them as the sounds of the kickball game filled the air. On the field, there was one main kickball game going on. About half of each team spectated, while others played tag or other games, enjoying the day.

John and Ian talked about many things on the jog, however, they kept a healthy distance from the problems at hand: Marissa, John's story, and Ian's guilt. They simply talked about everything else while forgetting the war ever existed.

At dinner Ian could not help but notice that the tension around camp had finally broken. The competition seemed to mark a shift in camp. Ian's failed jump was now behind them and he hoped that this feeling would carry over to his troubled dreams as fall began.

September quickly gave way to October and by the middle of the month the weather had also started to change. Old man winter was knocking at the door much earlier than anyone had expected and the tents were quickly becoming a little too cold for comfort.

The camp itself was unrecognizable from when they first landed on its shore. The dining hall had been in service for a few weeks, and Jerry and his team were working furiously on a wooden city erupting from the Eastern hillside (facing the lake).

Log cabin dorms and the massive decks connecting them were the main features of the new construction. One building was being built into the mountain and up towards the field, on top of the hill above the dining hall, a few other buildings, possibly a gym and maybe a new school, were far behind the now finished dorms, but were also under construction.

Ian's body also started to change. He had shed excess pounds of fat and replaced it with lean, limber muscle. The workouts had become progressively more bearable although Ian could still not best John or Marissa in a sparring match. And Rich and Evan were still faster than Ian ever hoped to be.

All the activity and distractions never sidetracked Ian from his mission. Every free moment Ian reminded himself of the war that raged on just beyond the beautiful skies. No news came from Earth and, while this was not a surprise, the lack of updates pulled hard on Ian's heart.

Fortunately, or unfortunately, the pace of camp gave Ian little time to focus on his pain. One Mid-October morning brought a huge change to Ian's, and the camps, life

"Has he said anything yet?" John asked as he sat down for breakfast.

"No. Now where did you get that?" Marissa said as she tried to grab something off John's plate.

The previous Friday Jerry had announced that: "An important change was coming Monday." Those six words invigorated the camp with gossip and excitement that had fueled the weekend.

Everyone was fairly certain the announcement was about the dorms. Some people thought it would be about why they were taking so long to complete, others speculated that it would be an announcement about what was hidden inside them.

For weeks the cabins had looked complete which let people's imaginations run wild about what was hidden inside these beautiful mountain side gems. Some people speculated that each cabin contained a hot-tub. Some thought they had water beds. A select few were convinced that Jerry had actually created secret passages inside the dorms connecting them to a hidden base inside the mountain.

Ian and his friends had some wild theories of their own. Evan thought an infestation of termites had postponed the opening. John on the other hand was convinced each one would come equipped with a training room, stocked with weights and other equipment. Michelle and Rich thought that the dorms had been completed for weeks and Jerry was waiting for Ian and Marissa to start dating before he would let them move in.

"Ian, it can't be done. John can't be beat in a foot race. Have you seen the size of his feet?" Rich joked. This joke came when Mikey had a mouthful of eggs that ended up all over the table.

"Come on man," John chuckled as he helped Ian and Marissa clean up. Cleaning the table in the beautiful cabin style hall. "We all know you are the fastest runner."

"Yeah Rich, stop being so smug. The real question is will Ian ever pin Marissa in a sparring match again?" Michelle joked.

"I may let him eventually." Marissa quipped with her mischievous smile.

Light conversation and laughter continued as they enjoyed and finished breakfast. Empty plates waited to be attended to while the group discussed their plans for the day.

Rising from the table Ian was about to clear the dishes when Jerry stood up on a table in the center of the hall. A table built around a large centuries old oak that supported most of the dining halls weight.

"Gather round, gather round," Jerry yelled from his high perch. "Come on everyone gather around close enough so you can hear me."

Jerry's arrival filled the hall with excitement and before long everyone was seated around Jerry, waiting for him to speak.

"First, last night was your final night in the tents. Tonight you will be sleeping in your new cabins."

Echoing off the high ceilings: cheers, high fives and hugs filled the warm space. With the announcement official a low hum of conversation started to rise as speculation about the dorms and roommates infected the crowd.

"Now, now, everyone quiet back down,' Jerry continued. 'There are some things you must know before you can move into your new homes. First there are going to be six to eight people in a cabin. And if you are over eighteen you can room with whomever you want. If you are under eighteen the dorms are not co-ed."

A few groans rose and died as Jerry continued.

"Stop complaining Andrew and David, no girls wanted to room with you anyway,' Jerry joked with the two most vocal groans. 'Even though the dorms are not all co-ed, you will be picking your own roommates and cabins.

"Each cabin has a living room, two bathrooms, a small kitchen, and a sleeping room. They are all nice, but are all different. You can do what you want with the space, but it will be your responsibility to keep it clean and livable. As always your linens and laundry will be done if placed in the proper receptacles now located on each cabin's deck.

"Today, we will be having a friendly competition to decide who will pick their cabins first. So find your new roommates and then we will have a day filled with events to decide who gets first choice. Every room is spectacular so even the final pick will be special. Again do not worry about the cabins. Think about who you want to live with, not who you think will get you first pick."

Students started shuffling and pairing up as the dining hall was engulfed with commotion. Small groups of two and three quickly transformed into families of six or more as students paired up, seemingly heeding Jerry's emphasis and finding people that they wanted to live with.

With everyone scurrying about Marissa, Ian, and their group stayed put knowing that they were already home. Looking back over the room Ian found a few other co-ed groups.

"I guess Mikey and I should go find another group then," Michelle surprisingly broke the friendly conversation with an upsetting thought.

In their group Mikey and Michelle were the youngest at 15 and 16 (their birthdays happening two weeks earlier). John and Evan were the oldest at 20, Ian was 19, almost 20. Rich and Marissa were a young 19 (birthdays in July and August), just at Jerry's cut off point.

"Don't worry about that. I'll talk to Jerry. I'm sure the rule is about maturity and I won't let him send you two away," Marissa confidently consoled the pair.

For some reason they all accepted Marissa's declaration as fact and the disappointment only lingered for a moment before melting back into laughter.

"You know we should probably find Jerry so we can run our little plan about these two by him," John reminded Marissa of her idea after looking around and seeing that most of their classmates had already paired off and were moving towards the field.

"Probably not the worst idea," Marissa agreed.

Splitting up, the group started wandering around the bustling building trying to find their lost leader. As he searched Ian took in the beauty of the hall.

The floors were deep, rich, hardwoods, wrapping their way around magnificent sequoias, which grew through and supported the structure. Along the far wall five stone fireplaces, complete with comfy chairs and couches, stuck out from the mahogany walls. Their morning flames had died as once grand logs were little more than glowing coals.

Each table and chair was a hand carved living canvas that changed a little everyday. Jerry, the workers, and some of Ian's peers used their off time to create, change, and embellish these wooden masterpieces.

The East wall held multiple food bars supplied by the kitchen just behind them. Above high ceilings, exposed beams, and brilliant skylights allowed the forest canopy to incorporate itself into this wonderful space.

After taking in the hall, for the hundredth time, Ian met John and Marissa at the back of the building before leaving together.

Unfortunately, Jerry was no where to be seen on the back deck either so they split up again. Ian walked towards the dorms, John the field, and Marissa stayed put, as a home base, in case anyone showed up.

Wandering to the cafeteria's southeast corner Ian was about to turn the corner when he encountered the hushed whispers of two people in a serious conversation.

"We lost another world.... Jerry... Jerry..." A virgin voice said. The voice stopped Ian in his tracks before he could round the corner.

"Jer-"

"-I heard you, I heard you..." Jerry, boiling over with frustration cut the other man off. "I know that this is the fifth world we have lost since Ian got here. I never expected his arrival to cause this type of ....Aggression.... But we all know he is not ready. Any word from Earth?"

"Cut off and stable," The man brushed off Jerry's question. "Jerry, you can't spend all this time worrying about Ian and Earth. We lost another dozen level three's. We have not sustained these types of losses since the-"

"-I know... I KNOW!!!" Jerry's voice, momentarily not a whisper, sent birds scurrying. "I remember that day quite well Blake. I lost my Godson that day; however, we can cannot lose sight of our end goal Blake. Last time we lost so many level threes was because of our pigheaded-ness. We will not make that mistake again."

"I understand that sir, but we have to be realistic. Without you we have two other level ones, both over eighty. We have a hundred or so level two's, and, with our recent losses we have less than three hundred level threes. That's a quarter of what we had a week ago, and I don't need to tell you that only 50 of them are not on long term assignments. At the rate the war is being fought we only have one option left."

Blake did not say it, but Ian knew Jerry could hear the implication: if you don't act now we are being pigheaded. No answer came from Jerry as the board Ian stood on begged to creak if he moved.

"If you want to give the kids a chance we only have one choice," Blake continued. "They need time. And if it works we can replenish the reserves a little. It starts with one or two, but the school is finished and if the program works we can really start recruiting and training again. In a few years we could be adding hundreds of special jumpers a year... If you want to have that chance then you have to give the command."

"I know, I know... Give the order to...." was all Ian heard a solemn Jerry say before Marissa's appearance broke his concentration.

"Ian you okay? You just stopped, and I was wondering what you saw?"

Turning Ian was happy the board didn't creak as he walked away from the conversation and towards Marissa. For the first time he was frustrated with Marissa's presence.

"Yah... Um... Jerry is busy... we can catch up with him later... let's... uh.. go this way," Ian answered absentmindedly as he ushered her back towards the cafeteria, not wanting to expose their presence.

Retreating into the dining hall Ian found a chair and was quiet as he sorted out the questions in his head.

What order did Jerry give? What happened to all the level threes and who was Jerry's godson? Why were things getting so much worse? And how many worlds were lost? Was he responsible? Why and how is Jerry protecting him? From what?

"You okay? What did you overhear?" Marissa asked the back of Ian's head as she sat down next to him. "Ian if Jerry is there-"

She started to say, getting up to go investigate when a question slipped out of Ian's mouth.

"Who was Jerry's Godson?"

Expecting some answer Ian was surprised with the silence that came. Marissa was stone cold, sad, and shamed as if she had seen a ghost.

"Marissa, are you ok?"

"I.. I..m... UH... I got to go..." Marissa muddled out as she jerked away from Ian's touch.

Before Ian could try again Marissa stood up and bolted out the back doors. Rising up Ian was about to follow her when John stopped him.

"John, I have to go after her," Ian said as he tried to push his way past his John. Trying to figure out where he had even come from.

"What happened?"

"I have no idea John. I just asked her who Jerry's Godson was and then..." Ian stopped short as John interrupted him with a hand on his chest.

Ian tried to push past, but that was fruitless and Ian did not know what to do. John was holding him back and Ian wondered if now was the first time for him to try to take on John.

"John either say something or get out of my way," Ian said after he failed to push past him once again.

"John I said-"

"-Ian hold on. It's time for you to hear my story."

CHAPTER SEVEN
Breakfast Stories

John took a seat across from Ian next to the fireplace. Ian wanted to speak but every time he opened his mouth only flies came out. He had been waiting for this moment for weeks and now that it was here Ian was conflicted.

"Shouldn't... we go ...after Marissa... to make sure she is... ok..." Ian finally broke the silence. John simply raised his hand to stop Ian's mumbling.

Ian felt powerless and trying to regain some control Ian started to speak again.

"But what if she..."

John raised his hand and Ian stopped again. After a minute of silence John gave Ian an answer, his eyes glued to the floor.

"She will be fine. She is probably running laps by now. Trying to run away from the past."

"But what is..." Ian started to inquire, his curious nature getting the better of him, when John raised his hand and brought silence to the room again.

"I know you are full of questions, but now you need to listen. I need your silence so I can tell you what you need to know. With any luck I can take some of the burden off you."

John finally made eye contact with Ian after raising his head from the hole he was staring in the floor. A few minutes later John's gaze shifted past Ian as he spoke softly into a space beyond this room.

"Six years ago I came to this world around the same time as Evan and Rich. Even though I feel for them the jump I made was much worse. The journey almost killed me and sometimes I wish I hadn't jumped. Other times I wish it had killed me.

"I replay that awful experience every day. I can never shake the feeling that I am responsible for everything that went and has gone wrong since..."

John trailed off as his demeanor changed. His body went rigid as he fought tears, fear, anger, and sadness. Ian wanted to comfort his friend, but could only stare. John didn't want to be interrupted now. He did not want pity or condolences.

"The war was a lot different back then. A lot different. I would maybe go as far to say that we were winning. Sure we had lost Evan and Rich's world, but that was a desperation attack it turned out. My home world Kelona, world 35, was dedicated to training non-special jumpers, soldiers, and staff. People from every resistance world were brought to 35 to train. We trained about half of the soldiers who helped defend and protect resistance worlds. Jerry was not the leader of 'the resistance.' He was just a junior officer and one of the head advisors on my world. He was young and ideological. He was an important leader and visionary, but not the head of it all. This young Jerry had a plan though. A plan that would change the war forever."

The room was still as Ian waited for John to continue. Crackling coals gave the room the perfect ambiance for the rest of John's tale.

"To this day the resistance's largest problem is that we are reactionary. To fight in The Dimension you need the right genes. To get new special and non-special jumpers takes a lot of time, effort, and planning. Jerry and a few others were taking steps to solve these problems and thought they had an idea that would change the fight. A plan that would allow us to go on the offensive.

"Jumps between levels 4-3 take a lot of resources to be successful. To have a successful first jump the jumper needs an escort, fake loops, fake jumps, among other things. They were and are, time sensitive, full time jobs that run our special jumpers ragged. If Jerry's plan, his invention, worked we could use non-special jumpers to coordinate these first jumps. We would gain new soldiers while freeing our current ones. If it worked we could send thousands of warriors to recapture a world instead of a few dozen.

"The plan hinged on Jerry's idea that he could set up passageways that went through The Dimension, but were closed to The Dimension's effects."

"I don't get it. Isn't that the same thing that Rich and Evan used?" Ian asked.

"For non-special jumpers and special jumpers once you have made your first jump creating the portal is like walking through a door, but, that first jump or trying to get a non-special jumper to a planet other than their sister world is much messier-"

"-John I still don't under-"

"-When a special jumper jumps, they do it in the safety of The Dimension. It is easy to create a portal inside there. Evan and Rich's jump used an earlier version of this technology that could connect two worlds through The Dimension. This technology required a special jumper and was easy to track. Jerry's idea would create a safe place, a hub of sorts, inside The Dimension. This temporary hub would be harder to track and would allow anyone to connect two worlds. In theory it would allow anyone to transverse The Dimension as easily as you walk through a hallway."

Wanting a moment John looked for clarity in Ian's green eyes.

"I think I get it, Jerry was trying to create a way for the tunnels, the worm hole, he sent Rich and Even through, to function as easily as portals do? He wanted to create a way for anyone to travel to through The Dimension, to any other world, without having to go into The Dimension."

John nodded.

"Exactly. He wanted to give non-special jumpers the ability to go to any world without the need of a special. If it worked the potential uses were endless. It could allow non-special jumpers to escort people on their first jumps. It was theorized that it could be used to create a pocket where non-special jumpers could fight in The Dimension. Hypothetically it could allow people who could not jump to travel between worlds. The possibilities were endless and I think Jerry's hope was this technology would eventually not only give us a leg up to win the war, but could be used to reconnect The Dimension."

Ian thought about what John had said. The idea was to remove The Dimension from the equation. If it worked it would have turned the tide of the war. It would let anyone travel allowing whole armies to be sent from world to world. Regardless of how powerful The Evil was, they could not deal with a mobilized force from all of the resistance planets. Especially if the resistance could bring the fight to them.

"What happened? What went wrong?"

"I was thirteen years old when Jerry hatched his scheme, fifteen when we did it. I had always wanted to be the fastest and strongest soldier in the fleet; however, I am a non-special jumper and knew that I would have limitations. I was Jerry's favorite student, his pet project at the center of his plan, and hoped that this technology would be the stepping stone that would allow me to fight in The Dimension and help win the war.

"After years of training and planning our strategy was set. My first jump would be World 103, my sister world, then, to test the technology, I would immediately jump to World 259, the other training world similar to my home planet. I was to be accompanied by four jumpers of which three were non-special who would join us on 103. Only one jumper, Lorne, was the unlucky special who would stay with me the entire trip." John became choked up as he fought the painful memory.

"Like any other first jump Jerry had planned decoy jumps and false leads. We did everything according to protocol and plan except for one thing. We started early. We jumped early for a variety of reasons, primarily because we thought jumping early would be to our advantage. We knew that the Evil knew about the technology, we knew they probably knew about the jump so we figured going early was best. If the jump went well it would take six seconds. We never thought so much could go wrong in six seconds.

"My first jump, to World 103, went fine. Once we reached 103 all hell broke loose. Out of no-where the skies opened up, and changed from a rosy blue, to a demonic twilight. More gates from The Dimension opened around us and before we knew it we were overtaken as The Evil flooded in. Above us, Dragons and darts rained down as Skeletal horseman and other unspeakable hor-rors came thorough the other portals. The day I jumped the gates of hell opened on world 103."

Ian could not imagine the scene that John was describing to him. Ian had thought that his first jump was bad, that Evan and Rich's were bad, but they were nothing compared to what John was describing.

"We had been set up and The Evil was coming with an invasion force. Lorne thought fast and activated Jerry's technology, which opened a portal behind us. There was not enough time for him to set up a portal to another planet, so he used Jerry's tech, and improvised a safe space inside The Dimension that he hoped we could hide in. For all my bravado and courage when it all happened I was a frozen teenage boy hoping not to die."

John stopped and took a deep breath. His eyes were somewhere else as he relieved the experience.

"Dying is an odd feeling Ian. I later found out that I was dying as The Evil broke down the protective bubble of Jerry's tech and The Dimension flooded in. I felt like I was drowning. I lost all my strength. I could not move my arm or legs, let alone breathe. I was losing consciousness and thinking about how Jerry's plan had failed. How it was all my fault that it failed. Then I felt a slight push and it all went black. After all of that I woke up in the infirmary of the old school building as if nothing had happened."

Ian sat silently hardly able to believe John's story; unfortunately he did not answer the question on the tip of Ian's tongue.

"I'm...sorry, but I don't understand. What does Marissa have to do with all this?"" Ian asked as he met John's eyes, full of anger, pain, and regret.

"Lorne was Lorne Laurenson, Marissa's brother. Another reason we left early was because he wanted to surprise her for her birthday."

John finally lost his composure as his face flooded with tears. Ian wanted to comfort him but was still struggling with what John just told him: Lorne was Marissa's brother and she lost him because he saved John.

Footsteps echoed through the hall behind Ian. Jerry was walking towards them. Solemn and sad Ian wondered if he was angry or upset about what John had just told him.

"It's okay John. It is not your fault," Jerry patted John on the back. "Why don't you get some fresh air or something to eat? Considering you heard the rest of this story second hand I think it is better I finish it for you."

Defeated and drained John gave a slight nod as he rose from his seat and walked away. Watching his friend slink away Ian was surprised when Jerry picked up the story where John left off.

"Unfortunately for us the attack was just the beginning of an awful couple days. That first day

I lost my wife Serena, along with many friends. In the end we lost three worlds. Even after the attacks I thought there was still hope for a counter strike and, unfortunately, so did everyone else.

"John was right, the loss of Rich and Evan's world did place stress on my mission; however, I never let that guide me. Unfortunately, some people used that logic against me, saying I waited too long, that I did not understand urgency and because of that I was banished from the rescue efforts and attacks. I was told that they wanted to give me space after my failed plan cost my wife and Godson their lives, so I was sent here to comfort Marissa and to grieve. The banishment is the only thing that spared my life.

"Lorne's quick thinking did two things for us Ian. First it saved John. Second, unfortunately, it proved that the tech worked.

"The bubble didn't fail because of outside force, but because The Evil was flooding it from its connections to all three planets. Lorne saw what was happening and used what he saw to open a portal to Esmerelda and save John. If the tech hadn't worked we probably would only have lost a single planet that day, but The UL used it to open all those planets to The Dimension."

"Jerry, if that was the case how was this bubble safer?"

"Ian, when we set up a wormhole between the planets we essentially send up fireworks inside The Dimension. Connecting two planets directly can be seen by everyone and lets us know what planet is open to attack. The technology gave us a safe space inside The Dimension anyone could jump from. The Dimension is vast and while the bubble could be found, it was the difference between finding the glow of a single coal in a dark forest compared to the light of a flare gun. We could safely set up passages that went from a world, to The Dimension, and to another world without being seen.

"Once we knew the technology worked we wanted to get our planets back and the attack was meant to go in two phases. The first phase was a scout mission, the second an all out assault. All of the special jumpers that we could afford were gathered, along with any non-special who could jump to the three worlds. In our haste we were sloppy and did not cover our trails. The plan was not one of skill and strategy but of passion and brute force. After losing two worlds earlier that year we were not about to lose three more. In our haste all the resistance leaders were on the same world to strategize and oversee. When stage one started and all was lost."

"What happened?"

"That day we remembered why our ancestors had respected *"The Evil"*. They let our scout teams succeed because they knew a bigger prize awaited them. The Evil knew where our leaders were, they knew how to track our jumps, and they knew our plan.

"Once the second phase began half of our leaders were supposed to come here and the others were supposed to lead the attack. It was a risk, we understood that, but it was supposed to turn the war in our favor. They used my tech to open portals, however, when the second phase started the ambush came. Anyone who jumped that day was killed. We learned the hard way, by losing all our level one and two jumpers, that The Evil had greater numbers than we ever anticipated. All were lost. but me..."

Ian's worst nightmare about this war never amounted to this. They lost five worlds and all of their leadership in a series of missteps and unfortunate events.

Sitting across from Jerry Ian saw a man whose plan to save the war almost destroyed the entire resistance he fought for. Jerry survived to see the mess he made and it was clear to Ian that Jerry would give anything to have sacrificed himself.

"How did they get overwhelmed like that?" Ian asked Jerry.

"We had become complacent and grossly underestimated The Evil's power. They knew how to track us, our communications, and kept that a secret until that day. They let us sabotage ourselves. The tech would have changed the tide of the war, but The Evil knew how to monitor it; they had infiltrated us, and until that day, we thought that, like ours, their major fighting forces were limited to a few worlds. We thought we were the same. Even after they had invaded five worlds in less than a year we thought that we were the same. We lost two more worlds and all of our leadership due to our pigheaded ignorance. We know better now, and, while we cannot confirm, we suspect that The Evil have discovered a way to alter people so they can survive inside The Dimension. We think that they have a way to turn an entire planet's population into soldiers that they can deploy in large waves. We have no idea how they do it, but it is the only thing that makes sense."

"Jerry why have you been protecting me and my planet? What order did you have to give?" Ian asked, wanting to understand why Jerry sacrificed so much to save him. After hearing about so much loss why was Jerry spending the scant resources of the resistance on him.

"Ian you are not ready to hear the information you seek. I thought you may have overheard something, but you must know that the information you seek is closely guarded. What you are asking about deals with our deepest understanding of jumping and The Dimension. If you must know something know that while we have sustained losses they will only be in vain if you let this curiosity distract you."

"But, three worlds? Half of our level threes?" Ian pleaded not wanting to be such a priority.

"Yes Ian that happened, but there are losses in war. While you may not think it now, you can make it up to everyone if you train your hardest and become a power for the resistance.

"Ian every sacrifice has a reward. Every failure, a silver lining if you learn form it," Jerry continued seeing doubt in Ian's eyes. "The technology I created, while not perfect made jumping much safer and easier. We cannot create them instantaneously or transport jumpers in large numbers, like The Evil can, yet, but we can get jumpers, non-special and special alike, between worlds much quicker and safer. That day has made fighting the war safer. We learned how to secure planets faster from those tragedies all but stopping invasions. It's not perfect, but those losses were not in vain. We have gone to extreme measures to keep the stalemate alive. Our measures are not ideal, but they will save lives and worlds."

Ian was about to respond when Jerry pushed on after a small breath.

"I need you to follow me. When I tell you that your family and world are very safe, that we are safe, I need you to believe me. I know that you are doing all you can but you need to train harder and to stay focused. What happened six years ago is already a burden on too many people and I cannot allow it to corrupt you or your training. Ian remember that six years ago a horrible thing happened, but it wasn't all bad. The Evil thought the war was going to end that day. The UL put all their resources into that and while it did hurt, it did not finish us and we have been growing and getting stronger ever since."

"Is there anything I can do to help Marissa?" Ian asked feeling selfish and wanting to help.

"Be there for her. I have known her for a long time and you are one of the best things to happen in her life," Jerry answered with a sad smile.

"Can Mikey and Michelle stay with us in our new cabin?" Ian asked the next logical thing that came to his mind.

"Of course they can. We planned on you seven being together and have a cabin built just for you," Jerry blurted out. His smile becoming more genuine as the conversation drew away from the war.

Waiting patiently for Ian's next question Jerry was actually starting to look excited, however Ian knew he had to tread lightly. His next question was on the line, but was probably one thing that bothered him more than anything else.

"Jerry, why are there so few jumpers my age? Are most of the jumpers already in the war?"

Any of Jerry's joy was washed away by Ian's question. Taking a second to gather himself, Jerry took a deep breath before answering.

"We have been rash. Many people joined the war before they were ready and that is why most of your classmates are so young," Jerry answered him the smile completely gone as a single tear flowed down his face. "Ian, please excuse me, but I think we should stop here for today. It has been a long morning and we all need time to digest and decompress. Go to your new dorm, I will have your lunch delivered there for you."

"-Jerry..." Ian tried to get Jerry to stay but Jerry did not stop. He simply rose and walked away. Alone in the hall, his mind a jumble of white noise, Ian tried to gather himself. Focusing on a smoldering log spitting its final flames Ian could not help but think about the resistance, like the flame, struggling to stay alive and striving to burn bright again.

CHAPTER EIGHT
Lost Love

A newly opened wooden bridge connected the dorms to the rest of camp. The settlement's eastern slope was now littered with a complex of buildings, walkways, and decks weaving themselves through the lush forest in a natural way. Lights, benches, and other amenities lined the spacious walkways welcoming people to their new homes.

As a whole the complex respected nature and used the trees and plants in their design. Taking advantage of their natural utility some plants provided shade and wondrous fragrances, others anchored structures or created a protective barrier to help stop erosion.

Raised from the damp forest floor the decks, dorms, and walkways would allow rain and snow to wash away into the lake and river. Even with the modern amenities, and incredible engineering, the forest was still the shining star in the newly erected city.

Taking a moment Ian looked around to see how the rest of camp was changing. The hill's north face was full of activity. Workers were busy disassembling the tents that had housed the camp until today, a few others were busy marking out the new construction that would be taking place there.

Opposite that, the southern face was filled with the sounds of construction. Behind the cafeteria new buildings, a gym, and other structures were well underway. Some next to the field they all called home. In all the change the lake was unique and unmoving. The thing that flowed and transformed everyday was the only thing that looked the same.

What difference can I really make? Jerry thinks that I can be special, but what am I? How can I make things better after everything that has gone wrong? Ian tried to escape his lonely thoughts as he wandered down the newly opened decks.

Before long Ian was in the middle of the complex's central, and largest, deck. The new deck, like everything else, was magnificent. Hand carved benches decorated it and lanterns hung delicately from the trees that anchored it. At the center of the deck, the center of the entire complex, was a fountain built around a centuries old sequoia.

Walking towards the fountain, the wooden deck gave way to short steps that led to a soft mossy field. Ian approached the magnificent fountain and found it was even more incredible than he thought.

The soft moss led to a short marble wall. Stepping over the wall Ian's feet fell into a shallow pool. A foot away a taller marble wall had water cascading over it, separating this shallow pool from the rest of the fountain. Around the tree marble pillars supported a golden halo that enveloped the tree itself. Water fell from the halo, cascading around the pillars and tree into the base of the pool.

Below the halo the tree had been delicately carved with pictograms. Dabs of paint brought the intricate stories to life enchanting Ian with an experience he could not pull himself away from. The fountain was truly a work of art, unlike anything he had ever seen.

"Ian is that you?" Laura yelled, emerging from a stone building that protruded from the mountain itself.

"Jerry told me he had a room picked out for us already. I was trying to find it when I got distracted." Ian responded, walking towards Laura and stepping out of the fountain.

"That makes sense. Jerry would never want to separate your little gang,' Laura commented as she approached. 'I think I know where your cabin is if you need help finding it."

"Really? Jerry told you where he was placing us?"

"Not exactly," Laura chuckled. "But there is one dorm Jerry asked us to have ready before the competition today. Considering you are not competing I think it is a safe to say that is yours."

"Is it far?"

Ian could not read Laura at all. She looked like she wanted to answer, but instead finally burst out laughing, no longer able to hold herself together.

"What's so funny?"

Laura continued to laugh unable to stop herself.

"Honestly Laura, what are you laughing at?" An irritated Ian demanded. Growing more frustrated as giggles turned into a hardy belly laugh.

"I'm not in the mood."

"If you turn around you'll find your welcoming party."

Following Laura's eyes Ian turned around to see Marissa, John, and Evan standing on the walkway above him. Marissa was waving to him while Evan and John appeared to be having a grand time of horsing and joking around at Ian's oblivious nature.

Eyes glued on his friends Ian waved back, leaned towards Laura, and whispered to her through gritted teeth. "How long have they been up there?"

"Since before I came out here," Laura answered.

"They have really been up there the entire time?" Ian asked, his voice much louder than he had intended.

"Yeah really," Rich grinned as he approached Ian from behind. "We thought that you had disappeared so Michelle, Mikey, and I were on a search and rescue mission," Rich joked as he patted Ian on the back.

"You really should come on up," John shouted down to Ian.

"Why is that?"

"Because there's a package waiting on your bed that says: '*From Earth*'," Marissa's mischievous smile excitedly answered for John.

Abandoning all other pursuits Ian bolted across the deck, up the stairs, and into the cabin. Ian flew through the cabin's common area and into the bedroom without taking time to bask in the craftsmanship and beauty of his new home. The bedroom had seven beds, all of which could be separated by a screen that pulled out from the wall. The beds frames were a rich cherry wood with lush linens on top of what were certainly some of the most comfortable beds in The Dimension. Ian did not see any of this and only saw a small package sitting on one of the beds.

Rushing to his bed Ian picked up the package as he jumped into the delicate linens. The package was plain, held his name, and the word Earth written upon it. Ending the suspense, Ian ripped it open.

Inside Ian was greeted by a familiar picture of himself: Ian as a toddler held by his father at the beach. He immediately welled up with tears. It was a scrap book that his mom had created for him years ago before he left for college.

Ian's eyes continued to water as he turned the pages and saw his life and family grow up before him. Baseball games and birthday parties. Concerts and Christmas. Family and friends were all right in front of Ian for the first time in months and approaching the final page Ian was hesitant to turn it. After months of silence Ian did not want this to end.

After a minute or so, and with a heavy heart,

Ian turned to what had been the last page to see three envelopes duct taped into the back cover. Ian laughed, there was no mistaking his father's handy work.

Opening the first envelope Ian was bathed in pictures that filled the gap where his mom had left off years ago. Some were of collegiate life; others were just a few weeks old of family and friends. Each picture was a bitter sweet reminder of what he missed from his life back on Earth.

Alone in his own world as Ian did not see his new friends watching him, not knowing whether to join their friend or let him experience this alone. After a minute or so everyone left except Marissa. Alone with Ian, Marissa wanted to share this beautiful moment with him, however, after what happened that morning she did not know how.

Opening the second envelope three papers fell out. Unfolding the first Ian found a typed letter from his brother. His brother had become engaged, because of Ian's disappearance, and wanted to tell him how much he missed him. Despite the happy tone, Ian could hear his brother speaking to him. Even in separate worlds his brother could still tell him what to do better, while being supportive, and telling him he loved him.

The second note greeted Ian with the blotched lettering of his father's scribble. A mixture of tears and his dad's penmanship almost made the message indecipherable.

Ian made it through the letter though and learned of the latest baseball games and some family events he had missed. His dad was trying to act as if everything was normal and okay even though he knew they were not. Putting down the letter Ian knew all his dad wanted was for him to get home to watch another game.

Ian took a minute to gather himself as Marissa watched. She had moved from the door to her own bed still waiting to make her first move.

Expecting a letter from his mother Ian was surprised to see that the last letter housed the penmanship of many authors. Messages from friends, teachers, and family dotted the letter, passing along well wishes and messages of hope. Like a birthday card, the messages length varied based on how well they knew him and how much they were told. Ian's best friend took up the latter half of the page, while other friends were a simple sentence or two.

After reading the last card Ian felt surprisingly hollow. After months of waiting he was finally getting the messages he craved and he was realizing how right Jerry was. These messages, while nice, did not bring him closer to home. He felt happy that his friends missed him, that they loved him, and that they were safe, but it didn't change anything about what had happened or what was going on. In the end Ian was still alone.

Picking up the final envelope Ian delicately opened the last duct tapped envelope Ian found two letters inside.

Ian,

> *I don't know what to write or even what to say. I miss you greatly, and life around here has not been the same. You never call any-more and whenever the phone rings I an-swer it expecting to hear your voice. Every time I'm disappointed and deceived. The only saving grace I have is that I have been told you are safe and being well cared for. Ever since the day you disappeared we all have been lost and miss you. We are all doing well and I don't want you to worry about us. Take care of yourself and come back safe. (Really we are fine your new friends know how to send help and protec-tion. It is like we have our own secret service detail!)*

> *R2 really misses you, like all of us, and I*

swear she wanders the house trying to find a way to get to you. I have talked to the rest of the family and told them the "cover" story, but everyone misses you and wants you to stay safe. The garden has been doing well and my thesis is in progress. We really are getting some good stuff done.

Ian... I know I'm rambling, but I want to let you know that I love you more than anything and only want to see you come home safe and sound. Please stay safe.... and come home.

Love,

Mom

Any tears that had stopped started again as Ian reread the letter. Ian knew she had slaved over this single page for hours and wished he could reach out and let her know that he was okay. Ian could not fathom how much harder it had been for her to write this letter than any paper or book she ever had.

Seeing Ian pause again Marissa decided to make her move. She wanted to help comfort him, to share his pain. Rising from the bed Marissa moved to join Ian; however, stopped short when Ian become rigid. Bracing himself, as he produced one final letter.

Ian, Blankow...

I hope you are well and miss you so much. I just want you back, but understand. Please stay safe and come home soon. I miss cooking with you, and walks, and cuddling, and everything about you. Everyone at school says hello, and I just want you to come home. I'm safe and you need to stay safe.

Hugs and kisses and cuddles love,

Tiny

The short letter was dotted with tears and as Ian read it only became worse. After reading it a few times Ian missed Nicole more than he had in months. This letter reminded him of how little he had gotten over her and wondered how far she had retreated into herself. Ian hoped that she had not shut herself off from the world and was as confused as ever about what they were.

"You still love her," Marissa commented. Placing her arm around him as she sat down next to him. She wanted to bring him back to reality before he became lost in sorrow.

Ian looked up at Marissa and nodded. Unable to speak, it was the only thing he could manage.

"She must be really special if your love can survive this. Even with the distance between you..." Marissa trailed off.

She was frustrated at herself. Ian needed support right now and all she could give him was disappointment. Marissa was being selfish, her only thoughts circling around how Nicole was interfering with their relationship.

"I still love her, Marissa," Ian answered her silent question. "These tears are not all related her. These letters may be the last communication I ever have with my life on Earth and for the most part I feel empty. I wanted this to be a conversation and hate to see them suffer," Ian said his green eyes glistening.

"I know it sucks, but you will see all of them again. You will find Nicole again and can grow old together after this is all over," Marissa smiled a sad smile as she felt herself start to lose something she wasn't sure she ever had. Trying to be the caring friend Ian needed right now.

"What about you?" Ian asked seriously. "You are as much a part of my family now. If I leave here I will be in the same position all over again. Do you really think I'm going to abandon you? John? Rich? Evan? Michelle, Mikey? What are the actual chances of me getting back there? And do I really want all of them to wait for me? Isn't it better for them to move on. Isn't it time for me to move on?"

Ian's words hit Marissa hard. He was lost. After months of waiting and wanting, Ian was lost as he tried to find meaning in the letters for everything he was going through. Every word made Marissa feel a little worse and she could hardly imagine the battle inside him right now. Even if she felt awful about it there was a silver lining, even if he couldn't say it Ian loved her too and if she were patient they could be more than friends.

"What is it?" Marissa asked Ian whose eyes changed as he flipped over the box everything had come in.

"The letters are a month old," Ian said pointing to the dates. "I hope they are all still okay-"

"-Ian, they are fine. It takes time to get packages

through The Dimension during the good times, right now, well let's just say, it's a lot harder," Marissa interjected to comfort Ian. "If anything, time should have helped everyone adjust and move on. They are probably doing better now then when they wrote them. Who are all of these people?"

Marissa tried to distract Ian and had opened the scrap book to a page filled with pictures of Ian and his cousins. Following her eyes Ian settled on a picture from one of his cousin's weddings.

"Those are my cousins on my dad's side. That's..." Ian started to explain the picture.

Ian and Marissa shifted to and took refuge on the room's oak floors for the rest of the afternoon. Flipping through the scrap book, sharing stories from their lives, Ian and Marissa worked through their pain together. Both of them hoping for a brighter tomorrow. One where the UL did not rip apart everything they loved.

CHAPTER NINE
A New Class of War

"What's wrong with you two? Can't you lay off Mikey just for a minute?" Marissa asked Evan and Rich as she, John, and Ian joined the dinner table. Half-wondering why Mikey and Michelle were so red. Half-wondering what Evan and Rich had done.

"We could, but you were not there today when little Mikey grew up," Rich said as he ruffled Mikey's hair.

"What happened?" Ian asked while starting to chop his grilled eggplant.

"Well, our little man, Mikey, inadvertently asked Michelle out today," Evan ribbed Mikey right before he cut into his steak.

Marissa's eyes darted between Mikey and Michelle. Her mouth opened and closed a few times as she searched for the right words before mumbling out "Really... and... Well," digging for more details with unbridled excitement.

"Today while you were enjoying your afternoon the rest of us decided to go up the field to enjoy the festivities," Michelle started to answer. "In-between one of the competitions Mary and her friends approached me about joining their room. They had one spot left and wanted to room near a group of boys they liked. We were joking around when Henry approached me and asked whether I was going to join their room so I could be closer to him. I was stunned, I mean he is kinda cute, but I didn't know what to do-"

"-Be honest Michelle," Rich interrupted. "You were not shocked, but you needed a reason to turn his and Mary's offer down."

Michelle went beet red as Evan, John, and Rich all started to laugh.

"As pleasant as Henry is we all knew whom I had been waiting for, but put on the spot I…. Uh…" Michelle trailed off.

"You didn't!" Marissa blurted out.

"She didn't know what to do," Evan continued the story for Michelle. "And that is when our little Mikey boy stepped up. Mikey heard what Henry asked her, walked up to him, and told him that: *'Michelle was his girlfriend, if he knew what was good for him he would back off.'* Our little guy even tried to look intimidating," Evan puffed out his chest with an imitation of Mikey.

"It wasn't until after Henry walked away that what Mikey said registered on both of them and they have been this like this ever since," Rich finished the little tale.

Ian and Marissa's gazes darted between Mikey and Michelle for some type of confirmation. Everyone in camp knew they had a crush on each other; however, no one was ever sure they would make that first step. Ian was certain there were bets between John, Rich, and Evan about which couple would start first and was sure Mikey had made someone a nice little profit.

Mikey and Michelle managed a slight nod through their embarrassment. A nod that broke the silence at the table with a round of applause and laugher.

The rest of the dinner passed with small talk and light banter. No one pushed Ian or Marissa on today's events and instead enjoyed dinner. When they had finished and were ready to head back to their new dorm Jerry climbed on top of a table for the second time today.

"Everyone gather round, gather round," Jerry addressed the crowd at large "Your plates can wait, come on please gather round and indulge me one more time today. I guarantee you will want to hear what I have to say."

A general murmur of discontent told Jerry that the students did not want to indulge him again. They were ready to pick and explore their new rooms.

"You know he really should get a podium, it is not sanitary," Rich joked as their little group joined the rest of the students around the table Jerry had chosen.

"First, most importantly we have the scores tabulated and my assistants will let you know who will gets to pick first. Tonight, the decks will be lit up in a way you have not seen and all of you will be able to explore and pick your new rooms, before creating a ruckus."

The room still did not die down and was not very excited at the news.

"If you quiet down I will personally arrange that you have all the drinks and snacks you could need to keep you going through the night," Jerry offered.

Jerry's last offer captured the students attention. Anyone who had been hesitant to listen now looked up giving Jerry their undivided attention.

"We are moving into a new phase of construction and teaching. Behind this building we have started constructing the gym and tomorrow will start on the staff's living corridors on the valley's north face, where your tents were. The gym will be a multi-story facility complete with courts for sports from all over The Dimension. Beyond the fields, weight rooms, and pools there will also be a large community room, lounges, and a food bar. This new facility will be open 24/7 and should open in early January. However, because winter is almost upon us, full time training will be coming off the fields and back into the classroom."

Jerry's announcement turned into groans as he announced the start of classes.

"Classes will be based on your jump level and educational development. An individual class list will be delivered to your cabin; however, because we have had to change a few things it will take some time to get those lists together. So this week stay up as late as you wish because your new schedule will start next wee..."

Pandemonium erupted before Jerry could finish giving the camp a week off.

Like the field day, seeing this pure joy from his peers gave Ian a glimpse of what the school was like before his arrival. This place had not been all about war and training. This place was a home, where people lived, grew up, and learned

143

together. A place where people fought, loved, dated, broke up, and spent time enjoying the growth that made life worth living.

This unbridled joy soured in Ian's mind as he glanced back at Jerry. He was not smiling, but instead he was struggling to accept the glee in front of him. No matter what Jerry said Ian knew that he held the secrets of the war and what really was going on. Ian wondered if Jerry and his staff really needed a week to get the classes together, or if it was his idea of a gift to the camp. Jerry was holding back something and looking at his group of seven he saw them wondering the same thing.

...

Morning rose on a sleeping camp. This was not a surprise considering most of the camp partied late into the night and now were resting for round two. Ian's cabin was plagued by a sleepless night after they found a note on their cabin door: Meet Jerry at 6:45 a.m.

"What do you think he wants?" John asked as the group prepared to meet Jerry.

"I think we all know what he wants. He wants to start our training," Rich chimed in taking a mug of koffela (a rich drink that was like a mix between hot chocolate and espresso from John's home world) from John.

"We all know that there is something special about our group, but what do you think it is?" Ian asked wondering if anyone else already knew.

"I'm not sure Ian why don't you tell us?" Rich responded. "I mean we all know something happened with you three yesterday."

Raised eyebrows greeted John, Marissa, and Ian as they quickly exchanged a glance not knowing how to answer. Ian did not like keeping his friends in the dark, but he did not want to give them a half story. Sinking into his chair, he took a sip of koffela when John spoke up.

"Rich, you know my story, so you know what we know. Lay off. We have to trust each other. You know that is the only way we can get through this."

"That was all. I'm so sorry." Rich apologized before taking another sip.

"Remember the plan: united we ask and get answers," John added reminding his friends of the plan they came up with the night before. Together they were going to ask Jerry questions. He could not avoid their entire group.

They left their cabin at 6:30 unsure where they were supposed to go. Shielding their eyes from the bright sunlight poking through the canopy it took a minute for their eyes to adjust. Once they did they found Jerry wanting at the the grand fountain for them. Coming down the stairs, they watched Jerry who had not moved or acknowledged their approach. Once the seven of them were at the fountain Jerry spun and started his lecture.

"The fountain behind me reminds us why we fight. On it there are stories from every world connected to The Dimension. From fairy tales, to epics, and biographies they stand here as an ever-present reminder of what the war is really taking from us. Some of the images here are the last remnants of places and cultures lost to this war and in that way this fountain is more than a simple decoration, but a monument, a reminder, to those we have lost."

Joyful, chirping birds fluttered in the dew filled air as the group looked over the fountain. Jerry had turned the halo off allowing them to examine each of the small pictograms covering the tree without getting wet. Each picture had a number underneath it representing the world it came from and the culture that might have been lost.

"This fountain is incomplete and does not hold a single image from World One or the war they have thrust upon The Dimension. We have no way of representing our recent struggles in pictures because the memories are too fresh. The pain, too deep."

Silence fell as Jerry gave them a second to reflect on the war and what it had done to each of them. This war had torn their families apart, destroyed lives, and brought many civilizations to the brink of destruction. Everyone let out a few tears as they remembered the circumstances that brought them before this beautiful fountain today. A fountain that ironically resembled an angel rising up from the gates of hell in the morning sunlight.

"As you examine the fountain remember that it demonstrates our greatest weapon in this war. Can any of you think of it?" Jerry posed a question to the group for the first time.

The group, once united and determined to get answers from Jerry, were mute when asked to speak. Each of them were touching and looking at a different part of the sculpture. Jerry let a song bird finish his song before answering for his students.

"Knowledge. Knowledge is our only way to overcome The Evil, The UL. They are more advanced and more powerful than us, so the only way we can beat them is by learning more. Ingenuity is also our friend, and we must use the resources we have to devise plans that they never would have envisioned. However, knowledge is better than any other weapon. It is how The Evil has done so well. They are not winning because of their weapons or their numbers, but because they know how to utilize their superior knowledge. If we are going to win this war it will be through uncovering The Evil's secrets and discovering things they don't know."

Jerry's bluntness surprised them. They knew that the UL was powerful, but none of them had ever heard Jerry admit to it like this. Standing there, in front of him, they did not know what to say and waited for Jerry to continue.

"Despite all of this we can still win because The Evil fights for the wrong reasons. They fight for power from a misguided belief about what they lost. We fight to preserve diversity and culture. We fight to save everything that The Dimension stood for before it fell into disrepair. If you ever feel down, unmotivated, or frustrated with your studies remember that this fountain, your families, are why we fight."

Without missing a beat Jerry and the group walked to the large double doors sticking out of the mountain side. A sea of white engulfed them as Jerry opened the doors. The walls, floors, and ceilings, were all made of white marble.

Not stopping for his stunned students Jerry walked down the corridor, passing every classroom, hallway, and office on his way to large marble double doors on the other end of the long hallway. Unlike the rest of the doors, which were wood, these massive doors blended in with the surrounding white. Struggling to keep up the group finally caught up with Jerry as he opened the doors.

Behind the doors the group found themselves in a large, circular room. A dome ceiling hung over twenty feet tall and three sets of doors decorated the remaining cardinal directions. Walking into the hall Jerry stopped at its center before addressing the group.

"This is the inner chamber of our school and is one of the most secure places within the entire Dimension. In time you will learn why, but for now all you need to know is this place is only for people directly training or fighting in the war."

Like usual Jerry's speech gave them more questions than answers, but before they could ask any of them Jerry continued.

"To your right on the South Wall is your classroom, behind me is the library, and finally on my right, against the Northern Wall, is the heart beat of our resistance effort. That area is off limits and requires additional clearance to enter. Please do not waste your time trying to get in."

Jerry paused letting the group catch up mentally

as they took in their new space. Behind Jerry a small group of plush couches and tables stood on top of an intricate, vibrant rug, which looked like two dragons intertwining on a red and green background. Wood and velvet chairs stood next to each door. These sparse decorations were the only things that were not marble in this grand room.

"Let's go to the library," Jerry said, just as the group was getting comfortable and before anyone could ask a single question.

Walking across the second half of the hall, Ian and his friends approached a set of black marble double doors, with ivory handles, opposite of the ones they entered through.

"You are the only students with access to this area, and I want you to keep what happens back here between yourselves," Jerry said after turning to address the group before entering the library. "Your cabin has a special entrance behind the fireplace that leads to your classroom and this inner chamber. All of the doors in this chamber are locked at all times; however, your watches will automatically unlock this door (the library), your classroom, and the passage to your cabin. Because of the delicate nature of this space, I once again implore you to keep them secret and treat them with care. In time more students will gain access to this space. For now you seven will be the only students in this space."

Jerry's last statement settled uneasily upon the group. They were not only being separated from their peers, Jerry was asking them to deceive their peers. That would not be easy.

"Yes, Mikey what is it?" Jerry addressed Mikey's raised hand.

"Jerry, why are we so segregated? I thought everyone was being trained to fight? Shouldn't we all have access to the same things?"

"Mikey, everyone on this world is important to this war, but right now my answer is no more than that."

The group groaned at Jerry's lack of a response. Knowing he would not get anywhere with this hanging over their heads Jerry spoke up again trying to appease his student's fears.

"Everyone is learning how to fight and survive; however, the rest of your peers are not in your shoes. Different situations have thrust each of you into the war in a way that cannot be helped. This is why your training is more direct. I understand your curiosity. I understand why you all are curious about Micky and Michelle being with your group, especially considering their age. I understand you trying to figure out why you are all special, but all that you need to know is that everyone is right where they need to be. A lot is riding on the seven of you and you need to stay focused on the tasks at hand."

Turning on a dime Jerry opened the magnificent doors before anyone could ask another question.

The open doors exposed them to a bright room that was a masterpiece in architecture and beauty. Oak couches and chairs were covered with delicate silk cushions. The floor was a mixture of red, gold, and white marble, covered with exquisite rugs from a variety of worlds. Past the couches, behind a white half wall, rows of bookcases stretched as far as the eye could see.

Taking it in the group waited patiently for Jerry to invite them in. Jerry smiled before giving them a slight nod, which sent them all off in different directions.

Mikey and Rich ran to the couches and grabbed a tablet off the oak coffee table in front of them. John, Evan, and Michelle bypassed the tables and went straight for the rows of books and priceless tomes. Marissa and Ian walked around the library's edges investigating the elaborate tapestries lining the walls.

"You guys must come back here," Evan yelled from the back of the library.

The other six quickly ran to the back of the room

and found, at the end of the bookshelves, a wall, half marble and half glass, dividing the library from what appeared to be a state of the art lab.

"I see you have found the lab Evan. Use caution, but this lab is open for your use and studies," Jerry said after following Ian and his friends to the back of the room.

"The tablets John and Rich found earlier, along with every other tablet and computer in this inner chamber have access to a digital copy of every text in here. If you want to find the original your watch can guide you right to the text's shelf."

"Do not get too comfortable my friends. We have another stop before you are truly free down here," Jerry tried to motivate his students.

After a half an hour of exploring the vast library, the group had reassembled in the library's lounge flipping through some of the things they found.

Mikey and Michelle put down books, Evan and John tablets. Rich was reading a comic book and Marissa and Ian set down two scrolls.

Following Jerry out of the library the group walked towards the South Wall's identical double doors and, without stopping, Jerry opened them and led the group into a much smaller, marble lined, room.

The room's front wall was blank where a projector could easily display an image or lesson. A podium, loaded with a computer, sat in front of this wall. A digital projector hung from the ceiling above them.

Three couches, one against the far wall, one facing the first, and the final was perpendicular to the two and dividing the room. A few end tables and a coffee table finished off the front part of the room.

The back of the room was mostly empty. On the back wall a singular door was flanked on either side with a counter area. Cabinets stocked with food and drinks were above and below the counter.

"Please get comfortable so we can speak," Jerry invited them into the new space.

Entering the room Ian and his friends got comfortable. Ian sat on the marble floor, his back against the leather couch that Marissa had claimed. Mikey and Michelle claimed the couch opposite them, closest to the door, and John, Rich, and Evan sprawled out on the remaining couch that divided the room.

"Now that you are comfortable I will give you a quick tour. In the back we have a counter area with food and drinks. The door opens to a staircase and your room,' Jerry said pointing everything out from where he stood at the front of the room. 'The phone in the back of the room is tied directly to the our complexes communication grid. If you need anything, medical attention, food, anything dial extension 770 and help will be on the way. Behind me, we have a projector for lessons and other events. Any questions?"

The group answered Jerry with silence. It was not that they were ungrateful, but the group felt uneasy about all the amenities they were being offered to stay down here and study.

"For tomorrow, I want all of you to pick a world you are unfamiliar with and research a battle strategy used there. Be ready to present it in any way you wish and feel free to move the tablets, books, and other material between the rooms down here. Beyond that every day, including weekends, you must get outside and exercise for a few hours. Go for a walk, run, play football, or shoot archery. I do not care what you do but do something that will take you outside of these halls. You need to stay in shape and energized. When the new gym is built use it.

"As I pointed out earlier, you can use the phone

to contact us. On each computer and tablet you will find a dedicated application that will reach me or one of my assistants. If you cannot reach us through these means hold the top right button of your watch down for three seconds and you will have a team there in a matter of minutes. IF your vitals go blank know that a team will be dispatched immediately. Enjoy the library, I cannot wait to see you tomorrow. Lessons start at nine." And with that, before they could ask a question, Jerry got up and left.

The rest of the morning and afternoon passed quickly. Rich and Michelle explored the lab while Evan and Mikey read as many texts as they could, regardless of how they applied to their assignment. Ian, John, and Marissa buried themselves in texts trying to finish quickly. After a quick dinner they found themselves alone in the cabin's living room.

"Why do you think Jerry has singled out Mikey and Michelle? It is obvious why he singled the rest of us out, but why is he dragging Mikey and Michelle into this?" Ian spoke a few of the thoughts piling up in his head.

"I don't know Ian, but he must have his reasons. He always does," Marissa responded with a voice full of doubt.

"But it doesn't make sense Marissa. We all know

that Mikey and Michelle are not that advanced. Their jump level is fairly low and, well to be honest, they are just young."

"They're not that young," Marissa countered.

"They are not even old enough to be in specialized classes yet. I talked to Kale at dinner and he has advanced infrastructure and economic studies. Nothing about the war or advance training has been mentioned to him or anyone else for that matter. For them it is back to classes as normal. Mikey and Michelle should be in basic classes for a few years, instead they are being trained with us. As though they will be battling tomorrow," John answered.

"Maybe Kale just has not heard anything because he is not ready?" Marissa rebutted.

"Then why did Jerry tell us that we were the only seven who needed to know about that back section?" Ian poked a hole in her answer.

"I don't know, but we all like them so what does it matter?"

"I know we all like them. And ever since Ian got here we have all been a little family, I get that, but something is up. Jerry even pointed it out." John responded to Marissa's exasperated tone.

John's answer troubled all of them, until Jerry had said something they thought Mikey and Michelle were with them because of their connection to Scoot and what had happened. Now however it was clear that all seven of them were here for different reasons.

Before they could continue their conversation Rich and Evan jubilantly burst into the room. Not stopping to say hello they continued to talk about their project when Mikey and Michelle entered right behind them hand in hand, talking about the experiment that she and Evan had performed.

Marissa tried to buy into the excitement her friends brought into the stoic room. Despite her best efforts, she could not fool Rich, after grabbing a drink from the fridge, he sat down and engaged them.

"Who died?" Rich asked Ian and John. "You guys aren't worrying about things that can't be helped are you? Because you know that will not be good for any of us."

Rich's words somehow released the pressure of the day as Ian, John, and Marissa smiled. They might not have forgotten their questions, but they could at least put them off until later.

"You're right Rich. Why are y'all so happy?" John asked, his mood noticeably improved.

"Wouldn't you like to know? You will have to

wait until morning since you bailed early," Rich commented with a smirk.

◆ ◆ ◆

The next morning each person presented their battle strategy; showcasing its applications, its traditional implementation, and how it could be adapted to their current conflict. Michelle and Evan each produced experiments showcasing the effects of chemical warfare. Mikey recited an epic from world 131's *"Battle of Galktia."* John, Ian, and Marissa's presentations were bland compared to these being no more than a short power-point. After seeing what their friends did the challenge was on and they were not going to be outshined again.

No ones presentation was as amazing as Rich's though. Rich dressed up as Napoleon for an inter-active play showcasing his battle techniques and strategies.

Jerry was fairly passive during the lesson primar-ily letting his students guide themselves only offering only a few questions here and there. By one o'clock everyone was famished so Jerry gave them their assignments before dismissing them to lunch.

Three or four hours of morning class quickly be-came part of their daily ritual. Unlike the rest of the school their group's classes revolved around the war, The Dimension, and how to fight within it. Their class was loose, free, and very different from what their peers were doing.

Morning classes were preceded and followed by exercise sessions. Most days after their afternoon session they had a late lunch, and researched until the night was half-done. Long days isolated them from the rest of the camp and they soon found themselves only seeing their peers in the mess hall or on the field. That was even hit or miss as they frequently skipped the mess hall and had food delivered downstairs or ate at off times.

October came to an end and November flew by as their schedule became an inescapable routine. Monday or Tuesday, Saturday or Sunday, it did not matter, as their classes became an monotonous daily agenda. The new gym opened at the end of November. This was welcomed because exercising outside had become a chore as winter descended. The magnificent seven were sometimes called the ghost seven by the camp as they became more isolated. Outside of the gym the only thing that changed was the tension between Ian and Marissa.

Ian and Marissa had many close moments where their relationship almost took the next step. One time Marissa fell into Ian's arms as she tripped down the stairs. A few times they fell asleep on each other in the classroom or library after a late night; however, they never had their first kiss or took the chance to explore where the sparks were going. As the months wore on near misses and interruptions built more tension that desperately sought relief.

December arrived and after a formidable dinner Rich, Evan, John, Mikey, and Marissa went out to enjoy a camp party. Despite their friends' protest Ian and Michelle turned in early.

In their cabin Ian went straight to bed and his scrap book, something he did at least twice a week. Michelle went to the shower and by the time she reappeared Ian was adding pictures to the new pages.

"What you working on?" Michelle asked as she ran a towel through her hair.

"Nothing... just putting a few pictures away..." Ian said as he tried to slide the pictures out of view.

"Cool..."

An awkward silence formed between the two as Ian poorly concealed the scrapbook and pictures in plain sight. Shuffling it out of sight led to a few pictures falling off the bed.

"I wish I could have known her," Michelle said

handing Ian a picture of Nicole.

"You would have liked her."

"Yeah she must be special. You know there is no need to hide these from us. We get it."

Feeling a little foolish Ian stopped trying to cover the pictures and then slipped the last few back into the places they had been.

"You must think I'm silly to hide this from you guys?" Ian said motioning towards the scrap book.

"No, we get it. We get that you still miss them all, but I guess I just wish I could know more about Nicole; she must be special if she can keep you from Marissa. I mean I can hardly imagine what the two of you must have had."

Ian put down the scrap book and looked back at his friend before answering her.

"We..." Ian started. "We had something special, but even I understand that it cannot, and probably should not, survive this."

"If you know that then why are you torturing yourself, Marissa, and Nicole? Why don't you just let her go?" Michelle pressed, surprised by Ian's understanding of the reality of their situation.

"I know... I wish I...." Ian tried to answer the

same question he had asked himself a hundred times.

"You know you're only hurting yourself," Michelle interrupted Ian's thoughts. "I know I cannot understand what you are going through, but you need to let Nicole or Marissa go. It's not fair to anyone to drag it on like this."

"I wish I could, but I just cannot let either one of them go like this. I need to talk to Nicole another time, but I cannot break up with her because of this Michelle. I must know she is okay. I have to let her know that she cannot live her life waiting for me to come home. If we are going to end it... I need to know she is safe, I can't leave her just to pursue someone else."

"Ian, that's not fair. I know things are bad, but you can't let that stop you. You know she's safe and you can't call what you and Marissa could have *'just to pursue someone else'.* We all know it is something more. It may take a while but I'm sure you will see Nicole again. You are right about one thing; you can't live waiting for that day to come. It will only distract you and hurt all three of you."

Ian knew Michelle was right and in his silence she took a chance to push, hoping to solve this issue.

"I'm sure Jerry could get her a message for you.

Loads of-"

"-He can't..." Ian cut her off. It may be possible, but Ian was not going to become more of a burden to Jerry.

"Even if we can't get it there write her a letter. Get the closure you all need. Maybe we'll get it to her, but at least then you can move on."

Sitting across from Michelle Ian thought about her idea. Michelle's words were full of wisdom beyond her years and everything she said had been true. What he and Marissa had was special. The situation was creating more distractions than solutions. More pain than relief.

"I know you must be tired of talking about her and your old world, but I'd love to know more about where you come from. We have been together for a few months and I would like to know more about the person who replaced one of my best friends," Michelle said changing the subject as she moved next to Ian.

Michelle's last statement brought Ian back to reality. The tear running down her face reminded Ian about something he usually forgot: Mikey and Michelle lost their best friend, Scoot, someone they grew up with, the day he arrived. They lost him because of him. Ian had never apologized to them for what happened and he didn't often give it a second thought. Michelle and Mikey were not going to ask him to spill his heart or apologize for something he could not control, however, seeing Michelle now, Ian knew he wanted to.

Since the day the scrap book arrived Ian had hoarded it. Outside of an isolated incident with Marissa, he had not shared the stories or pictures with anyone. He thought that he was protecting them that he was not burdening them. In reality he was hurting them. Michelle was not asking for much. Considering how much Ian had changed her life it was the least he could do. Michelle had the right to know more about the person who replaced her best friend.

"Her name is Nicole," Ian started his story in the same place he had with Marissa on a beautiful autumn morning a few months back. The story was not as hard to tell this time and Ian used the scrap book to help him along the way. It took a while, but what started as an early night in turned into a late one as Michelle and Ian talked for hours about their lives.

As the night wore on the rest of their friends joined them and by the wee hours of the morning everyone was sitting together reminiscing about the good and bad times of their lives before Esmerelda and the war. For the first time Ian could talk about Earth, his life, without breaking down. The ghost seven were becoming a family.

CHAPTER TEN
Missle-Toe

The next morning was brighter. Ian's cabin woke after a few hours of sleep and went to the great hall for breakfast. After taking the morning to play kickball with the other students they leisurely wandered down to their classroom where Jerry eagerly awaited them.

"Nice of you to show up," Jerry welcomed them in with a joke. "Hey... hey you guys quiet down... down... Hey Moe, Larry, and Curly sit down. Settle down you three I have some important news."

They were late, however last night they all agreed that they needed a little break. So they had a leisurely breakfast and decided to exercise with their classmates. Jerry had figured this out and was not actually angry.

After the late night and fun morning, the group arrived full of life and energy. Led by the antics of John, Rich, and Evan it took everyone a minute to get cozy before John replied for the group.

"Come on Jerry, you know that we are the Three Musketeers," John said with a grin. (Rich had dubbed themselves that ever since discovering the group in an Earth novel)

"Until you learn how to behave you will be the stooges to me," Jerry retorted. "I know these past few weeks have been busy, but today we will be adding something new to our studies," Jerry continued as he powered up the computer normally reserved for presentations.

"In case you didn't know we have been using that thing for months. So if the computer is the big addition we may need to check your memory Jerry," Rich joked as the group laughed with him.

"Thank you Rich for noticing that we are using the computer, but did you notice that the coffee tables are missing?" Jerry countered with a wit of his own.

"If by missing you mean moved to the side of the room. Then yes, we noticed," Rich responded pointing to the oak tables lining the walls.

"Do you know why they were moved?" Jerry asked and a silence fell over the group for the first time.

"You don't Rich?" Jerry joked with a slight smile. "Why don't I show you?"

Jerry flipped a switch and the floor between the couches started to separate as the lights in the room dimmed. Ian jumped into Marissa's lap and Mikey and John jumped onto their respective couches next to their friends in surprise.

Rising out of the middle of the floor was a marble table with a large glass top. The fixture kept rising until it was a few feet off the ground. Once settled the marble drawers, housing tablets, pushed out from the table and each student took one.

"This is the latest in battle strategy simulation," Jerry announced to the group as he flicked another switch and the overhead and table whirred to life. The words: "Battle Ready" projected behind him.

"This technology is the first of its kind and is the first of three steps in preparing you for battle. Behind me you will see all the input options available in creating a battle scenario. In this software we can choose from countless variables to create an ever challenging and evolving program. We can choose the number of enemies, the number of friendly forces, topography, world, weather, time of day, weapons available and much more. We can test what you have learned these past few months while also having the ability to handicap you, change your goals, and even input what battle strategy or strategies we want used for or against you. This software has access to the entire library and is fully customizable. It is the perfect tool in teaching you how to fight against The Evil. Any questions?" Jerry asked, beaming with excitement and pride over the new software.

"What battle strategies do you have for The Evil?" Ian's hand shot up with the question he had just asked.

"The Evil's battle strategies are based on personal observations and a random generator. The generator generates battle strategies by utilizing and combining battle strategies of every world along with battle strategies they have used against us."

Jerry's answer appeased most of the congregation that was too distracted by their new toy to pay to much attention to Jerry's answer. Ian, however, was concerned that Jerry had skirted a question about The Evil again.

"Any more questions?" Jerry asked superficially before moving on. "Good, everyone pick up a tablet and let's begin."

Without hesitation everyone grabbed a tablet, except for Ian.

"What's the problem?" Jerry asked Ian seeing his hesitation.

"I just don't get it. I don't get why everyone's so

excited and how this is different."

"Ian, before to train they would bring people up to the field and have them spar against soldiers," John answered for Jerry.

"John's right. This software is miles beyond the old training methods. It is also only a single tool. I did not tell you guys this before, but you seven are part of a new training regiment we are trying. It is part of the reason we choose you and separated you, if it works how we want it to it will give us a better chance at training this entire camp for the war. Ian just give me a chance and if you still have a question I will answer it afterwards."

Taking the tablet Ian was not convinced, but reminded himself of his promise: He was going to trust Jerry.

"I will be programming our first scenario; however, you can start a new scenario from Battle Ready's start screen. You can program and save as many battles you would like so don't be shy and try your own scenarios as often as you like. If you do not want to program a scenario there are thousands of pre-created challenges and if that does not fit your fancy, the computer can randomly generate a scenario for you. I took the liberty of creating our first scenario. Also in case you were wondering the program has a random infinity generator as well, so no two scenarios will ever be the same," Jerry finished as he clicked *"proceed"* and a new screen popped up.

Two things appeared on the next screen: a drop down box for difficulty and a *"finalize"* button. Once Jerry clicked on the difficulty box, a menu opened and revealed over 50 different levels.

"What level are you guys at?" Jerry asked as he ran his cursor between difficulties. "Novice, beginner, or simply easy?" Jerry challenged the group to answer him.

"Jerry, we have been studying, give us a challenge. We can do this on hard."

With a raised eyebrow Jerry answered John's challenge "Are you sure you are ready for that?" Jerry surveyed the group and a nervous nod told him all he needed to know. "If you insist, we will compromise on normal."

After selecting normal, Jerry hit the *"finalize"* button and the scenario began.

A mountain and its surrounding valley buzzed into existence over the marble table. Trees covered the mountain as wildlife ran through the three dimensional environment. So enthralled with the mountain in front of them, no one noticed their tablets buzzing to life.

"In front of you is our battle field. We are on

world 73, and you should take that into consideration as you plan your strategy. If you have not noticed yet your forces are represented by the blue humans on the mountain and your enemy the red."

Looking closer at the mountain, what they thought was blue and red dots were actually intricate, detailed soldiers. Using their tablets they zoomed in on them to see armor, weapons, and even scars, on the soldiers face. The student's force was about twice the size of the enemy.

"Your mission is to get to the base of the mountain and reach the river at the edge of the map. Your jump point is at the river. Understand?" Jerry finished his explanation.

The mission seemed simple. The river ran down the side of the mountain and getting to their jump point seemed easy enough. They had the upper ground, and the number advantage, for all intents and purposes, it should be a fairly simple task.

"You will use your tablets to program your strategy. You have a variety of information available to you there. Advance scouting, weather patterns, world information, etc... it is all at your finger tips. Before we start this simulation I want you to devise a strategy. Your troops have been placed, so it is your job to figure out how to get them to your goal. Once the battle has started, you can use the tablet to deliver orders on the fly and adjust to the ebb and flow of battle. With that said do you want to do this first battle together or do you want to make it a competition? Do you want to share the glory or do you want to see who can beat the other battalion first?"

"You know the answer Jerry. I will finish off the enemies fastest," Rich answered for the group.

"If that is the case please begin planning your strategy," Jerry answered with an untrustworthy smile.

The room went silent as everyone directed their attention from Jerry to planning a winning strategy.

Looking down at his own screen Ian saw that he had two hundred troops in one group at the top of the mountain, the enemy two groups of fifty at the bottom. Ian had them outnumbered 2-1, but was hesitant about planning his attack. All indications showed that he had the upper hand. He had the numbers, he had high ground, but Jerry's smile worried him. After 45 minutes Ian was the finally ready to proceed to the relief of the group.

"Done?" Jerry asked politely.

"Yeah Ian? You finished? Because I think we are all a year older now," Rich teased Ian, ready to see his own strategy unfold. Ian nodded and laughed confirming that he was ready.

"Now that everyone is done we will begin. Once the simulation is finished we will replay each battle and review them as a group."

On the table the mountain broke into seven smaller examples, one for each of them. On their tablets the screen changed. They were in command mode ready to direct their forces. Quickly scrolling through the options they had the ability to micromanage everything, from what type of weapon a single soldier was using, to whether he should walk, run, or jump.

"Remember your mission is to escape. If you can beat the enemy, great, but escape at all costs. Just like in a real battle there is no pause button. Good luck. Let's begin."

The mountains buzzed to life and in an instant each person was on their heels trying to respond and regain the upper hand.

It took only a few minutes before Mikey and Ian were defeated. Mikey was thrown off by a tremor that caused chaos in his ranks. Ian was caught off guard with his opponents long-range capabilities. John, Marissa, Evan, and Michelle fared a little better, but ten minutes later found themselves in similar predicament: surrounded by enemy troops, trying escape. At the end of

25 minutes Rich's final commander went down, officially ending the simulation.

"What just happened?!? We didn't stand a chance, I thought we had learned more than that!" Rich blurted out in disbelief and anger as the mountains disappeared from the table.

"I expected this," Jerry answered nonchalantly. "This program is designed to simulate an actual battle. It is not a theory or a book. You have all done very well these past few months, but it is time you put your knowledge into practice. You can read every book about war from now until you die, but without practice it will mean nothing. The only way to get better at anything is to practically apply knowledge. The only way we can win this war is if you start learning the rules of war, the first being that anything can happen."

"But, what could we have done better? Where do we even start trying to figure out how to improve?" Marissa spoke up, a little lost on how to overcome this defeat.

"How many of you took the variables created by the planet into account?" Jerry asked the group. Their confused looks giving him his answer. "That's what I thought and because of that you lost this battle before it began," Jerry said as he scrolled over a bar at the top of the screen

"Look here," Jerry started pointing at a tab at

the top of his screen. "If you were looking you would have seen the information scrolling at the top of the screen giving you insight into natural phenomena and weather patterns found on the planet." Jerry continued as he highlighted the word *"tremors"* on his screen. "If you had used this you would have seen that tremors and tectonic activity are common here. You can also tap here to get expanded information on the planet or if you are completely lost all you have to do is ask the computer and it will tell you without a click."

Sitting in humbled ignorance the group realized that the information Jerry told them was hiding in plain sight. All of them had been throw off by tremors that killed their strategy from the beginning. Scrolling through the options they found more than weather forecasts, including advance scouting about their enemy and possible capabilities.

For the rest of the class Jerry individually reviewed and explained each person's strategy with the class, giving them tips on how to improve while he did. Not giving them the answers, but suggestions and advice Jerry's guidance kept the class at full attention as they soaked up his wisdom. Around five they finished with Rich's strategy ready for a break.

"I know this has been a long class, but I must ask

you to indulge me a bit longer before I let you go," Jerry said to the exhausted group as the afternoon turned to dusk. "You all know that knowledge is our best weapon and with that in mind I will be asking you to hold class on your own for the next month."

Their fatigued attention dissipated as the group's faces fell and collectively wondered: *How can Jerry leave us when we are just starting to learn how to fight?*

"Do not worry," Jerry said trying to comfort the group before anyone could raise a question. "Evan, Michelle, and Mikey I still want you running your experiments. I still want all of you reading and learning. Nothing else changes except that you will be adding the battle ready program to your daily routine. You are in the early stages of your development and I think you should explore it on your own without anyone deterring your creativity and growth. If you need help my aids will be here. I must leave to proactively rectify a problem our resistance has encountered."

The mood cheered a little bit with Jerry's reassurance. It would be a rough month, but they knew they could handle it, especially if it would help the resistance take the upper hand in the war.

"Take our class time to utilize this new technology and practice. I will be back before you know it and in January I'll show you stage two of this training, which is more amazing."

After a week they had all beaten the original program and started to move on. During the morning they ran battle simulations and studied on their own. At night the group created, reviewed, and ran battle strategies and scenarios together, helping everyone master the new program. Somehow they crammed the rest of their exercise and meals around this new software.

Time flew by with their new software. Everyone strived to make Jerry proud and redoubled their training efforts. They studied harder, exercised more, and did everything they could to grow. All this training brought Ian a new respect for what they were fighting for. Everyday he learned more about each world and the culture there.

Beyond studies December was a time of holiday and celebration all over The Dimension. Every day Jerry's staff celebrated holidays from worlds scattered far and wide. Food, education, and celebration filled the month as Jerry's staff led traditional holidays and their celebrations.

Traditions of lost worlds were given extra care and everyday the staff made it very clear if the world was still free or not. The communication silence from Earth had Ian eagerly awaiting Christmas. Not only would he get a taste of home, but he would find out if Earth was still a sovereign planet. For a month that was flying by it also felt like Christmas took its time to get there.

Christmas Day started with a present settled on the end of Ian's bed. It was nothing more than a little card with a message that read: *"Merry Christmas, your home is safe. Earth is free."* Written in Jerry's scribble the little letter was the best gift Ian could have received and gave him peace about two things: Jerry and Earth were both safe.

Ready to celebrate and Ian decided to make everyone a little eggnog. Walking into their living Ian found that Jerry's staff had gone above and beyond and decorated their living room with lights and a tree.

"What is all this?" Ian heard Rich mutter as he walked out into the living room. "Did someone get drunk? We have a tree in the living room, and it looks like someone threw up green and red lights everywhere. This is kind of ridiculous," Rich added as he crossed the room and took Ian's specially prepared drink.

"One of Santa's elves was a little sick last night. Isn't it wonderful," Ian retorted with a chuckle as he basked in the warm comfort of his home world.

"Who is Santa and why was he here?" Michelle asked as she wandered in with sleepy eyes.

After Michelle, the rest of his friends wandered into the living room and took a seat on the couches. Passing out drinks Ian took his own seat before answering Michelle's question.

"Santa is a mythical man from my planet who brings toys and gifts to the good children and coal to the bad."

"I guess that means that John isn't getting that new bow he asked for," Rich joked.

"So this is an Earth thing?" John said as he pointed around the room with laugh.

"Well yeah..." Ian responded happy to discuss his home world.

The day began with sleepy questions and quickly evolved into one of the best on Esmerelda for Ian. Beyond his first note, the group found a second on the door informing them that their group, like the rest of camp, had from now until New Year off. Throughout the day Ian and his friends discussed Earth and enjoyed the new gym's lounges while catching up with friends they felt like they had not seen in months. Much to Ian's relief Jerry's support staff presentation about the Earth re-confirmed Jerry's message that it was safe.

"Ian... Be honest with me. What was your least favorite gift you ever got?" John asked as he, Ian, and Marissa made their way back to the dorms after an amazing holiday feast.

Stopping by the fountain Ian could not come up with one and laughed as he responded "I really don't know, but probably one of those combined gifts."

"What do you mean?" Marissa asked.

"As you know my birthday is two days away, so many times people would combine the two gifts into one. Heck, sometimes they would even wait until the after Christmas sale to get it. I used to hate that, but right now I would give anything for one if it meant seeing Earth again."

Before anyone could reply Mike and Evan ran out onto the balcony and yelled down to John. They were starting a card game and wanted a fifth. Before John could refuse, Marissa volunteered him.

Alone with Marissa Ian teared up for the first time today as he thought about Earth, his family, and what he was missing out on right now.

"I'm sorry about this. I just really miss them," Ian said wiping the tears from his eyes as he looked back at Marissa, alone with her for the first time in a long time.

Marissa was lost for a response. Instead of words Marissa reached out, wiped away a tear, and nodded. The touch sent sparks through them as a familiar tension settled in place.

Placing his hand on hers Ian looked into Marissa's eyes and was transported back to his first morning here. The morning they were lost in emotion not knowing what to do. He wanted this tension to end, but he was still with Nicole.

"What is that?" Marissa asked breaking their contact, but not the tension that had settled in the crisp air.

Following her gaze Ian found a red and green piece of holly hanging from the light above them. Golden Christmas lights illuminated the holiday treat.

"That is mistletoe," Ian chuckled, wondering if this spot were destiny or a cruel twist of fate.

"What are you laughing at?" Marissa poked Ian. A moment ago he had been solemn and now he was laughing uncontrollably. "Stop laughing Ian, come on what is it," she continued, her pokes turning into slaps.

Catching her hand Ian started to explain.

"On Earth when you are caught under mistletoe with someone you are supposed to kiss them."

All the feelings they had been fighting for months were battling to get out and an Earthly plant was becoming a calling card of fate. Against their better judgment they both started to lean towards each other, eyes closed as Marissa broke the silence.

"I would not want to disgrace one of your traditions Ian. That seems so disrespectful," Marissa said softly as they got closer.

"We wouldn't want that," Ian softly replied. Their lips less than an inch apart.

"No, we wouldn't," Marissa whispered back a moment before it happened.

In a single moment it happened. One little kiss, a peck. When their lips met the tension they had built for weeks, the emotions they had fought for months, melted away.

As the moment passed they backed away slightly, for a second, as they held on to each other. Then they embraced in a more passionate kiss. One that would should have signified a new beginning until Ian jerked away.

His eyes full of fear Ian grabbed Marissa's hands and tried to reassure her. "I am sorry Marissa. This is not fair to either of us."

"I understand," Marissa said dejectedly not needing an explanation for what had just happened. The reality settling in that: this relationship between them was never going to happen and it was time she gave up.

"Marissa don't go. It is not you or this moment. This is beautiful and wonderful, but it is premature. We cannot be together yet," The words dribbled out Ian's mouth, sounding worse than he thought they could.

"And why not?" Marissa snapped back as she pulled her hand away from his. Anger and frustration that had festered over this situation for months was finally boiling out. "Ian why not? We have been doing this song and dance for months and nothing has changed except that our feelings have grown. It is now or never. Nothing else will change so it is now or never. Do you want this? Will you ever move on from her?" Marissa finished with a fire burning in her chestnut eyes. There was no mischievous grin and Ian was sure he now knew what Rich and John had faced a few months back.

"Marissa I need a chance to let Nicole go."

"I thought that is what these past few months were for. You can't take that moment back and at this rate you will never get the chance for closure that you really want," Marissa responded. "Either you will never get to say good bye or you will see her and not break if off. How can I keep waiting for you to do something your being thinks is impossible?"

Her cold question cut through the heart of the issue and reverberated in the brisk air. Ian knew Marissa was right. He was using Nicole as a crutch, a shield to opening himself up to Marissa and everything that would mean. Ian did not want to loose Nicole and despite everything he knew it was time to move on. Ian had to say something before he lost Marissa forever.

"Marissa you have been patient, but please give me a little more time. I will find a way to tell her. I will find a way to get closure so I can be with you. Marissa please. I don't want to lose you."

Ian knew his words were inadequate and hollow before they came out of his mouth. They were the same message he had been telling her for months and in this moment he needed something more. Marissa's eyes told the true story: Ian had lost her.

"Okay.... Ian... Okay.... I'll... I'll be around...." was all Marissa said as she disappeared into the night.

Ian wanted to follow her, but couldn't. The tension had broken and Ian messed it up. He had to act now if he wanted to salvage this. A little mistletoe made him realize that it was time he let Nicole go.

CHAPTER ELEVEN

A Birthday Card

Climbing into bed with pen, paper, and a heavy heart Ian stared blankly at a piece of paper, trying to figure out where to begin. After Marissa left, Ian flew through the dorm, determined to use Michelle's idea, to write a letter, to try. Ian and Nicole had a lot of history; however, they needed to move on. That realization, this decision, did not make any part of this reality easier and in the end Ian fell asleep full of pain and sorrow. Failing to write a single word.

The next morning came quickly and Ian woke to find his friends sleeping soundly. Everyone except for Marissa whose bed was empty. Marissa had left a note telling them that she would be gone today and not to wait for her. Worried he had lost her Ian used the note as motivation and was determined to write the letter that day.

Despite his determination, the 26*th* went by without incident or progress. Ian had not been able to write a single word and spent much of the day in a daze trying to figure out where to start.

Ian ran into Marissa twice during the day: at lunch and dinner. These meetings were not helpful and only scared Ian more. Marissa was not upset or mean, but eerily cordial and friendly. She was having fun and reconnecting with Jen and Jill, her two best friends, from before Ian showed up. Ian would have preferred she showed some emotion towards him, but her lack of emotion made him worry even more.

The next day sunrise came and went, along with breakfast and lunch, as Ian spent his birthday alone in library. Going through multiple drafts Ian was not going to leave his isolation until the letter was finished.

After several hours, and many tears, Ian had finished the letter to Nicole. Ian had the closure he needed, hoped it would be enough for Nicole, and was concerned it may be too late. Realizing only now that Jerry may have given Nicole the same advice he had given Ian and, however unlikely to Ian, she may have already moved on.

Ian had the library's oak doors ajar when he heard a voice, he had not heard in a few weeks beyond them.

"It is time to make our move," Ian heard Jerry's voice fill the grand atrium.

"Are you sure? Is it safe to jump yet? We cannot risk losing you," Lance asked.

"That is unimportant. We have to move and I have to make sure everyone is okay. We have to get out there and check The Dimension. We have to reopen communications and we need to make sure everything is okay."

"But..."

"-The scrambler is ready and the plan is sound," Jerry said as he began to recite his plan again for Lance. "I'm going to jump to my sister planet for a final test. When that goes well I will begin move to each free, safe, or resistance planet I can get to and set up the scrambler. If all goes according to plan I should be back before you know it. Two, three weeks max."

"What about the group? What if it doesn't wor-" Lance started to challenge when Jerry interrupted him.

"-Lance the group has been fine. If anything they have been doing better since I left. Beyond that, we know the scrambler works and I am the only one who can place all of them. We are completely shut off from each other right now and we need to restart communications. This is our first chance to be offensive in years and we have to take it."

Ian could imagine the look on Lance's face. He was sure it was one of disbelief and fear based on what Jerry said next.

"This plan will reboot communication and our ability to fight. I am the only level one left, so I am the only one who can do this. You know that knowledge is the key to this fight. To get knowledge flowing again. We have to do this."

It was time to reveal himself so Ian stepped into the hallway. Not wanting to miss his chance to deliver his letter Ian yelled to Jerry and watched him turn with a look of shock, as if he had heard a ghost.

"Ian... I had no idea that you were down here... I assumed you were celebrating your birthday.... Or doing work....I checked the classroom, and no one was in there... I know you must have questions, but we do not have time and I need you to keep this to yourself..." Jerry rambled on, trying to regain his thoughts after Ian's surprise.

"I was in the library," Ian answered Jerry.

Ian had a list of questions, but he knew that agenda would get him nowhere. Questions would have to wait for another day. Right now

Ian had a more important mission to accomplish.

"Jerry I wanted to see if you could deliver this letter for me?" Ian asked now face to face with Jerry. Trying to sound as innocent as possible. "If you're going to Earth, it is the least you can do." Ian knew he had a little advantage and would not give it up.

"I can try to deliver this under two conditions. First, you did not hear anything down here today. Secondly, you leave without reciting a list of questions," Jerry presented his offer as he opened his hand to take the letter.

Ian knew he could live with these demands. He also knew that, for once, he had a little leverage and countered Jerry.

"How about this. You deliver this letter for me and I can tell my friends that you are checking up on other worlds. I'll save my questions for when you get back," Ian said starting to hand over the letter when he pulled it back as he amended his offer. "And when you get back, you answer all my questions. All the ones you have avoided during our lessons, meetings, and talks."

Ian's counter offer resonated off the marble walls as he presented the letter to Jerry once again. Jerry knew he had little leverage. Silence encased the three of them before Jerry's stern look transformed into a smile as he offered to take the letter.

"Fair enough, but you must keep what you heard here a secret," Jerry added as he took the letter.

"Agreed, but remember-" Ian started as he released the letter.

"-Yes, I remember I will answer your questions when I get back," Jerry answered to seal the deal.

"Who is this letter for Ian?" Jerry inquired as he weighed the small envelope in his hand.

"It is a long overdue letter to Nicole," Ian said looking down at the letter one last time.

Jerry, with a sad smile and nod, understood what the letter was. After wishing Ian a happy birthday Jerry and Lance turned to leave. Ian was halfway to his own exit (the classroom) when he realized a fatal flaw in the deal they had struck.

"Jerry... Wait..." Ian yelled from across the room. Running to reach Jerry before he disappeared into the forbidden area.

"What is it?" Jerry asked, stopping so his frantic charge could reach him.

"I need a copy of that letter..." Ian let out as he began to catch his breath. "I need a copy for Marissa."

Without saying a word Jerry walked to the library and made a copy. Handing Ian the copy Jerry wished him good luck. Watching him leave Ian realized that the easy part was done. Now the hard part would begin.

Not wanting to open the hidden door, behind their fireplace, Ian stood behind it as worries and fear plagued his thoughts.

Was this letter enough? Did Marissa still love him? Would he even be able to find her and would she listen to his plea?

Thoughts swirling, Ian noticed for the first time that this door was also marble. Dismissing any curiosity he would normally have about the door Ian reached for the handle and slowly opened the door into a dark, still room.

Startled by the darkness Ian's eyes took a moment to adjust, before he surveyed the room to find his friends hidden behind couches and chairs. They had not heard him.

"Are we playing hide and seek?" Ian whispered in Mikey's ear after sneaking up behind him.

Mikey jumped into the air with a startled squeal.

"Quiet down," John yelled back at Mikey without looking to see what startled him.

"But John-" Mikey started

"-Mikey come on quiet down... He could be here any minute."

"But John..." Mikey tried to continue when Evan spoke up for him.

"John your surprise party idea is not going to work," Evan said after seeing what startled Mikey.

"SHH...Come on guys be quiet. Why do you say that?" John asked Evan as he waved them off.

"Turn around."

John and the rest of the group turned around to see Ian waving back at them, while Evan turned the lights back on.

"You had to ruin my surprise," John joked as he passed Ian a drink.

"Sorry about that," a distracted Ian replied. *How do I get Marissa alone?* Was all Ian was thinking as they settled onto the couches.

"We wanted to surprise you for your birthday. Where were you?" Rich piped up with a question as John finished passing around drinks.

"I was in the library finishing up some work," Ian responded, looking up at the clock to see that he had been gone for over 14 hours.

"Classes are out though?" Rich pushed.

"I have to catch up...." Ian answered, which everyone seemed to buy.

The next hour went by in a blur as the group gave Ian his birthday punches and pinches, ate cake, and celebrated his birthday. At the end of the hour, almost as if her social requirement had been fulfilled, Marissa excused herself to bed.

Palpable tension filled the room as Marissa departed. Everyone painfully aware of the rift between Ian and Marissa.

"Go talk to her," John broke the silence as the door shut behind her.

"Lead with the letter, she will understand," Michelle suggested pointing to the envelope in Ian's hand.

"You sure?" Ian asked Michelle

"I am." She answered him, the rest of the group feeling a little out of the loop.

The delicate sound of rain greeted Ian's ears as he entered the room. Marissa had jumped into the shower, so Ian took a seat on her bed and waited. He was not willing to let this opportunity pass him by. He had to get her back.

A half an hour had passed when Ian heard the lock click and watched the door open. Marissa's stunning beauty hit him harder than normal as she walked out.

Marissa wore a red nighty with matching pajama pants. The cute top flattered her, while her blonde hair cascaded across her shoulders and back.

Marissa did not acknowledge Ian. After messing with her hair and dresser Marissa looked towards Ian before averting her gaze. She obviously wanted him to move off her bed, but knew he was not going to.

"Ian I didn't mean to leave early. I got up pretty early and am exhausted," Marissa justified her departure, trying to conceal her slightly blood shot, freshly cried, eyes from Ian.

"I know. I got up around six and you were already gone," Ian answered her ready to work this out. "Marissa we really need to-"

"-Talk," Marissa interjected, taking a seat across from Ian on the edge of his bed. *We need to talk* that's what they all say. Ian what happened the other night was rough, but now we can move on. I know how we feel, but you agree that this game of cat and mouse isn't working. So let's put it to rest and be done with it," Marissa finished her rehearsed statement as her eyes fought back tears.

"We both know that you do not mean that Marissa. You and I want this to work more than anything in the world. And-"

"-And nothing," Marissa cut him off again. Her tears of sorrow replaced by those of frustration. "*'Wanting this to work'* or *'wishing for this to work'* is a great idea, but it is not working out. We both knew this relationship was doomed to fail. There is no communication between worlds and without that we can never begin. One of your beautiful qualities is how caring and loyal you are. Without really ending it with Nicole you would not be you. And I want to be with you not someone you change into."

Marissa's frustration simmered off towards the end of her answer. She wanted to be with him, but had given into reality.

Ian knew he was fighting an uphill battle. Marissa had come to terms with their situation and if he was going to win her back now was his only chance. Standing up Ian went to join her on his bed, but before he could sit down Marissa stood up to meet him. She was beginning to fume again, and with her hands on her hips Ian was beginning to see why no one crossed Marissa.

"Don't sit," Marissa ordered him in a cool voice, her eyes burning red. "I love you Ian, but I am done with this back and forth struggle. I know I told you I could wait longer, but I can't. As long as you can't see her, can't end it properly, you will never be mine. If you could go home, we would never be together. I'm over it Ian. So please just go away, I don't care where, but I just can't do this right now."

Ian could see Marissa fighting with herself as she screamed at the person she loved. It was now or never. Ian had come too far to back down now. This was his last chance and he had to get this right.

"Please Marissa. As a birthday present, please read this. Please," Ian offered her the letter. "If you read this I will go away and never come back."

Fear, anger, love, and sadness clearly ran through Marissa as she looked down at the letter and weighed her options. She knew Ian would not leave unless she read it; however, she had no desire to drag this out any longer. After what felt like an eternity Marissa sighed and took the letter from Ian. Ready to indulge him one last time.

"For your birthday," Marissa told Ian as she sat down on her own bed. Opening the envelope she took out the letter and began reading:

Dear Nicole

After these first few words I'm sure you will know what this letter is all about, but, I implore you to continue reading to hopefully understand why I must do this.

Nicole, my Tiny, you know that I love you. I love you with all my heart and all I ever have wanted is for you to be safe and happy. I always thought that would mean growing old with you, but recent events have changed those plans. I'm sure you understand how difficult this is for me, but I hope that you can forgive me for this.

Over the past four years we have grown up together and formed a bond that I thought could never be broken. And while I will love you forever it is unfair for us to live our lives as if we will be able to get back together. Circumstances have forced us apart. Our lives are now filled with uncertainty and I know now that no matter what I say here you will worry about me. While I cannot ask you not to worry I have to ask you to start living again.

As much as we do not want to admit it, we know putting up the charade that we are still together is only harming us both. This is more than distance or a slight hurdle. This is a schism inserted in our lives by a fate out of our control. The distance from one another has been rough and has been like losing a part of ourselves.

Our ability to cope with this has not been adequate and while I have not been there I know you well enough to know that you, like me, have not moved on. Knowing you, I know that you have given everything, wishing for me to come home. You have not found someone else to form this bond with, you have not truly been there with your family and friends. I know you have been a hollow shell as you deal with this and knowing I am causing this pain is something I cannot accept. I am certain that amidst all of the uncertainty and pain the best remedy is to allow ourselves to move on, trust, and love someone as much as we love each other.

Nicole I will love you forever, and I hope that one day we can rekindle our sacred bond. In person. In some way, shape, or form. For now though we both know we must move on, live, and love again.

You are too beautiful a person, inside and out, to die for me and this war. The war we are in has caused too many casualties, and I cannot let you become one of them. With a heavy heart and apologetically I tell you that I am breaking up with you, my tiny, my little one, my life.

Knowing the person that you are you will understand this, others may not, but you will. I am not breaking up with you for any reason other than what I have said above; however, I hope it can bring you some solace and joy that I have found a new group of people here who care about me. There is one person in particular who I think you would approve of who wants to care for me in the same way you do.

I hope you can spread my well wishes and love to my family and friends on Earth. I also hope that in time you can forgive me for hurting you. Unfortunately, this was the only way I could ever know that you were safe and getting the love that you deserve.

Your true friend and love forever

Ian

"I am sorry about everything. I never wanted to hurt you or make your life harder, but...."

Standing up Marissa placed a finger over Ian's lips cutting him off again. There was no need for words right now. There was only one thing left to do.

Removing her finger Marissa threw her arms around Ian's neck and began to embrace him. In a moment of perfection they met in a gentle kiss, one free of attachments, pain, and struggle. A pure kiss marking the beginning of a new day.

CHAPTER TWELVE

From Seven to Six below

Ian woke abruptly with the rising sun blinding him through the slatted oak blinds. Shielding his eyes Ian wondered why this was happening for the first time this morning. He had been living here for half a year and it's not as if the sun decided to rise differently today.

Ian sensed Marissa before he saw her. She was in a deep, peaceful sleep and after the last few mornings Ian knew she needed it. Watching her sleep it took a minute before reality dawned on Ian: this beautiful girl next to him was more than just a friend. After months of cat and mouse, they were finally together.

Half an hour after he woke Ian emerged from the beautiful marble bathroom to find everything the way that he had left it. Marissa's bed was the only one occupied, the others still sat undisturbed, the sound of chirping birds had replaced his friends' snoring. Ian laughed as he prepared for the day, wondering if his roommates' absence was out of respect or self preservation.

Leaving the bedroom Ian found the rest of his friends sprawled out across common room. Michelle and Mikey cuddled around one another on the couch next to the fireplace. John's large frame filled another couch. Rich and Evan were sprawled out on either side of the coffee table.

Walking over to their en-suite kitchen Ian pressed Koffela machine's magic button and leaned against the marble counters as he waited for its elixir. Despite how uncomfortable they looked Ian was grateful for what they had done. They were good people. That sometimes got lost in the drama of the past few months.

A creaking door showed the first signs of life stirring in the room. Standing in the doorway, complete with bed head and groggy eyes, Marissa was awake, searching for Ian and, more importantly, the elixir that gave them all life in the morning.

"Good morning," Marissa sleepily said to Ian, as she took her first drink of the day.

"Morning beautiful. Did you sleep well?" Ian responded in a delicate tone. With one arm around her hip Ian kept Marissa on her feet as he poured himself another mug.

"I slept wonderfully," Marissa answered becoming human again as she gave Ian a kiss on the cheek.

"Did you now?" Ian responded in a flirty tone as he returned the present.

"I did," Marissa responded with another kiss.

"Is that so-"

"-Thank God that is finally over," Rich broke the two apart as he sat up on the floor.

"Rich, looks like you and Mikey will be showering last this week," Evan commented as he got up to help Marissa and Ian pass out mugs.

"Fine with me. I'm just happy that's over," Mikey spoke up.

"Me too. Considering how Marissa has been acting I thought we would be spending the better part of the day cleaning up body parts," Rich joked.

Laughing with Rich the room settled into comfortable chit chat. The drama finally over, everyone could actually look forward to spending the final days of their break together. The group was ready to be young, alive, and have some fun.

"Come on in," John yelled towards a knock at the door; as the morning turned into early afternoon.

Opening the door Laura entered. Waving her in John asked her to join them as their day of fun was about to begin.

"As much as I want to, I am here to deliver a message. We are doing construction and until further notice the basement library is closed. Your classroom is the only room you can get to. Only use your entrance to get down there and if you need to reach the library materials use your tablets. Most of it's archived there."

The group was befuddled. Other than telling them the library was closed, the rest of the information was redundant. They always used the secret entrance as well as their tablets. The real books were preferable, but they could tell something else was on Laura's mind.

"Any questions?" Laura asked still looking concerned.

"What is it Michelle?" Laura inquired to Michelle's hand that shot up.

"What about our experiments?" Michelle asked referring to her and Evan's lab work.

"They are on hold for right now," Laura responded.

"But we have some time sensitive stuff," Evan

complained.

"Can Carmen finish it up?" Laura asked.

"Well yes. but I mean, I would rather..." Evan trailed off. Carmen was a smart and hard working resistance scientist who was a few years older then them. That is really all they knew about her aside from the fact that she always came from the forbidden hallway.

"It has nothing to do with the quality of your work. Just let Carmen know and we'll get it done. We are doing construction downstairs and I'm sorry to tell you, but your break is being cut short, and tomorrow you will be starting back with a few changes to your routine."

Laura's face relaxed as her announcement brought personal relief and a collective groan from the group as they saw their plans disappear.

"The assignments I'm about to give you are subject to change; however, you will all be exercising outside for at least three hours a day and we will be doubling down on your studies and specialized training."

"Are you crazy!!!" Ian exclaimed.

"You can't be serious?!?!" Michelle complained.

"Really???" Rich said in disbelief.

Like every other planet in The Dimension winter on Esmerelda equaled cold. Winter started in late November and recently temperatures had started to dip into the low teens at night while not breaching the high teens during the day. This was just the beginning of winter and the all knew the weather was going to get worse.

"What about the gym? Can't we keep using that?" John asked for the group.

"You can and will. This training is on top of the time spent in the gym. That does not change."

Disbelief turned into blank stares. Laura said she had a few changes; however, this was not a few changes, but a complete overhaul of their life. They already spent everyday, dawn to dusk working. Their new schedules would require they plan out every minute of their life.

"I know all this is a lot. I know it is cold, but you will be fine. Y'all will be having so much fun out there you will not even notice the cold," Laura tried to play off the situation with a laugh. "Also, y'all will be meeting Lance and Sara soon. They are Jerry's right hands and will start running your training since Jerry's gone."

...

The next morning the group of seven found themselves bundled up, at the field, fulfilling

Laura's new assignment. For the first hour, they ran around the track surrounded by a few other students getting their daily exercise in. At the end of the hour, instead of retreating inside, Ian and his friends broke off in to different activities while their peers retreated to the warmth and safety of their dorms, mess hall, and gym.

Ian and Rich shot archery, trying hone their skills in the harsh conditions. Every shot felt like a knife cutting through their fingers. The bow's vibrations sent pain through their frozen arms and spines.

Michelle and John were sparing with joe's, (a long wooden pole). The cold slowed their reactions, as every hit stung more than the last. Evan and Mikey spared in hand to hand combat. The soft snow cushioned their landings; however, the frozen earth soon made them numb. Marissa spent her time on the track trying to outrun the frigid conditions in vain.

After struggling for an hour the group found their way to the middle of the field and collapsed in exhaustion. Unsure how they would survive the third hour.

"It is really cold," Rich commented through chattering teeth.

"I do not feel the cold any more," Michelle responded rubbing a sore spot on her arm.

"What do you think Lance and Sara will be doing to us?" John asked trying to distract his friends from the cold.

"Well if it is anything like our current schedules, probably kill us..." Rich answered him. "Don't forget that after this wonderful exercise we have a half an hour for an early lunch before an afternoon of study."

"Yeah and why did she mention meeting Sara and Lance? I mean I think we have all met them... except maybe Ian, Mikey, and Michelle." Marissa added.

"I met them, I think." Ian said remembering his first night in Jerry's tent.

The group felt uneasy and full of doubt at these new changes. For over a month their training had been self-guided and they were told that they were doing well. Now they were told to redouble their efforts and found themselves freezing to death with an afternoon of study to look forward to.

"I think I was doing better than the rest of you guys," Marissa clutched herself trying to get warm and distract the group.

"That's why you collapsed with us?" Ian took the bait.

"I was doing just fine. I collapsed so you guys would not feel as bad," Marissa smiled back as she sat up in the bed of white.

"Is that so? So, you still think you can run?" Ian challenged her, forming a small ball in his right hand as he sat up to face his sweetheart.

"You wouldn't," Marissa threw back at him, nodding to the snowball in his hand.

"Wouldn't what?" Ian replied as tried he put on an angelic smile, jumped to his feet, and threw the projectile.

Marissa dodged, the snowball went wide, and hit John in the face. Marissa fell back to the frozen earth laughing with the rest of the group. Wiping the snow from his face John looked back at Ian ready to respond.

"You know what this means man... It's on...."

With that John threw a snowball that missed Ian and hit Michelle, starting, what would become, an hour long snowball fight. Chasing each other, throwing snowballs, and general roughhousing filled their final hour with fun. Out of breath, their frozen fun was interrupted by Laura running across the field shouting at them.

"Are y'all insane!!!" Laura yelled as her feet crushed through the snow. "We said we needed you spend more time outside. Not freeze to death!"

Checkups by a group of doctors lasted over an hour. As they left the medical staff reminded them to lay low and rest. Alone with Laura the group of seven found themselves wrapped in blankets trying to get warm.

"I told you we were fine," a disgruntled John spat at Laura.

"I'm sorry, but we were worried about you. We do need you to train outside more, but we were hoping you would do it in a few hour sessions or even six half an hour sessions. We never intended you to stay out in that weather for three straight hours," Laura apologized to the group as she took a sip of tea. "Being out in that could get you really sick. In a few weeks that cold will kill you."

"What about The Dimension?" John asked. His question zapping out what little life was left in the room.

"What about The Dimension?" Laura asked him; hoping he would move on.

"I thought you wanted us to train in the cold to prepare us for the conditions in The Dimension. You know as well as I do, Laura that The Dimension isn't a breezy, balmy 75. It is a cold, desolate tundra that drains life. I thought you wanted us to train for that, but apparently I was wrong. All you want us to do is to spin our wheels."

John's heavy accusation settled on the group and reminded them of the troubles that had plagued their lives for months, for a few of them, years. The fear of the war, the lack of information, and now their enhanced schedules. From a certain perspective it could simply come across as a lot of busy work.

"John that was one reason we had you out there," Laura backtracked from her previous answer. "Our goal is to have you carry out missions on worlds. Not to fight in The Dimension."

"Oh really? So now that I mentioned something different it is 'part of the plan?'" John responded arrogantly. "Let's assume that you are telling us the truth now and at some point you plan for us to fight on other worlds. Don't we have to be prepared for when our safe portals start to break down. Shouldn't we be prepared to survive there?"

John and Laura were locked in battle as his friends let him speak. While more pronounced, they all shared John's feelings in some way and wanted answers.

"John, one step at a time," Laura answered with the wrong answer.

"Not one step at the time. No speaking around this. What are we supposed to do in The Dimension!!! I want to know," John exclaimed, his body tightening as his anger grew. "I'm not willing to die out there; I'm not willing to be a weak sidekick. Laura what am I supposed to do? When my body is starving for oxygen and the cold is enveloping me what good is an extra study session going to do? When my strength is being zapped because I do not have the right genes what am I supposed to do? Huh? What should I do as I die? How should I welcome death?"

"John, calm down," Evan finally interjected trying to diffuse John's anger which had clearly taken a turn.

"Calm down!!! Calm down??? Really Evan??? I thought you and Rich would understand my position better than anyone else. Maybe you don't since you have not been in The Dimension," Rising from the couch John's voice rose as he began to tear into everyone in the room.

"We are lackey's. Extra's. You, Rich, and I. We are not special jumpers. At best, if we are lucky, we are trained monkeys who can run a few missions. Most likely we will be stocking shelves or taking inventory like Laura."

"You are not being fair-" Rich started before John cut him off

"-You guys know deep down inside that little Jeffy, the eleven-year old level 29 special jumper three cabins up, would survive longer in The Dimension than us. He is more important to Jerry and this cause than we are. The rest of them will never know, because they can fight," John said as he pointed to Marissa, Michelle, Mikey, and Ian. "Hell, the second Ian fell into this world he was more important than the rest of us. I live to train so I will never feel that pain again. Everything I do I do to appease Lorne's death."

John's statement hit the group like a ton of bricks and their stunned silence only fueled his burning rage. The sound of shattering ceramic filled the air. Pieces of the cup, koffela, and blood spilled onto the floor from the mug John had just crushed.

"Don't you get it Laura? I do everything because I trusted that you and Jerry had a plan for me. It is not that cold out there. The only thing that is really cold is The Dimension and your demeanor. Your orders for me are nothing but bull shit and busy work. I can finally see what you and Jerry think of me. I guess I'll just have to show y'all that I'm not some weak piece of shit. That I'm ready for this."

Rushing to the front door John slammed it as he left the cabin. Marissa tried to stop him, but was stuck to the couch in shock. Laura and Michelle ran to follow their belligerent friend; however, when they opened the door they were greeted by the seasons first blinding snow storm. A storm that had picked up since the medics left.

"Stay here you six. I'll alert the camp. We will find him," Laura told the group as she bolted to their secret door.

"He'll come back right?" Mikey's timid voice squeaked into the silence left by Laura.

"Of course... He always comes back," Marissa responded, trying to convince herself as much as Mikey.

Their happy world was shattered and laid among the pieces of ceramic on the floor. Just when everything had started to get better, they got worse. This time though they were not wondering if someone would get together or about a little fight, instead, they wondered if they would ever see their friend again.

CHAPTER THIRTEEN

Presents

Searches for John were fruitless. A blinding storm destroyed his tracks and made it impossible to see. Without any tangible leads, trying to find John turned into a frivolous, proverbial, needle in a haystack, search. Three days into the search they found a piece of his coat. A few days later a piece of his pants. A week later a fruit core and a small animal skeleton popped up at the main field.

After two weeks official search parties were called off. Some people still tried to search a few hours a day, but were met with little success. With early January turning into mid January, the weather became bone chillingly harsh and three weeks after John left searches had all but stopped. Most of the camp had given up on finding anything but a corpse once the winter thawed.

Marissa and Ian's honeymoon period ended with John's disappearance. Marissa became a shell of her former self, and Ian did his best to find her again. John was her protective shadow, her savior, and, without Jerry around, her last connection to her family was gone. On the verge of mental collapse Ian did all he could to comfort her. They were growing closer through this, but there were two things that really kept Marissa sane and moving forward.

The first was the ritual between Mikey and Marissa. Every night, before bed, Mikey asked Marissa the question he asked the night John left:

"He'll come back right?"

Marissa would always respond:

"Of course. He always comes back."

This was the only time John was mentioned and was the last thing said before Marissa's sobs filled their sleeping quarters.

The second thing that kept Marissa going was the discovery of a missing tent and supplies a week after John's departure. Most people thought that the missing supplies were simply misplaced inventory, but they gave Marissa hope. She refused to accept that explanation and thought that the missing supplies were John's way to survive.

John's departure brought changes to camp and shook the magnificent seven to their core. The field was banned and with the weather so rough staff escorted students between buildings.

The magnificent seven went from a cohesive family, to three couples living and working together. They still lived, trained, and attempted to joke together, but their linchpin was missing. Their group's heart and soul, its protector, was gone. Without John no one was safe. Without John they had lost their family.

John's departure had not shut down their classes or training. If anything his disappearance had reinvigorated them. During the day they studied and trained as a group, at night Evan and Rich sparred in the living room, Ian and Marissa practiced yoga, and Mikey and Michelle doubled their study times trying to research everything they could about the planets and the war they were a part of.

Sara and Lance had formally introduced themselves three days after John's disappearance. Their meeting was little more than introductions, apologies, and the plan to find John. No one mentioned that they had met before and let them talk in vague platitudes about what they were doing to find John and what was coming. Surprisingly outside of this meeting they never saw Lance or Sara and continued to guide themselves through their studies and training.

After John's departure time became nothing more than an entity that demarcated waking and sleeping. It was not until the 21st of January did their lives change again.

A knock at the door grabbed everyone's attention away from their morning drinks. No one drank kofella after John left. The only kofella left in the cabin was on the stained couch cushion and rug that Marissa would not allow to be cleaned.

"Mikey could you get that," Ian yelled from the dorm's kitchenette as he fixed his morning tea.

"Yeah, no problem," Mikey answered as he rose from the couch to answer the door.

Opening the door Mikey found Sara and Lance bundled up and carrying packages in the frigid weather. It had been weeks since they had seen them and Mikey invited them in and offered warm drinks. Soon, everyone was warming up by the roaring fireplace ready to talk about what was coming up for the group.

"Sorry we have not been around much, things have been a little crazy," Sara started as she sipped some tea. "We are here today because it is time for you six to start the next phase of your training."

The news got little more than a nod. The group had been so embroiled in training since John disappeared that adding something new would be little more than a distraction before it became habitual.

"To start, I need everyone to take off their watches and put on these," Lance said.

Pulling out a cedar chest Lance placed and opened it on the table in front of them. Inside were seven matching watch boxes. Everyone took one except Marissa, who took two.

Opening the boxes black screens gazed back at them. The watch's band was carefully crafted marble that melted seamlessly into the watch. Gazing at these masterpieces no one could figure out how to slip them on. The watches were a closed system, with no visible buttons, cracks, or locking mechanism.

"What do you think?" Sara asked the group. Her eyes sparkling as she watched them examine their new gifts.

"They are beautiful," Marissa said emotionlessly.

"Impressive," Evan added flatly.

"How do we put them on?" Mikey asked the question they all had, as Marissa failed, for the third time, to get her watch on.

"Of course," Lance said as he rose and approached Marissa and helped her slip on and secure the watch.

Over the next few minutes, each person had their new watch fitted and locked into place with Sara and Lance's help. Even though they were primarily made of marble, the watches did not feel heavy or obtrusive. They were so comfortable the group quickly forgot they were there.

"Why did we get the new present?" Ian asked, the mood brightening in the room as he examined how snug, flexible, and comfortable the band felt around his wrist. Realizing that it would probably never come off again.

"Like we said earlier you need to start your new training regiment, which means fitting you with a new watch and heart rate monitor," Lance started to explain as Sara pulled out another chest.

Unlike the watches the new heart rate bands were a blend of white and black marble. Just like the watches though they were a closed system that would not come off. It took ten minutes before Ian heard Lance click the final lock in place.

"What exactly do these do?" Michelle asked as she, Marissa, and Sara rejoined the group from the bedroom.

"Everything," Lance answered with a grin. "These watches have the capabilities of your tablets and much more. They have access to the battle ready software, most of the library, and will even allow you to set up portals between worlds."

"The watches are linked to one another on a single system so you will always know how each other is doing. In battle, you can have it monitor anyone on the system, your generals or a specific soldier. Beyond standard vitals, it can test your blood for most anything. You will always know what is going on inside of you," Sara continued where Lance left off.

"In battle it will keep you up-to-date on everything: give you access to maps, area scans for enemies, and even help you monitor your own troops. The watch is voice and touch operated, solar powered, and can last up to four years on a charge," Lance finished his and Sara's little tale.

Looking at their wrists the group inspected their new watches wondering how all this was possible. Slightly doubtful of Lance and Sara's claims the group knew one thing: these watches were never coming off.

"For now the jumping mechanism is locked on the watch," Sara jumped back in after watching their watch screens pop to life.

The screen showed each person's vitals for a moment, before melting away to be replaced by a screen where they could access a myriad of apps.

"Your new training starts on the field tomorrow. We originally intended this training to be done in the renovated basement, but it is not finished. Take the rest of the day to rest and get comfortable with your new watches. We will see all of you at 8 a.m. tomorrow morning, suited up, and ready to train."

Lance ended the meeting like Jerry: abruptly. Before anyone could ask a question Lance and Sara had risen from the couches and left.

.   .   .

Around five a.m. everyone rose and showered. Waiting for Mikey to finish his shower, Evan, Marissa, Ian, Rich, and Michelle eagerly waited inside the bedroom to see their new gifts. Last night a note had been delivered informing them that a surprise would be delivered this morning.

"I hope the gifts are warm," Ian said as they heard the shower stop running. "It's barely five degrees out there today."

The group nodded in agreement. Lance and Sara left so quickly yesterday that Ian and his friends did not have a chance to ask "how they were supposed to stay warm." In the end, they had spent much of the day trying to figure out warm outfits that they could move in.

A few minutes later, when Mikey was ready, they entered the living room to see seven tall wardrobes standing in the center of the room.

"This is creepy," Rich commented as he inspected their new furniture. "They slip in here at night and set this stuff up without us noticing."

Mikey, Evan, and Ian nodded in agreement while, Michelle and Marissa laughed under their breath behind them. Last night they had let Laura and a few others in to deliver these packages.

"They must have secret fairies," Marissa sarcastically chimed in making Michelle laugh again.

The wardrobes stood as seven-foot mahogany armoires. Each one was four feet wide, two feet deep, and came complete with beautiful ivory handles and an engraved black marble name tag inset on a white marble base. Enthralled with their beauty no one dared open them and instead stood, for many minutes, taking in their beauty.

"At some point we should probably open them," Marissa broke the silence after a quarter hour.

"On three," Evan said reaching for the ivory handle. "One... Two... Three"

Together they opened the armoire to find weapons and armor staring back at them. The armor was jet black, marble, and looked as if it could become the darkness at night or the shadows during the day.

The weapons were exquisite. Gleaming blades were a mixture of compounds that no one could name. Black marble handles topped each piece and after an initial once over everyone disappeared into their wardrobes to explore their weapons and armor further.

"What is it?" Rich asked after Ian had broken the silence with a barely audible "no way."

Turning to the group Ian was holding a simple longbow. The leather grip was unprofessionally wrapped around what looked like a very unfinished, rural bow. A recent coat of varnish might have been applied, but outside of that no one understood why Ian was so enamored with this lack luster bow.

"Want a challenge?" Evan asked searching for a reason to Ian's excitement.

"This is my bow from Earth," Ian replied in disbelief as he turned the bow over in his hands, checking it against his memory. Inspecting every inch Ian was trying to confirm what his instincts were telling him.

The natural two tone wood, with all its imperfections, was the same. The leather handle still had his hand print. Across the front of the bow was the same woven cloth that helped add to its strength. The only thing different was that the bow shined back at him with a lacquer that he did not apply. As similar as the bow felt it felt different, stronger, than it was before. Ian would now be fighting with Earth at his side.

"String it up so we can test the weight," Evan suggested as he walked closer to examine the bow. Everyone now sharing in Ian's excitement.

Looking inside the bow's long, green, sock-like case Ian found a familiar stringer. Placing the stringer's loops at either end Ian instinctively took his stance. Anchoring himself over the stringer to create the required resistance to string his bow. Gripping the heart of the bow's leather handle, Ian started to pull up only to find another surprise.

The bow resisted him. After the past few months of training Ian never expected this. Pulling up the bow fought back with a strength it had never possessed. This was his old bow, Ian was certain of that, but Lance, Jerry, Laura, Sara, or someone had done something to strengthen his bow. They had done something to make it more powerful and indestructible than it ever had been on Earth.

With a deeper stance and a deep breath, Ian pulled up on the handle again. This time Ian looped the new string into its waiting grooves. Their fit locked the bow in place.

The string had been changed and was a weave of a few unidentifiable materials. Under this closer inspection, Ian could tell that his bow had been reheated and re-bent. It had been coated several times with a new finish and, while he did not know *how* exactly, his bow had been turned from a hobby into a tool of war.

Taking the bow in his left hand, Ian took his stance, and began to pull only to have his suspicions confirmed. His 50 pound bow now drew at least at 80.

Passing it around Evan and Rich were the only other people who could get the bow to full draw. Surprised by its strength everyone gave the bow its praises before returning to their own chest of goodies.

The morning moved along quietly. Weapons got passed along every so often as they found ones worthy of praise or that raised questions. Through the morning, the group found that many of their weapons were heavier than what they should be. This would have been the worst problem, but when Mikey dropped a knife and caught it by the blade they discovered something much worse.

"Mikey you okay?" Michelle and Evan jumped to his side as soon as he grabbed it.

"Show me your hand," Evan started. "Rich, use the phone we will need someone to look at his hand. Breathe Mikey."

Mikey was concerned, like his friends, but shocked everyone when he opened his hand to find a bruise, no blood or wound.

"What…" Evan said in disbelief.

"What is it?" Rich asked, phone in hand about to dial.

"Put that down. Ian hand me the knife."

Rich put down the phone and Ian handed Evan the knife and after looking it over for a minute Evan spoke up again.

"Check your blades," Evan announced to the group, leaving Mikey in Michelle's capable hands.

Going to their weapons they found a surprise. The weapons were not only heavy, but dull. They could break bones, but were not sharp enough to cut through cardboard, let alone a suit of armor.

They did not have much time to focus on this because, before long, it was time to don their armor. Unlike their weapons the armor was light, strong, and, more important, battle ready. Laying out the pieces the found a little note attached to each piece explaining how to put it on.

The first step was to put on the armor's under suit. It was jet black, like the rest of the armor, and was made of three pieces: a hooded long sleeved, gloved shirt, pants, which covered the feet, and a belt. The under suit hugged the body like latex, but breathed like silk. Being so tight the suit exposed everything about each student's body. They each could see the months of hard work in the mirror. They could also see the work left to do.

"This suit is crazy," Evan exclaimed, as he contorted his body in every possible way. Trying to stretch the suit to its limits. "It's snug and moves. It is warm, but not smothering."

The non assuming black leather belt was smooth too and finished the under suit. Mikey explored the belt and found a place where it turned from leather into marble. With a tug, he pulled out a knife. Showing the rest of the group they all found this same knife in their belts. At first, it was difficult to find and draw. After a few minutes of practice it became second nature to draw this sharp, battle ready blade.

With their under suits on the group was ready to put the armor on. They pulled on an extra pair of socks over the pants. After that they put on heavy, armored black boots. The boots had thick soles and were reinforced at every angle. Even with this strength they were remarkably pliable. Their glass like surface appeared as if they could stop a blade all on their own.

The leg armor stacked up their legs, each piece covering the one before all the way to their waist. The back piece went on next and locked into the suits bottom half. Like dragon scales, the back piece stretched to keep them covered when they extended their body and contracted when they crouched, allowing full movement.

The arm pieces went on like the leg pieces and locked into the back piece, and finally the chest plate snapped into place, locking it all in.

All the pieces fit snuggly together, did not limit movement, and locked together as a single strong unit. The armor was cold to the touch and was some infused mixture of marble, steel, and kevlar they suspected. It would take some getting used to, but was not as heavy as they thought it would be.

Running his fingers over his suit Ian found that his backplate had an attachment for his quiver. Below this groove Ian found a compartment that ran the length of his back. Fiddling with it, in the mirror, Ian opened the compartment to find arrows tipped with the same compound as his armor. Outside of a few arrows, the compartment was surprisingly empty.

Each suit was a tailored fit, which included specialized places for their weapons of choice. As a group they found several knives, same as the one on their under suit belt. All expertly hidden.

"Do y'all have these?" Mikey asked pointing to a few spots. One on his ankle, thighs, and breast plate.

"What do you mean?" Evan asked, unable to see what Mikey was pointing at.

"These spots. You must have them too," Mikey responded a little frustrated that Evan was not taking him seriously, something that had gotten worse since John's departure.

Using their armored hands they felt the areas Mikey pointed out to find small empty openings. Running his finger through space on his right thigh Ian knew, in an instant, what was missing.

"There is even a small one on the back of the helmet," Mikey announced before Ian could speak.

Without responding Ian went back to his cabinet and found five marble boxes in the back. Retrieving them, Ian opened the boxes to have his suspicions confirmed. Five handguns of various size, with numerous clips, started back at him.

Examining the clips he found they held a variety of bullets.

Taking them out Ian snapped the guns and clips into place, before bending down to put the final gun in its hidden ankle holster. Standing up Ian felt their weight, but did not see the guns. Tucked into the armor, there was just enough wiggle room to draw the weapon.

"Ian what these holes are for?" Mikey asked.

"Guns," Ian said emotionlessly as he placed his helmet on the table. "They are the most common weapon found on my planet and are in the boxes in the back of your cabinet. Be careful, they are loaded, but I can help you all put them away if you like."

Over the next fifteen minutes, Ian helped his friends holster their guns and clips. Exploring the armor this intimately lead to another discovery. While Ian was helping Michelle (the fourth person) put her final clip away, Ian found a hidden compartment that held additional clips. Curious, Ian removed one of his own clips to find a hidden compartment underneath.

His mind racing Ian helped Evan get his guns in place and decided he had to know.

"Guys get John's armor out."

The group laid out John's armor and Ian began

methodically searching every groove trying to find its secrets. Ian looked for anything that was out of place. His meticulous search paid off as Ian found one hidden compartment after another.

Under each gun there were extra clips. Other compartments held empty water bladders, while others held knifes and rations. All in all there were fourteen on the arms and legs, but this paled to what he found in the breast and back plate.

The back compartment, which Ian had found earlier, was larger than he initially thought and could be stuffed not only with arrows, but had marked spots for first aid and ration kits.

The breast plates' compartment was filled with first aid supplies, food rations, another water bladder, and other survival gear. Using John's armor as a guide, each person reached around their own armor, found the compartments, and realized that they were all within reach without ever having to take off a single piece of protection.

"Now, we know why it is so heavy," Rich joked. A little curious how all these compartments stayed shut, knowing that they would never open unless he wanted them to.

"How do they expect us to fight in all this?" Mikey asked the question they all wondered as they put

John's armor away. "I am getting fatigued just wearing it. I can't imagine fighting in it."

"I am sure we will get used to it. They would not create something we cannot fight in," Ian responded. Personally wondering why there was so much marble integrated into the suit.

"But what about the weapons?" Mikey asked the other thing they were all wondering.

"I have no idea," Ian answered. He, like everyone else, was wondering why his weapons were not battle ready, but the armor was.

The weapons were heavy and dull. Together, each person's collection of weapons was possibly doubling the weight of their already heavy armor.

"Its almost 7:30 guys," Marissa spoke as she put John's helmet away. "I'm sure Lance and Sara will have some answers for us."

"We should probably get moving considering how heavy all this is. So let's grab our helmets, weapons, and head out," Rich added.

Nodding in agreement each person went back to their cabinet and finished suiting up. Ian attached his quiver and bow to their intended grooves. He also strapped his scabbard sword into place. Looking at himself in the mirror Ian pulled on his under suit hood and realized that the war was real. He was a soldier and whatever Lance and Sara had planned for them would re-inforce that.

Taking a look over his armor one final time Ian was surprised to see his under suit poking out on the fingers of his right armored hand. It was too obvious to be a flaw, and Ian knew his exposed fingers were waiting for something.

It took a second, but then an idea hit Ian. Rum-maging around in his bow's sock Ian found his finger guard from Earth waiting for him. It too had been covered with something to strengthen it, but was as pliable and form fitting as ever. Tak-ing off his right gauntlet, Ian fitted the glove be-fore replacing his armor.

"Come on sweetie, let's get going," Marissa whis-pered to Ian as she gave him swift kiss on the cheek before joining the rest of their friends.

Ian took one last look at himself before flexing his hand and grabbing his helmet. With over a hundred pounds in additional gear, the group knew that the war had found them.

CHAPTER FOURTEEN
Battle Ready

Lance and Sara waited for them in the middle of a snow white field. Despite the armor's weight, the group of six soon found some its benefits as they trudged to the middle of the field. First, they would be in better shape than they had ever intended in no time, and even walking through the brisk $-10°$ air everyone was warm and cozy inside the amazing suits.

"I see you found your new armor," Lance commented as six soldiers stopped in front of him "What do you think?"

"It's a little heavy, but I feel unstoppable in it. I feel like I am my own mini army," Michelle answered for the group who nodded in agreement.

"It is the best armor available and is being moved out to all fighting level three and above special jumpers," Lance said. A sense of pride beaming out from him underneath his heavy winter coat.

"This suit is not standard issue then?" Ian asked one of the questions that had been bothering him all morning. Flipping his helmet in his hands as he did.

"Not at all. The suits are made up of our strongest and lightest alloy and are designed for fighting in and across The Dimension, and the worlds attached to it. These suits are climate controlled through your under suit and watch. Outside of keeping you safe they will keep you comfortable as well," Lance continued as he started to bask in the glory of his team's genius.

"Have you tried on the helmets yet?" Sara asked the group. "You really should; they showcase the suit's best feature," Sara finished as the group shook their head "no" to her first question.

Taking Sara's advice the six students donned their full face, midnight black, helmets. The helmet fell into the armor's neck piece, and with a small twist, clicked into place and whirred to life. The vitals of the six of them popped onto the visor along with a targeting screen, scanners, night vision, weather conditions and more. All the options of their tablets, their new watches, were available at a glance.

"What is going on!?!" Mikey screamed trying to

regain his composure from the visual assault.

"Don't yell Mikey.... We are mic'd up," Rich said as he tried to recover from Mikey's squeal. "Although he is right. What is going on?"

"Your helmets are tied into your suits and your watches. All the information gathered from both is at your disposal with a glance and voice controls," Sara started to explain. "With this helmet, you will have real time battle information and can communicate with anyone on the planet you are on. The helmets are equipped with X-ray, infrared, night vision, and a variety of other sensors and scanners. Over time the computer will adjust to your glance commands and preferences, but for now your best option will be voice commands."

"The tubes at the front of your helmet will keep you running during the battle," Lance took over for Sara as he began to explain the suit. "The one on the left will provide water, the right a nutritious supplement. Your suit continuously absorbs and filters water through the soles of your boots and will hold a few gallons of water. The food is a protein mixture designed to keep you moving and alive. While there is a two-week supply, I would personally use rations and find other food when you can."

Under the motorcycle style helmet each person took a quick sip and found that Lance was correct. Anything would be better than the "supplement" Lance had provided.

"These suits are designed to be lived in. That is why all your rations are hidden within reach."

Lance waited for the group to nod. Once they did, he knew that they were all on the same page. His students had found the hidden compartments.

"Finding food will not be that difficult because as you explore worlds, edible and nutritious plants, grubs, and substances will automatically be located and indicated."

"As Lance said these suits are designed to be lived in for months at a time and, unlike your weapons, the suits are battle ready. We want you spend a day out of them at least every two weeks, but need you to wear them as much as possible. We want you to live in them as much as possible so you can adjust the weight and get used to moving in them," Sara continued.

"So these weapons are not our final ones then?" Rich asked the question they had all wondered since they found their dull blades this morning.

"The weapons you received, except the guns, knives, and possibly bow or crossbow will all be replaced. These practice weapons are heavier than the ones you will actually use in battle. Training with them will give you strength, mobility, and agility. Perfect your skills with these you will have more facility than you could ever dream of with your actual blades," Lance answered Rich's question. "Your under suit, along with being extremely comfortable, is also designed to keep you safe. It will regulate body temperature and keep track of your vitals, among a few other things. Always wear it with your armor and you will never have a problem. Any more questions?"

It took a minute for the group of six to take in what Sara and Lance said. They were getting answers and wondered what Lance and Sara had in store.

"Until now you have run simulations, sparred, and trained on your own. While that was good you have not had to fight. You have not personally experienced battle. That changes today," Sara said. Snapping her fingers she brought the barren field to life.

Instinctively the group took defensive stances, reaching for a weapon, as hundreds of enemies appeared around them.

Some enemies held axes, some swords, and others weapons that they did not recognize. The enemies were not heavily armored, but their skin was scaly and intermittent armor was grotesquely detailed with skulls and skeletons. The ghouls were quite ragged and detailed. Crooked noses, straight noses deep eyes, and shallow eyes, strong bodies, and ones with more fluff than muscle filled out the army. Even with the variety of bodies and weapons each enemy carried an evil expression that, even while frozen, expressed their only desire: to hunt and kill Ian and his friends.

"The goal of these simulations, of these enemies,' Sara started motioning to the army around them. 'Is for you to learn how to fight with your swords, bows, knives, and other weapons."

"You should know that your guns will not harm these creatures,' Lance commented to Ian whose hand already rested on one of his firearms. 'Firearms are not very effective in The Dimension. They do not consistently work between worlds and are useless in The Dimension itself. Guns have a purpose, they work well on some planets, but you cannot count on them. Many of your missions will require you to fight in close quarters so we need you to be ready to defend yourself with reliable means. History has shown us that simpler weapons are better."

Removing his hand from the pistol grip Ian reached for his bow instead.

"You should also know that while your enemies will use a variety of weapons, The Evil's best soldiers use swords and axes. They are well trained and if you do not know how to wield these weapons, equally well, they will destroy you before you could ever draw a gun."

With Lance's last warning the group looked back at their frozen enemies with their suspicions confirmed: These things wanted to rip them apart.

"Today, your goal is simple: We want you to escape from the field and find Laura. She is at a camp, in the surrounding woods, three miles from where you are standing now. After you escape the field you will need to lose your enemies and find Laura. She will feed and give you the next part of your mission. Out in the woods all wildlife is real and anything that attacks you can kill you. Stay alert and behave accordingly."

Thinking Lance was finished; everyone began to brace for battle when Sara piped up one final time.

"Beyond that, this field and the surrounding forest, for about five miles, have been laced with projectors. The projector creates your enemies and while their blows may not be fatal, I guarantee, they will hurt. Do not get lazy once you have left the field. They will be coming after you. You must always stay vigilant!!!"

"So do you understand? The enemies are real. Escape them and find Laura. Understand?" Lance asked the group who nodded. "You all must reach Laura, so don't leave anyone behind. Good luck."

Without another word Sara and Lance left the field as the magnificent six prepared for battle.

Rich swung a mace impatiently, while Mikey chose matching long knives to start the battle with. Michelle held a trident like spear. Housing nasty looking blades that arched back that looked as if it could rip through anything. Evan and Marissa had drawn their swords. Marissa's Broadsword was smaller than average, while Evan's was a Greatsword that should be wielded with two hands, but could be handled with one. Torn, Ian's hand was on his trusty bow, but acknowledging the situation he drew his own broadsword and prepared for battle.

How am I ever going to wield this? Ian wondered to himself. The heavy sword clunky in his hands as he rethought his choice.

Bouncing the blade in his hands Ian, started to adjust, and knew that he did not have a choice. He had to learn how to use it and now was as good a time as any. Adjusting his stance Ian addressed the group, like John would have, through their intercom, as they waited for their lifeless army to animate.

"Let's battle towards the Southern Woods."

"Sounds good," was the response Ian heard as the inanimate army sprang to life.

In an instant the cold air was filled with the sounds of steel, war cries, and death as the opposing army began their assault. Mikey and Marissa were facing the Southern Woods and became the groups de facto leaders as they started moving through the opposing force.

Moving steadily through the enemy the magnificent six was finding out first hand that, while they may not be lethal, their enemies were out for blood. Arrows flew towards them and after deflecting them they realized this enemy would do anything to win. After a few minutes they were all feeling the pain of the battle taking place.

The enemies were unending as axes, swords, maces, and more were being thrown at them from all directions. Some blows glanced off their armor, while they parried others into their own strikes.

"How close are we?" Ian screamed over the intercom as he removed his knife from a gruesome ghoul. Parrying a spear away with an axe he had picked up a second earlier.

"We are getting close, but I do not know how we are going to lose them," Marissa chimed in as she decapitated an enemy that was about to hit Mikey's blind side.

"I agree," Mikey said. Removing his dual blades from a downed foe as he prepared for his next encounter.

Looking at his heads up display Ian saw what they meant. The battle field map showed their progress and while they were getting close to the Southern Woods, once they broke through the enemies southern flank, they would not be home free. The woods would offer cover; unfortunately, without some sort of distraction, they had no chance of escaping their enemy. If they could not make a clean get away fighting in the woods would be all but impossible.

Facing the North side of the field Ian saw downed enemies slowly getting up. If the ghoul had not been killed it was rejoining the fight. The ones that were down for the count, were being scavenged for anything that could help their fellow soldiers. This was confirmed for everyone on their heads up display as their enemy started to flank their sides.

"Mikey and Marissa you guys break up into the woods going South-East. Evan and Michelle you follow them and break off South-West after about fifty yards. Rich follow my lead," Ian said through the headset.

"Sounds good,"

"Okay…"

"I'm with you," Rich confirmed after Michelle and Evan chimed in.

"Ian what are you doing?" Marissa asked, not ready to accept his plan.

"Just go…" Ian said, as their group of six breached the enemy's southern flank.

Mikey, Michelle, Evan, and Marissa started to take off for the Southern Woods as the fallen soldiers flanked and followed.

"Rich you got this, follow me…" Ian said before running back towards the enemies.

"I'm right behind you…" Rich said, swirling his mace in glee as Ian's plan started to take shape.

"Ian what are the two of you doing?" Marissa screamed over the intercom as she looked back to see Ian and Rich running to rejoin the fray.

"Giving you a distraction so you can escape. Now get moving," Ian responded as he started slashing blindly at the oncoming attackers.

"How exactly is charging the enemy going to

work?" Mikey asked. His heads up display showing their opposition following them into the woods.

"Yeah how?" Michelle's voice broke through the intercom with the woosh of an arrow. She had put away her trident and laced a few arrows as they waited for Ian to respond.

"Like this."

Running to the Northern Woods Rich and Ian were slashing their way through the weakened forces with ease. They caught the enemy off guard and had divided their attention.

"You idiot!!!" Marissa screamed over their shared channel. "What were you thinking," her anger rising as she started to run down the mountain side back to the field.

"I was thinking that you four better be running for cover for this maneuver to be worth anything," Ian said as he stabbed another enemy on his way across the field. Rich saved Ian's six by bashing an enemy over the head with his mace.

Glancing at the heads up display, Marissa, like everyone else, saw Ian's plan unfolding in front of their eyes. Their path to the Northern Woods was littered by the weakened, fallen, injured, or dead. The remaining enemy was frozen, divided on who to follow. Ian's charge caused pandemonium as the enemy tried to readjust their lines and strategy.

"Start moving," Ian yelled over the intercom to his friends on the hill.

Without hesitation the four used Ian's diversion and escaped into the woods. Within thirty-seconds, the enemy had lost track of Michelle, Evan, Marissa, and Mikey. Ian's brazen maneuver had worked and the enemy was going to make him pay.

Back on the field Ian and Rich were reaping the benefits of their new gear. Their boots crushed through the snow and downed enemies easily. The suits extra weight propelled them forward.

Close to the battle's starting point Ian looked at the battle field display and saw that his and Rich's luck was running out. The enemy had adjusted and closed ranks around them. After losing the other four in the woods the soldiers had turned all their attention on Ian and Rich. His friends were too far away to provide assistance. They were on their own without a clear way out.

"Ian, what now?" Rich's voice crackled through the intercom.

The snarling enemies had stopped rushing them. Rich and Ian were completely surrounded and enemies were starting to close in carefully.

Watching their breath break the cold air Rich knew that they had no way to overpower this army.

"Rich you were a track star right?" Ian asked. Slicing at the enemies who dove forward.

"Yeah... Why?" came a nervous answer from Rich along with the sound of a cracking skull.

"I will drop to my knees and let them converge on me. I need you to use my back as a springboard and jump the last few rows of enemies separating us from the Northern Woods."

Looking at his display Rich saw what Ian saw. The enemy had converged on them, but the northern side was weak. Using Ian as a springboard Rich could jump to safety. He would be able to escape. However this plan would leave Ian stranded and Rich unable to help.

"I can do it, but I will be unarmed going into the jump. You're on your own until I can redraw," Rich informed Ian.

"That's fine by me. If this works all I need you to do is keep running once you land," Ian responded as he sheathed his sword and prepared to drop. "I'm dropping in three-seconds Rich. All I need you to do is draw your guns and send off some warning shots as you go over." Ian said as he dropped to one knee and braced himself.

"Your funeral," Rich said as he stowed his mace, bloody with gore, and began to run at full speed. Hoping Ian had a plan.

Closing the distance quickly, enemies started converging, when Rich planted on Ian's marble quiver, propelled himself up and over, drawing two pistols as he went. The soldiers closing in on Ian stopped and watched Rich flip over them, firing off warning shots as he went.

Rich holstered his guns as he prepared to land a few feet beyond the enemy's final line. Sliding to a stop in the snow, Rich fought his momentum as he drew his mace. He was about to rush back for Ian when he saw soldiers falling down like trees in a storm. Wondering what hit them Rich saw, smiled, and took off towards the Northern Woods.

Ian broke through the last line after using his bow as a battering ram. Enemies fell to either side as Ian's bow struck them in the abdomen and sent them head over heels.

After breaking through the final row Ian quickly knocked an arrow and released it back into mass of foes as they tried to catch up with him and Rich.

"Put away your bow, Ian, and run!!!!" Rich yelled, as Ian caught up with him. They had done all they could and it was time to make a beeline for the waiting woods.

Putting away their weapons they galloped through the snow as they tried to cover the final forty-five yards.

"How did you know the guns would work?" Rich asked Ian as they ran.

"I didn't," Ian answered honestly. "I was just hoping it would distract them. What is going on!?!"

Their heads up displays were flashing with hundreds of red dots rushing towards them.

"I'm not sure?" Rich responded, fighting the urge to stop and wonder what surprise these holograms still had in store for them.

Twenty yards from the woods the red dots were closing on them faster than they were on the woods. Ian and Rich were not going to make it. Deciding to go down fighting, they were about to draw their weapons when Michelle's voice rang through the intercom.

"Split off in opposite directions and start weaving. You have projectiles coming in."

Without a seconds hesitation they took their hands off their weapons and followed orders. Weaving for as long as they could, Rich and Ian both jumped into the snow as they drew their mace and sword. On their backs, they used their helmet's incredible software to assist them to harmlessly knock away the incoming projectiles.

"Good job guys. Now get up and run for the woods before they catch you. Keep weaving and don't give them a clean shot. Once you reach the woods you will have a minute or two to lose them. Arrows incoming momentarily."

Ian and Rich had darted off in opposite directions, as soon as they heard Michelle say *"Good job,"* weaving as they went. Fortunately for them their enemy had changed tactics and stopped chasing them entirely when the second deluge of arrows were launched.

The arrows reached their crest and started to fall back to earth, but this time Rich and Ian were only a few feet from the safety of the woods. Diving into its glorious shelter, Rich and Ian heard a shower of arrows fall just short of them, a few drifting harmlessly into the majestic canopy.

"Rich, you good?" Ian asked over the intercom, as he got up and wandered to his friend.

"Yeah," Rich responded with a tone so happy you could see his grin through the helmet.

"You two should be moving. Not hugging," an annoyed Marissa came over the headset. Without another word Ian and Rich started moving again.

They had survived their first battle.

CHAPTER FIFTEEN

Hiking Through Pain

"Never again, but that was awesome," Rich admitted as he and Ian wandered deeper into the forest.

"It worked," Ian replied. Letting his muscles relax as they walked. "Now we have to think of crazier things to do. The software learns and we don't want to become predictable."

Rich and Ian laughed together and after not seeing an enemy for over a half hour they took a seat on the bank of a river to rest while they waited to hear from the other half of their group.

Their bodies may be relaxing, but sitting on the river's edge Ian and Rich kept a keen eye out and their minds alert. They were not going to be surprised and refused to solely rely on their suits amazing sensors.

They sat there for an hour and felt fairly safe until Marissa's voice broke through their jubilant laughter.

"You two better not try that again!"

"Sorry sweetie?" Ian apologized nervously. "It did work though and everyone is fine."

"This time...." Marissa hissed. "And you are not out of the woods. Follow the river toward the Mountain's east side. We will find you there," Marissa ordered over the intercom.

"So you, Mikey, Michelle, and Evan are back together then?" Rich joked as he and Ian began moving again.

"We are looping around in a zig-zag pattern to avoid any trouble; something you two should learn about." Marissa growled.

"We will meet you at the river's fork in about twenty minutes," Evan answered Rich's question. "Mikey thinks Laura's camp is most likely a quarter mile up the mountain from that fork. You will be at the fork in two minutes. I suggest you get there and take cover."

"We found out our boots are designed to decrease our tracks by 80%. Once you reach the fork take high ground and you should be fine," Mikey chimed in for the first time in a while. His voice noticeably happier than Marissa's.

Taking their time Ian and Rich walked up the river and knew better than to question Mikey, Marissa, or Evan right now. They all had skills and had learned that Mikey had an uncanny knowledge of the woods and tracking over the past few weeks. The suits amazing sensors did point out all the useful things around them. Fish and ways to catch them, medicinal plants, poisonous plants, and edible ones. It was quite a feat for their suits and was something Mikey knew by heart.

Reaching the river's fork Rich and Ian followed Marissa's advice and took up posts in the trees.

"Ian, what do you think those tracks are?" Rich said over the intercom as he motioned to tracks about forty feet from their location.

The tracks did not register on their computer and, looking back at Rich, Ian shrugged. Ian wanted to investigate the tracks, but acknowledged that the chances of them being related to John were slim. The search parties had scoured this area.

"Probably something stupid," Ian said trying not to encourage Rich.

"Yeah. Or it could be…"

Rich did not have to finish his statement, they

both were thinking the same thing.

"You think we should check them out?" Ian asked. Despite his better intentions, he was ready for another challenge. Ian felt invincible and a little cocky from their earlier success.

"Ian, I will shoot you in the leg if you get down from that tree before I am there," Marissa hissed over their group channel before Rich could answer him.

"Mikey will check out the tracks when we get there."

Looking up the hill Ian was barely able to make out four shadows moving through the woods; certain that one of them had a bow trained on him. Waiting in their trees, as ordered, it took a few minutes before Marissa, Evan, Mikey, and Michelle met them at the river's fork. Mikey took a look at the tracks, even followed them for a few minutes, before deciding they were nothing of consequence. Making a mental note Ian decided he would have to investigate the tracks another day.

...

"Nice going Ian," Laura congratulated Ian on his successful plan as she passed around warm drinks and biscuits to the newly arrived group.

"Thanks. But I couldn't have done it without

Rich," Ian said patting his partner on the back as they sat down to rest for the night.

"I wouldn't get so cooky," Marissa spat cooly across the flames. "It was stupid, irresponsible, and dangerous. You could have been killed if those weren't holograms."

"You just wish you had been with him instead of me," Rich defended Ian.

Silence grew until Marissa's scowl turned into her mischievous smile. Laughter broke the tension as the group began recounting the day's events and what each group did after Ian's bold move.

"Do y'all have any questions for me?" Laura asked the group as the conversation started to die down.

"Who designed these suits?" Evan asked first.

"In all honesty, I don't know. All I do know is that these suits are designed for prolonged battle in The Dimension. We hope that these suits will be able to help non-special jumpers like Rich and Evan survive longer in The Dimension. With any luck they may allow them to fight. Everything is designed with survival and battle in mind. The undersuit is pure genius. It not only keeps your body temperature regulated and monitors your vitals, but also applies healing solutions to minor wounds. It will heat and cool your body to heal minor aches and pains."

Now that Laura pointed it out Ian and the others noticed that parts of their bodies felt cooler and hotter as the suit tended to their sore muscles.

"What's next?" Ian asked. Wondering what mythical beast they would have to fight tomorrow.

"In the morning your mission will be to find your way back to your cabin. Y'all will leave the camp at dawn and can relax with whatever time you have left in the day."

"That's it?" Rich blurted out in disbelief. The task was too simple after what they faced today.

"That's it," Laura answered. "Eat up and get some rest you guys. The morning will be here before you know it."

The next day, around 4:30 in the afternoon, Ian would have loved to have another go around with the enemy holograms. At dawn they woke to find that a fresh layer of snow had covered the ground and any tracks they had made. This was the least of their worries because Laura had packed up the camp during the night. They were alone on a mountain side, in the snow, and, to make matters worse, Laura had also taken their valuable helmets.

Without their helmets they had to navigate using natural markers. The sun would have helped, but a cloudy day made it almost impossible to see.

Of course the helmets offered a lot more than direction. Without them they had no prior warning to the dangers around them. They spent the day on watch for anything mother nature, Lance, Sara, or Laura could throw at them. As the day wore on they became tired, irritable, hungry, and lost.

"You don't think they would let us freeze? Do you?" Evan asked trudging through the snow at the head of the group.

"No," Marissa snapped back, her exhaustion finally coming through. Leaning down she started investigating a broken branch. Trying to find the clues that it held to their survival.

"That's good to know that they won't let us die, but Marissa the only secret that branch holds is that Evan tripped over it a minute ago," Rich informed her sarcastically as he walked past her up the hill.

"Any ideas?" Evan asked irritably, his frustration mounting as he led the lost group.

"The field is at the top of this hill," Mikey informed Evan yet again.

"You sure?" Rich asked questioning Mikey's expertise after saying that statement a few times today.

"What is that supposed to mean?" Michelle questioned Rich's tone.

"I thought that was obvious. Why are we still listening to the youngest person here who apparently does not know his ass from a hole in the ground."

The group was exhausted and Ian had to grab Michelle as she started to jump towards Rich.

"Calm down, calm down," Ian said to his enraged friend.

"Let me go. Let me at him."

"Rich didn't mean it. We are all tired. The weather is just getting the better of us," Ian interjected to diffuse the situation.

Rich and Michelle quickly apologized to each other before Mikey had a chance to answer Rich's original question.

"There is smoke rising from the hill. If I'm not mistaken I think that is camp," Mikey answered Rich as he pointed to the smoke billowing behind him in the sky.

Walking over the crest of the incline Mikey was

correct. Laura, Lance, and Sara were at the center of the field waiting to congratulate them. When they reached Laura she gave each of them a hug before returning their helmets with a wink.

Two hours after arriving home Marissa exited the bathroom. She was the final person to shower after the last two days. Their new armoires had been moved into the bedroom, between their beds. Their armor now hung inside, while the undersuit hung on the doors to air out.

They were all dressed to relax. The boys in boxers and undershirts. The girls in nighties and shorts. Exhausted as they were they were trying to enjoy their free time after spending the last two days inside the suits.

"Looking good," Rich shot Marissa a wink as she left the bathroom.

"Don't you wish," she chided back as she went to Ian's bed and planted a kiss on him.

"Real nice," Evan laughed back. Excited to be back in his own bed after last night.

"Do you think they meant to take our helmets?" Ian asked as everyone began to settle in for the night.

"Yeah, why?" Rich asked wondering what Ian was getting at.

"Sara and Lance looked a little surprised to see us without them. I just wonder if it were originally planned or if… if-"

"-If what Ian? So what if it wasn't planned. Laura probably thought it would be a good way to get us extra experience," Rich answered him.

The room seemed to agree with Rich. Ian knew he was probably right so he shrugged off his suspicion as they got back to enjoying their night.

After the excitement of the past few days everyone's adrenaline and base instincts were running high. Any walls they had set up melted away as they lounged in the cabin's sleeping quarters.

"So, Michelle have you and Mikey moved on to bigger things?" Rich asked directly.

"I do not know what you mean Rich?" Michelle answered with an innocent joke.

"Real funny. I mean, have you two explored the forbidden fruit?" Rich pushed.

A little embarrassed, Mikey started to glow red, but Michelle, calm as ever, answered Rich.

"Not yet, we haven't had time considering you two stags are always around."

Michelle turned the tables on Rich and laughter broke out at his and Evan's expense.

"She's right. Stags like you two mess up every-thing," Marissa chimed in from across the room as she gave Ian another kiss.

"That must be it," Rich rolled his eyes as he sat up.

Conversation lulled and an uneasy tension set-tled in the air. A few attempts fizzled as their sa-cred spare time ticked away.

"What now?" Rich asked. Shifting uncomfort-ably as he tried to escape the tension in the room.

"I have a question. Why haven't you two found someone?" Marissa asked.

Her personal question was innocent and sat in the air waiting for an answer that neither one of them wanted to give. Despite how close they had become Evan and Rich's love life never came up. Evan responded with a question of his own try-ing to break the impetuous silence.

"Is there any reason you want to know?"

"Outside of training for the war, we are all pressured find someone. Jerry pushes it here, es-pecially with the girls who cannot jump. We all know how hard he pushed for Ian and me to get together. I am just a little surprised he did not push you two," Marissa answered Evan's ques-tion with an answer he did not expect. "Plus I may know a girl or two who are interested." Marissa added as Evan and Rich rolled their eyes.

"I don't know about Rich, but I'm taken," Evan revealed something new.

"Who?" Michelle exclaimed.

"Her name is Evankila and she is still on my home world. We were separated when I jumped. She is a special jumper, but was not allowed to jump with me for some reason," Evan tacked on as tears formed under his brown eyes. "I have asked Jerry hundreds of times why she couldn't jump with me? Why we could not try to save her? But all he ever gives me are vague answers like:" *Her double is not ready*" or "*it's too big of a risk.*" For years, I have tried to find her double. I want to help them train so we can save her, but all my efforts have been fruitless and in vain."

"What have you tried?" Michelle asked wondering if there were anything she could do.

"I have checked all the jump records. Her name has been removed or marked in a way I do not understand. The mark appears across various names, mostly on lost worlds. As far as I can figure out it is something marking that they are not safe to save or jump to."

"I'm sorry," Marissa let out to her friend searching for hope. "But the mark shouldn't stop you from finding out who it is. Maybe we can help."

"Thanks but that is the thing. Once a name is marked their information is encrypted, stored, or deleted. It may be on a separate server, I don't know, all I know is the information is lost."

"That's... awful... I'm so sorry," Michelle commented with a few tears of her own.

"It's fine. I just hope that one day she will stop suffering."

Rich tried to comfort Evan but his despair was infectious. Everyone felt it. A single question lingered in the air a question that Marissa pushed her friend a little further by asking.

"But Evan...If your world was lost, how do you hold onto hope? How do you know she is alive?"

Marissa tried to be as delicate as possible, but the question was harsh and cut through the air like a knife. Looking back at Marissa, Evan shook his head before answering.

"How do you keep hope that John is alive?"

Evan's retort was rhetorical and while empty of any malice or anger hit hard. It also was the only time John had been mentioned outside of *"the ritual"* in months.

"I am not trying to be mean, but I thought you

would understand why I am hopeful," Evan continued. "In some ways I pity you. John's situation relies solely on the hope that he is either alive or dead. We all acknowledge that if he has survived this long he must be somehow taking care of himself. If not, we know he is not in pain."

His statement did little to lessen the blow of his question. Evan did not let the air hang as he finished his explanation.

"How would you feel if you knew John was alive but suffering? Which would you take? What if it were Ian? What if you had the choice to know, for certain, that he was somehow surviving or dead." Evan waited a second for an answer before continuing.

"I know it is not a fair question, but it is my reality," Evan finished as he pulled a necklace out of a box on his dresser. It was half of a charm and a glowing sapphire lit their little room.

"What is that?" Michelle asked. Enthralled with the beauty of the charm that Evan had just produced.

"These are our betrothed necklaces. On my world each person gets one at birth and when you find the person you want to be with you exchange them," Evan explained holding it up for all to see.

"As long as the gem glows, it means, the giver is still alive."

The sapphire filled the room with an eerie glow. Marissa never answered Evan's question and knew that she couldn't. No one in the room could make that choice. The room was silent watching the little charm glow.

They all felt for Evan as they tried to understand the horrors that he experienced every day. The only thing Evan knew was that Evankila was alive and probably suffering. Ian thought back to his first days on Esmerelda when he worried that his family had been captured and tortured for information they did not know.

To make matters worse for Evan, Evankila could escape. She was a jumper, a special jumper at level four no less, but he was not allowed to help her. No one was allowed to save her.

The group's silence turned into prayers. Some sent to Evankila, others to their loved ones, and missing comrades. A few to the victims of this war that they had never met and to all the worlds they had already left behind.

After what seemed like an eternity Rich looked up, found Marissa's gaze and answered her un-asked question quietly.

"I'm single because the person I cherish has

never been available for me to pursue."

Holding eye contact, neither one of them could turn away from each other. Ian wondered what Rich meant. Ian wondered if he had interfered with something that he hadn't known existed.

Silence fell after Rich's statement and would not be broken that night. Evan's story weighed on all of their hearts as they fell asleep one by one; reminded of the loved ones they had left behind.

Unable to sleep Ian looked at John's undisturbed bed and wondered if he was safe. Marissa tossed and turned as he looked at Rich's bed wondering if he and Marissa were responsible for breaking Rich's heart.

CHAPTER
SIXTEEN
Gifts

"Earlier this week you ran a simulation with some success," Lance said after the group of six reached the snowcapped field. "However, it is time you actually learn how to fight. Today each of you will be fighting various sized groups, individually, on the field. The combat will include everything from archery to knife fighting, hand to hand combat, and everything in-between. The field has been divided into five zones. While five of you train the sixth person will run the track to keep warm. Everyone pick a spot and let's begin."

Lance's speech was short and serious. They were no longer students, but warriors in training. No one talked as they picked spots. After five minutes of training they all wished they could have had a few more days, or months, to prepare.

Battling one on one, three against one, ten

on one, every member of the magnificent six found themselves out matched and beaten. The training wheels were off and they were feeling the pain. The holograms hit with just enough restraint not to break bones or cause serious internal damage. This was a small blessing after everyone found themselves, doubled over, fighting to continue and master the forms Lance, Sara, and Laura were forcing on them. Their three drill sergeants did not find any value in acclimating them to their new task. They felt the six of them should learn from the school of hard-knocks.

As the day progressed each person began to relish their laps. Even with armor weighing them down these laps were their only reprieve. After eight hours of this, the sun was abandoning the sky, and they were allowed to leave. Retreating to their cabin, battered and bruised, they ate, showered, and went to bed. Their sore bodies following them into their dreams.

Lance, Laura, and Sara gave them the next day to rest and recuperate. The following day they spent training on the field and after ten hours of work they began to wonder if their wounds would ever heal. After the third day, the weekend was upon them along with their new schedules.

Saturday and Sunday were dedicated larger group missions like the first one they faced.

Some missions were cooperative; others were competitive. Sometimes they had to defeat an opposing force. Other times they snuck into a strong hold or faced each other as opposing commanders. Search and destroy missions, rescue excursions, and full scale war filled their weekends.

No matter how long the mission took Laura, Sara, and Lance filled the day from dawn to dusk and sometimes beyond. A few times a single mission lasted the whole weekend. Other times they ran three, four, or even seven missions a day. The group knew Saturday night would be spent outside in the woods and frigid snow.

Monday and Wednesday were days of rest in a sense. They still trained for over six hours, on the field, but it was done alone. Beyond that they leisurely pursued their other studies and rested.

Tuesday and Thursday quickly became the bane of their existence.

Starting at dawn and going well past dusk these days featured intense one on one training where Sara and Laura pushed them to their limits and beyond. Every day became harder, the techniques more complex, and the repercussions for failure more severe. Beaten and bruised the magnificent six were pushed harder to succeed than ever before.

Friday was a day of guided study, battle preparation, and planing. And was the only day not spent in armor. What used to be a week's worth of study was mostly crammed into these Friday study sessions. Sara and Laura did not run these study halls, but instead sent generals, medics, and others directly involved with the war to grill their students.

Beaten, tired, and battered this new schedule became their life. Their life passed in such a fury that it gave them very little time to breathe let alone acknowledge the idea of time.

"Rich you can't hit Mikey that hard," Michelle screamed violently at Rich as she threw her helmet across the room, after a long weekend of missions in early March. Missions that had not ended so well.

"Michelle he needed to get down," Rich defended his actions. "He would have been smashed from behind, and it was the only option considering no one else had his back. We all know I have to have all of your backs because you can't cover them. Plus there is no way this crappy weapon would go through this," Rich finished his defense by striking his chest plate with his mace.

"You can't bank on that. You could have killed him," Michelle screamed at Rich from across the room, keeping her distance to avoid doing something she would regret." I guess you don't realize that this stuff is not always going to be fun and games. Soon enough our weap-"

"-You think this is fun and games!?!" Rich yelled as daggers flew from his eyes cutting her off. "You two don't have it half as hard as the rest of us. Every Tuesday and Thursday you go off with little Lancy to do who know's what. You escape half a day of training and leave the rest of us with the heartless sisters. Without you there we don't get to run laps. All we do is get battered until they decide we are done."

Tensions had been running high for weeks and was finally boiling over. For the past two weeks on Tuesday and Thursday afternoons Michelle and Mikey would disappear for special training with Lance. Michelle and Mikey's silence about their training divided the group even further. It added another layer of secrets and shadows to a group shrouded in mystery.

"Don't bring that up again," Michelle spat back. Showing Rich that he was not the only one who could shoot daggers with his eyes.

During the exchange Ian and Marissa helped Mikey out of his armor and onto one of the couches. Evan was in the kitchen fixing plates for everyone. Evan hoped sustenance would diffuse the situation.

"Why not Michelle? You are the only two people who keep secrets here. There are only six of us here, and you know, as well as I do, that the rest of the school does not exist to us. We have not seen any of them in over a month and if you two want to keep secrets then what do we really have here?" Rich asked pressing the issue farther than he ever had before.

"We have each other," Marissa said as she rose from the couch. "And you cannot forget that Rich. We are all here for each other and we have to trust each other. We are a man down and have more important things to do. We have to find John and cannot keep bickering like this."

The stalemate in the room changed as Marissa and Michelle switched places, physically and metaphorically. Sinking into the couch Michelle checked on Mikey as Marissa and Rich started their own standoff.

"We are all here for each other.... Really Miss Laurenson? How is that?" Rich goaded her on. "Evan and I will never be able to jump like you four and no matter how much we dance around it or how much we train with you, we all know the damn facts. We know that Mikey is fine or the doctors would not have released him. We know that Evan and I are lackeys and are not really a part of this family. And we know John knew the truth before any of us," Rich finished with a flurry of accusations.

"You mean as John knows," Marissa corrected him in an unwavering cool tone, giving Rich a clear warning to watch his step.

"Stop denying it Marissa, you know John's de-" Rich started to say when Marissa cut him off.

"-He's not dead!!!" Marissa's tone sizzled as she ended Rich's thoughts.

Tension settled uncomfortably in the room. The attack directed at Marissa seemed to be about more than what had happened today or John. It all seemed to stem back to the night where Rich exposed that his lover's heart was taken.

Ever since that night there had been an uncomfortable tension in the group. A tension that got continually worse between Marissa and Rich.

Evan passed out dinner plates hoping to diffuse the room. As dinner wore on the tension between Marissa and Rich did not disperse and was hard to distinguish from the current fight or Rich's confession a few weeks earlier.

After many minutes of silence Rich spoke in a delicate tone, hoping to say what he needed to say.

"Where are they Marissa? Where are John and

Jerry? Why haven't we heard from Jerry in months? Why are they running us into the ground as if there is no tomorrow? You know as well as I do that something bad happened, is happening, or is coming. If that's the case all indications say we are the only ones in the dark."

In one succinct statement, Rich hit the core issues that none of them had been able to state: If they were so important why were they being left in the dark?

No one could answer Rich's question except one person, but Ian kept silent on Jerry's whereabouts, keeping his promise to Jerry. With everything out in the open the tension started to wane. Unfortunately no one had anything to say that would satisfy the morbid situation.

"Guys, sorry about fighting. Rich I'm really sorry about what I said and I know you never meant to hurt Mikey. If it's alright with you I think it's time this guy went to bed," Michelle broke the silence as she gathered Mikey and brought him to the bedroom.

Michelle's apology cleared the air. Looking up from her tea Marissa found Rich's eyes and apologized by mouthing a silent "I'm sorry," to him. Rich sent her the same. Both apologies about more than a silly fight.

With the dishes cleared the room finally relaxed. Evan, Rich, Marissa, and Ian had gathered around the fire to play cards when their watches came to life. A violent progression of beeps interrupted their peaceful night.

"What is going on?" Marissa asked as she looked at her watch.

"I have no idea," Evan said, tapping his watch hoping it would respond.

Looking at their watches Mikey's vital signs had taken over the entire screen. His blood pressure was rising and his breath was short. Panicked they all ran to the bedroom door wondering if the medics had missed something serious.

"I hope I did not rupture anything," Rich prattled on. Worried that he may have actually wounded his friend.

Reaching the door first Marissa opened it, started to peak inside, and abruptly pulled the door shut.

"Marissa we need to get to Mikey," Rich said as he reached for the doorknob.

"No, we don't," Marissa knocked Rich's hand away. "Michelle has everything under control."

"What if he's hurt?" Rich countered. Still worried that the life of his friend rested in their hands.

"Rich, he is not hurt. I can guarantee you he is

doing just fine. In fact I'm sure he is doing great," Marissa answered him with her sly smile.

"But you only went in their for a second how are you so ..."

Before Rich could finish his statement their watches went insane once again, this time with Michelle's vitals. Without finishing his sentence, the watch answered Rich's question.

One by one they all looked to Marissa who confirmed their suspicions with a slight nod. Walking back to the couches they made themselves comfortable. Tonight they would be sleeping in the common room .

...

After breakfast, the group was settling into a relaxing Monday alone as they waited for Mikey and Michelle. The air was light as the group joked and relaxed, trying to decide what they should do today. Once they started to make plans they heard a knock at the door.

"Who could that be," Rich said in an exasperated tone, not wanting surprises on their day off. "Don't they know today is Monday."

"Maybe we're being punished," Marissa joked as she sipped her tea and reclined further into the couch.

Reaching the front door Rich threw it open to be greeted by a picturesque snow-covered land-scape.

"Huh?" Rich asked the thin air as he peaked out into the cold. Trying to figure out where the knock came from.

"I guess someone is playing pranks on us now," Evan irritably said. Perturbed that they were being hassled on their day off.

"Maybe the rest of the camp is just trying to make sure we are still alive. I mean I haven't talked to Jen or Jill in a month," Marissa added to the conversation.

"Maybe? Whatever the reason it looks like pranks will be added to our list of pain," Rich remarked as he sat back down.

"As fun as that sounds I am here to bring y'all some presents," Laura said as she emerged from their secret door behind the fireplace.

Giddy with happiness Laura looked like a puppy that had just received a new toy. The rest of the room did not share her excitement. They looked at her with reservations not convinced they liked Laura's idea on their off day.

"Laura, we didn't see you. Why don't you come and join us," Rich hesitantly offered. Clearly hoping to coax a longer stay and more information out of her, before they agreed to abandon their glorious day of rest.

"No time Rich, I need y'all downstairs as soon as possible," Laura responded. "Get your gear on and come downstairs."

No one budged. They knew better than to move before getting a valid explanation.

"Laura we're not ready for anything and two of us are still in bed," Ian rebutted motioning towards the bedroom where Mikey and Michelle slept.

"Yeah, we have barely eaten or had any time to recuperate from yesterday's debacle," Rich slightly lied with breakfast plates strewn around the room.

"And we have studies this afternoon," Evan lied considering they had just discussed how to avoid them a minute earlier.

"I'll see you at ten," Laura offered after checking the clock that read 8:45.

"How about you give us the morning and we will see you at one," Ian countered trying to salvage some time to themselves.

"I'll see you all at eleven."

"Noon."

"Eleven and I will bring lunch," Laura finished the negotiation the same way Jerry used to end a conversation, before leaving through the secret door.

As Laura left applause and cat calls erupted from Rich and Evan. Mikey had finally emerged from the bedroom. Grabbing his breakfast Mikey tried his best to hide as he slid onto the couch.

Five minutes later Michelle emerged rubbing her hair dry as Evan and Rich welcomed her. Instead of hiding she turned to the crowd and curtsied before grabbing her breakfast and joining them.

"It's obvious you all know what happened with us last night. What happened out here?" Michelle asked as she took a bite of her toast.

"Nothing much to be honest with you," Rich said. "Once we found out you two weren't dying we did our best to get comfy and went to sleep. We just took those off this morning," Rich joked as he pointed to their armor haphazardly stacked into the corner.

"Well at least you're out of them now. Hopefully we can stay out of them," Michelle said as she thought about the day ahead.

"Not so fast, Laura just informed us that we are

due downstairs at eleven. Mikey you may want to duck a little faster today."

The air tensed as the group waited to see the couple respond to Rich's joke.

"Sounds fair. Although you may want to watch your own back. I'm not nursing you back to health," Michelle joked as the room exhaled.

...

"I'll be out in a minute, I want to help Ian get his last piece of gear on," Ian heard Marissa call out to the others as they left the living room.

At a quarter till eleven Ian had just strapped his last piece of armor on when when was pushed flat onto the bed behind him. Breaking away from a kiss Marissa was looking at Ian with something obviously on her mind.

"Ian..." Marissa started in her flirty and seductive voice. "I think we should take a page out of Mikey and Michelle's book."

With her sly smile Marissa started slowly walking her fingers up and down Ian's chest piece.

"Do you now?" Ian responded as he sat up and pulled her as close as their armor would allow, kissing her again.

"I do," Marissa whispered pulling away to steal

quick breaths.

As Marissa reached for one of the clasps on the back of Ian's armor Ian laid down pulling himself out of reach.

"What about Laura?" Ian teased Marissa by stroking her beautiful hair.

"What about her?" Marissa challenged Ian as she began reaching for the clasp again.

Even in her armor Marissa was breathtaking and tempting. Ready to blow off the day Ian waited for Marissa as she shifted her weight to get closer to the clasps separating this beautiful moment. As Marissa's weight shifted their helmets fell off the bed and onto the floor with a resounding clank. Startled Marissa rolled off Ian and, before they could regain the moment, the bedroom door flew open.

"Come on you two," Rich announced as investigated the source of the sound. "It's almost eleven and we don't want to be late."

Leaving the door open, Rich left as Marissa picked up their helmets. "I guess not now..." she said handing Ian his helmet as an angry Rich left.

"But soon I hope," Ian responded. Checking to make sure his bow and quiver were still in place.

...

The magnificent six barely recognized the basement classroom. The couches were gone, the holographic table put away, and the podium was missing. In their place were seven tables littered with weapons.

"What is all this?" Mikey asked in awe. Wandering through the tables. Gazing at the new arsenal.

Swords, knives, and a variety of weapons littered the tables along with new supplies. Marble sword blades were perfectly blended colors of white, gold, and black. These swords clearly were not dull but instruments of death.

Deadly arrow tips, maces, and axes matched the new swords and their old knives. The maces had sharpened spikes, the Jo's were steel, completely retractable, and had hidden blades at either end. Each table could arm a small army.

Stepping up to the first table, his table, Mikey spoke up with the question on all their minds. "Are all of these are mine?"

For the first time today the group eagerly acknowledged Laura who waited patiently, in the corner. When everyone was focused on her Laura gave them nod and an inaudible "yes".

Rushing to find their tables, no one needed name tags. They knew their table based on the weapons.

Marissa's table was highlighted by a brand-new recurve bow alongside a real Shortsword. Mikey had two stunning knives, but more importantly two Sai that he had been asking about for weeks. Michelle had a new Jo, with retractable blades at either end, instead of a new trident, and a new long bow. Rich's crown jewel was a new mace, along with a bow, and long sword. Evan received a new trident he had been asking for ever since using Michelle's old one a few times. Vicious, with jagged blades, the trident had Evan so distracted he did not notice his new crossbow or Greatsword.

Walking up to his own table Ian was immediately drawn to his Broadsword. It was longer than Marissa's, shorter than Rich's, and had a beautiful pure white blade that illuminated his table of black and gold. A new quiver and arrows sat next to the sword along with a new bow string. Dozens of boxes filled with what appeared to be darts sat next to his quiver. An entirely new back and chest piece, a new sheath for his sword, med-kits, food rations, and a few other survival items rounded out his table.

Lifting it Ian examined the sword's glistening

white blade as he grasped its pure silver handle. The marble blade was light, perfectly balanced, and engraved with dragons running the length of the blade. Delicate scales and sharp claws blended into the swords sharpened edge. The blade was flawless, perfect, and ready for battle.

"What do y'all think of your new arsenal?" Laura interrupted their exploration of the new toys.

"They are fantastic," Rich blurted out. "Amazing,"Mikey chimed in. "Lighter," Marissa commented as she manipulated her new blade.

"Ian you are quiet did you find your new axes?" Laura asked trying to bring an answer out of his silence.

Ian nodded to Laura. He did find his axes once he moved his new back piece that was on top of them.

One of them was a black marble, double bladed battle axe with the perfect mix of gold veins running through it. Perfectly weighted Ian could see this axe coming in handy when he needed power.

Next to the battle axe was a smaller, different style axe. Almost like a fireman's axe, it had two spikes protruding from its top and back, along with a curved axe blade opposite the back spike. As sharp as everything else this smaller axe looked like a cousin of his larger one. It would have its uses and Ian looked forward to trying these new axes alongside his new sword.

"Why is everything marble?" Ian asked the question that had been bothering him for months.

"Ian they are not marble, but a composite mixture designed, by Jerry, for performance within and outside The Dimension. All your weapons have an edge that should never dull."

What is she hiding? Ian thought to himself. Something bothering him about her. *I have to know what she is hiding.*

Unsatisfied with Laura's answer Ian wanted to push the topic further when Laura preempted him with a question.

"What do you think of your new arrows, quiver, and string?"

"Umm...."

"Let me show you how these things work and I guarantee you *'umm'* will not be your response."

Ian had not paid the new archery gear any attention until Laura walked over and removed a single dart from one of the cases on his table. Taking it in her hand Laura showed it to Ian before pressing a button on it. Springing to life the dart became a full size arrow that was the perfect size for Ian's bow.

"These new arrows are designed for each of your individual bows and bodies. They are designed to be accurate, compact, and deadly. By collapsing in on themselves you can carry six times more than with standard arrows. They are hollow and made out of a metal compound that is sturdy, light, and strong enough to hold five hundred pounds of dead weight. Best of all they automatically store and deploy themselves. In other words, they will automatically keep your new quivers full."

With a smug look Laura handed Ian the arrow that had sprung to life in her hand. Ian inspected it and found that everything she said was true.

Like his new blade, the arrow was flawless. The engineering, the simple design, and the abilities of these arrows made them incredible. The tips were coated in the same compound that made up their armor and other blades.

It will be a shame to lose these, Ian thought while looking over the masterpiece a few more times.

"Each arrow carries an identifying isotope mixed in with the compound itself. When you are within a mile of an arrow, you will be alerted of its general location on your heads up display. If you are within two hundred yards an orange dot will lead you to the arrow. This way, if you are going back through an area, run out, or have time you can recollect your arrows without any difficulty." Laura answered Ian's thought. "Ian why don't you take off your chest and back pieces so we can get your new ones packed up. I really want to show you the difference your new equipment will make in weight, among other things."

Ian agreed and removed his chest and back pieces as Laura started setting up his new ones. Filling it with the new arrow darts, med kits, and rations it only took Laura a few minutes to get everything in place. Once the back piece was closed, Laura showed Ian how to attach his new quiver and loaded up the chest piece before helping him put his new armor on.

"Ian when you use your arrows they will automatically fill from a reserve in your armor. When you reinsert an arrow, into the quiver, another will automatically retract into the armor," unlatching his quiver Laura turned it upside down showcasing its final trick. "Also, all the arrows are held in magnetically. You will have an easy draw, but never have to worry about them falling out. I know you like your wood and carbon fiber arrows so I will left some in your reserves and quiver."

Ian felt Laura snap his quiver back in place and thanked her with his astonished silence. Looking at the mostly empty table Ian was surprised to feel so complete and light.

Taking off his old sword and Ian began suiting up with his new weapons. Sheathing the marble sword Ian placed it where the old one had been before storing his axes. The smaller axe opposite his sword, on his right hip. The battle axe slid onto his back, under his quiver. Ian was even given a retractable Jo (without blades) that stored in a groove on his lower back.

Ian restrung his bow with his new string and placed it in its slot. With all his new gear in place, Ian stole a glance at the full length mirror on the wall as he put his helmet on.

His sword's silver handle shone out from the black and gold accents that his armor glistened with. Still black as night Ian thought that the hints of gold made the armor more realistic and would help it blend. It was not reflective, but would give life to the darkness. Allowing people to pass him thinking he was nothing more than a shadow.

Ian started to move and could not believe his body or his eyes. After all the changes Ian not only looked fiercer and moved better, but his new back and chest pieces were more flexible. Even with two, new, additional weapons, more rations, and arrows, Ian felt at least thirty pounds lighter.

Over the next twenty minutes, Ian watched

Laura and his friends gear up. After checking themselves over in the mirror, they all ate a catered lunch and were ready to head upstairs when Laura stopped them.

"Where are y'all goin?"

"Back upstairs. I can't wait to try the new gear, but it is still our day off," Rich answered for the group as they took another step towards the door.

"I get that but where are you going?" Laura asked again

"I thought that was obvious: to the field. You know to try it out. Without you." Rich said.

"Yeah and as much as we hated you guys for it I would like to take a second to thank you for letting us train with the heavy gear. This new stuff feels amazing, and I can't wait to try it out," Evan thanked Laura as Mikey reached for the door handle ready to leave the room.

"Oh you're not going anywhere. These presents are only the beginning of today's fun."

The group stopped cold not wanting to know what Laura's idea was fun was. They were ready to try the new gear, but they wanted to do it on their own. Not with one half of the heartless sisters.

"What do you mean by fun? Isn't today our day off?" Ian asked Laura as she stepped towards the door to the entrance hall.

"Starting today days without us no longer exist. Today your real training starts."

"Our real training? What do you think we have been doing?" Rich blurted out as Laura placed her hand on the doorknob to the great room. "You guys have been beating us up for weeks. What could you possibly have in store for us that would be more *'real'*."

With an excited smile Laura motioned the group towards the door as she answered them.

"I'm glad you asked Rich. If you think you have been training then, y'all are in for a little shock."

Throwing the door open the magnificent six were left with their mouths open, lost for words.

CHAPTER SEVENTEEN

July Eleventh

The group followed Laura into the next room cautiously. The central atrium had been turned into a lush rain forest.

Tripping over roots, fighting through vines, and trying to take everything in was impossible as their senses were assaulted. Sounds of wildlife filled their ears, the air was humid and sticky and any wildlife they saw responded accordingly to their presence. Their helmets and visors buzzed with excitement. They knew that they had a large learning curve ahead of them.

"Pretty impressive. Right?" Laura said smugly to the awestruck group. "This is the final stage of the Battle Ready software. In here we can create and transport you into any situation. Any scenario that you created with Battle Ready can be run in here, letting you be front and center. Right now; for example, we are walking through world

73, home to your first battle simulation."

"Laura this is incredible, but if this is a battle scenario where are the enemies and our allies?" Ian asked as he tripped over another rock.

"We haven't started that part of the program yet. Once we do the place will be teeming with them though. For this first run it will just be the six of you against the enemy. However before we start the simulation I must explain the program and its emergency features. Your new enemies are harder and will do more damage. They are not designed to be lethal but broken bones, bruises, and sprains are possible if they hit you right. We have a team of medics standing by if something happens. It should go without saying but you have to be more careful with your new weapons. They are designed to kill and if you are not careful they will."

The group heeded Laura's warnings. They did not need the reminder about their weapons as they wondered how much punishment their bodies could actually take.

"Once a program is running, it will not stop until the mission is complete. When not running the room will return to normal and the projectors will be turned off. If you are knocked unconscious the program will automatically stop. The emergency stop is done by saying: stop alpha protocol 1,2,3."

With her words, the vast forest disappeared and

was replaced by the white hall they had walked through hundreds of times. The doors, walls, and floors were immaculate and pristine as ever.

"Use the Battle Ready software as you always have. The only difference is that once you are done programing you will be given the option for *'real life projection.'* That option will transform this hall into the simulation. To start the program say: *'begin simulation'* inside this hall. Any questions?"

The group was silent. Still trying to take in what had just disappeared around them. They thought they understood what Laura had told them.

"I will join Lance and Sara in the library. Once I'm in there you will start your mission on world 73. Your mission objectives will be displayed on your visors before you start. Good luck."

Finished, Laura walked to the library, her steps echoing off the walls as she went. The magnificent six were left standing in the middle of the room ready for their next challenge.

"This is incredible," Rich interjected as they listened to Laura depart.

"It really is," Marissa confirmed waiting for the forest to form around her.

As soon Laura entered the library the dense forest reappeared and their mission goals started scrolling across their helmet's visor screens.

"You guys ready?" Ian asked the group smiling. Their mission was the same one they had that first day with Jerry.

Looking around Ian saw a collective nod of approval and without hesitation yelled: "Begin simulation."

The rest of the week was spent running simulations in the newly improved hall. Sometimes once a day other times three or four. They ran missions in different sized groups and their old classroom became a place for rest and recuperation between missions. Their dorm was a safe haven to nurse bruises, sprains, and a few minor breaks.

The physical stress of the new training was twice as intense as what they had done before. Dealing with different weather patterns, terrain, enemies, and worlds made everything more challenging. From the forests of world 73, to the dense city scape of world 98. They faced heavy rains, hail, snow, and more inside the simulation chamber.

Even with their amazing armor and under suits doing its best to protect them they struggled to succeed in their new missions. The challenges pushed them to their limits and made them all question if they had what it took to face the challenges the basement would throw at them the next day.

The training was so grueling that it pretty much stopped everything else in their life. They no longer went to the field, gym, or the dining hall. Research was done in-between simulations. Outside showers and sleep life revolved around their cabin and the basement below.

Life became a blur, and with so many things stopped by training only three things changed during this new time.

First, Mikey and Michelle's special training with Lance picked up. What had been twice a week was now five days a week, leaving Evan, Marissa, Rich, and Ian to fend for themselves against the terrible two.

Secondly, John and Jerry's absence became a natural afterthought. Too busy to spend energy on it, John's empty bed and wardrobe were the only physical reminders of their absence. Mikey and Marissa's ritual the only cognizant reminder that they were missing.

Finally, in mid April Michelle became quite ill. Every morning she would wake sick as a dog only to have it pass through out the day. Everyone had a suspicion, but no one dared ask. Michelle and the doctors knew, but were not saying a word. Her missions and more strenuous activities were replaced with a cardio regiment.

This was how days and in the end months passed. When they were not running a simulation, they were doing research or creating a new scenario as they waited their turn. There was nothing else in their lives that mattered. The camp, families, friends; everything had taken a backseat to the war.

For the first time they understood what Jerry meant about distractions. To succeed, they had to set everything aside. They had one objective: Train. And that is what they did. They trained harder than anyone until July eleventh.

"Ian! We need you downstairs now!!!" Laura yelled up to him for the fourth time on the morning of July eleventh.

Ian was dragging his feet this morning. Still trying to recuperate before another hard day started. He was sore, battered, and looking outside his window he wanted to go enjoy the sunshine. Spring had been spent in the basement and Ian wanted to enjoy the summer. However, he couldn't. Ian had to train and even though this was the first morning he had been late it was becoming quite an ordeal.

Dressed in his armor Ian adjusted his helmet and looked at the reflection that had not changed in months. His armor had become his birthday suit. The surface, despite months of use, still looked new and glass like. Looking deep into this reflection Ian was reminded of the real reason he was running slow this morning.

Last night a tent was found floating down a river

towards the lake. It was the first sign of John in months and Laura offered to lead search parties that were leaving today. While Ian wanted to help, the tent was more of a reminder of the ever growing list of unanswered questions.

Where was Jerry? He was supposed to be back months ago and I still have held his secret. Ian thought to himself. Despite his better judgment Ian had kept Jerry's secret. He did not want to worry his group, especially Marissa, any more. She had lost John; she didn't need to lose Jerry too.

Why is everything Marble? What have Mikey and Michelle been up to? And why had they been lumped into their troubled group in the first place? Why is our group being trained and why haven't any of their peers joined them?

Lost in his own thoughts, the morning was turning into one of reflection as his mind continued to run away on him.

Was there something between Rich and Marissa? What are his true feelings? That was nothing compared to Evan and Evankila. Would Evan ever get to see her again? I wonder what Nicole's up to? Ian thought as his mind wandered to Earth. *I wonder how the school year went? Did she get my letter? Wouldn't his friends be going back soon? What is my family doing?*

Ian longed for his mothers fresh strawberries and watching baseball with his dad.

All of these questions paled to the largest, omnipresent, questions about this war: What were they being kept in the dark about? What was really going on? What was The Evil up to?

"Ian if you are not down here in the next minute you will be running solo suicide missions all day," Laura announced her final warning to Ian.

This worked and Ian rushed downstairs to join the group. If he had to be hit today that was fine, but he refused to be the only one.

"Nice of you to join us," Laura said as Ian took a seat in front of Marissa.

When Ian entered the room he was surprised to see everyone inside. Mikey and Marissa were on one of the couches, Michelle and Rich on another, and Evan was standing at the doorway. Laura, Lance, and Sara were all standing in front of them. Seeing the three of them together was never good.

"Now that we are all here we can begin," Lance said slightly perturbed as Laura hit the lights.

In front of him was an illuminated simulation projected from the marble table. The mission looked more complex so the group waited for Lance to explain.

"I would like to introduce my newest simulation. It is designed for two people and takes place on Evan's home, Telvena, world 205," Lance's mention of Evan's world brought everyone's ears up. "This mission is designed to test your ability to survive and escape from one of the most hostile planets in The Dimension."

Lance's last words hit Evan hard. He grasped his chest where his necklace hung, reminded of the reality of the situation.

"The mission is simple: find a jump point and escape. The catch is that you will have to find a jump point without using software. You all know how to find the natural signs of jump points, so as a pair you will have to sneak across the planet searching for clues to find your exit."

The mission seemed pretty simple even with Lance's restriction. Especially considering they had Evan at their disposal. He was the master of portals and knew the world.

Regardless of if he was in the group, he would be on the intercom to bounce ideas off of and help whichever pair was inside the simulation.

"The planet is relatively small and densely populated. Evan can tell you, it is primarily one large city and while you may not run into difficult adversaries, we do not want this mission to become a blood bath. Getting to an extraction point will be difficult and we want limited casualties. With that said the mission may not take too long if you are efficient and careful."

Lance's continued explanation made sense, but it

was too simple. They all knew there was another catch.

"Because this mission is designed for two, we have created individual plans for everyone today. Mikey and Michelle will be with me training," Lance started with little surprise. "Evan since you know the world inside and out you and Rich will take the day and lead your classmates in their first field day of the summer. Classes are out for a few weeks, and we are a little understaffed. Take the day without armor."

"Marissa and I are running the simulation then?" Ian interjected sarcastically; wondering how he and Marissa got stuck training yet again.

"Well... Yes... But once you are done you will have the rest of the day for yourselves. Call it a date day if you will, " Lance answered his sarcastic pupil.

It was a gift and Ian knew it. There was no way this mission would take all day. Their group had not had a day off in well over a month and in a few hours he and Marissa would have the day to themselves. The smile on Lance's face let Ian know that he wanted to give them a day off as much as they needed one.

Fifteen minutes later Marissa and Ian sat alone in the classroom waiting for the simulation to load. It was fairly complex and would take at least another quarter hour. Mikey and Michelle had disappeared with Lance. Evan and Rich changed and stopped by for a few minutes before leaving for the field. Sara and Laura took refuge in the library to load the mission. All this left Ian and Marissa alone for the first time in a long time.

"What do you want to do?" Marissa asked Ian as she removed her helmet and released her beautiful hair.

"You know what I want to do," Ian said as he removed his helmet. His hair not nearly as perfect as Marissa's.

"We could get started," Marissa suggested, straddling Ian's lap as she joined him on his couch.

"We don't have the time for that," Ian answered her with a small laugh and a kiss.

"Is that so?" Marissa chuckled back as they kissed.

Drifting into a blissful state Ian and Marissa were finally enjoying some peace and quiet when a sonic boom knocked their world apart. The entire building shook as the power flickered.

"What the hell was that?" Marissa broke away from Ian. More annoyed than worried.

Putting on his helmet Ian asked Laura and Sara what had happened over his intercom.

"No idea, but we will have to start the load over. According to Velena they didn't feel it at the field. Although, if you guys wouldn't mind, we could use a hand in here getting everything back up and running as we check it out." Sara chimed in.

"Of course," Ian responded relieved. If they didn't feel it on the field that was a good sign.

Inside the atrium Ian and Marissa were about to reach the library when the hall's forbidden doors burst open.

Someone, exhausted and wearing a battle worn suit like theirs, had just entered the hall. The person did not have his helmet on, but Marissa and Ian did not notice their face, eye color, hair, height, or weight because as they entered the hall they screamed "Jerry's hurt....."

CHAPTER EIGHTEEN
Answers

Bursting past the foreign party Ian and Marissa sprinted down the unfamiliar hallway with one goal in mind: find Jerry. Surrounded by sterile, white marble walls, they passed what appeared to be large bank vaults on their right. On their left they passed a mixture of offices, labs, and hallways.

At the end of the hallway, a group had formed around an open vault door. Ian and Marissa picked up their pace knowing who was in the center.

Approaching the wall of people Ian knew he had to make it to Jerry and started to shouting out:

"Level three jumpers, coming through, excuse me... Level three coming through," Not knowing why or even if it would have any effect on the large crowd.

His message resonated with the group and as soon as he announced himself people parted, allowing them to penetrate the circle. Reaching the final rows the sight and smell stopped them in their tracks before they could reach Jerry.

Jerry was lying in a pool of his own blood on the now stained marble floor. A nondescript lab tech was sitting with him. Trying to keep Jerry there until the medics arrived. Dressed in a very light suit of armor Jerry struggled for every breath.

Looking around Jerry spotted Ian and Marissa whose helmets sat on the floor in the classroom. Reaching for them Jerry needed them at his side as he fought for his life.

"Jerry... it's okay... you will be fine...." Marissa stammered out in a scared voice. Replacing the lab tech as Ian fell to Jerry's other side.

Jerry caught Ian's eye and started talking. Blood spilling from his mouth Jerry was a horror show struggling with broken ribs and a myriad of other internal injuries as he tried to speak. Unable to hear Jerry, Ian leaned closer to the man who had introduced him to his new life.

"We've been betrayed... Protect Mikey and Michelle, Mission Virgin E needs to be commenced immediately ... Mikey and Michelle..."

Jerry coughed up more blood as his eyes rolled back in his head. Sitting in Marissa and Ian's arms no more words emerged from Jerry as his painful existence came to an end. Ian and Marissa were full of tears as a medical team pushed them aside and loaded Jerry onto a gurney.

An hour later Ian and Marissa sat in silence on a couch in Jerry's office. White walls and floor mocked them with a sense of purity and security they just lost. They could not forget Jerry's last words knowing that he fought death to deliver it.

"Lance is on his way with Evan and Rich," Sara spoke as she and Laura reentered the room they had left an hour ago.

"What about Mikey and-" Ian started

"-They are in a safe room with extra security. Until we know who betrayed us they will not be left alone. If we lose them The Evil might have finally won," Sara answered Ian before he could ask his question.

The door opened for the second time as Lance, Rich, Evan, and the man who had burst into the great hall entered the room. Lance took the seat behind Jerry's desk and, like he had done so often during Jerry's absence, broke the silence by diving straight into the heart of the issue.

"Everyone this is Blake. He was accompanying Jerry on his journey and was with him when they were ambushed in The Dimension."

Lance's statement was short, succinct, and left an echo in the room as they all absorbed what he said. Turning to Marissa, Lance made eye contact with her.

"I'm so sorry, but Jerry has passed," Lance directly apologized to Marissa who had broken into tears before he said anything.

Ian took her into his arms and held her as she was consumed with grief. Though he had died in their arms, they were holding out hope that he would be okay.

For the first time in months Ian felt the extra layer of his second skin and wished that it was not there. Ian wanted to hold her close and comfort her for as long as she needed. Addressing the group as a whole Lance continued to speak.

"Jerry's death has hit all of us hard, but the circumstances have forced our hand. The time is upon us to carry out Jerry's last orders."

"No Lance it isn't. Not yet," Ian responded shocking the group that had just nodded in agreement.

"Ian time is of the essence. We must-"

"-We need answers. And Jerry would agree," Ian stated. Resolved they would have answers. "You were there when Jerry promised to answer all my questions when he returned. Jerry is back and it is time for the truth."

The tension in the room rose as the mention of Ian, Jerry, and Lance's meeting came to the surface for the first time. Marissa did not notice, but Rich and Evan became very confused wondering when this secret meeting took place and what they were being kept in the dark about.

Lance sat quietly weighing his options. Ian, Evan, and Rich were no longer focused on the mission at hand. Jerry had promised them answers and Lance knew there was only one way that they were going to get anything done.

"You're right. What would you like to know?"

Prepared for a fight Ian took a deep breath before jumping in with questions that had been bothering him for months.

"Where has Jerry been?"

"As you know, Jerry left to reestablish communication."

Annoyed by Lance's short response Ian pressed him with more conviction. "Why did he leave?"

Lance could see how perturbed Ian was and knew they would not accept his answer. Acknowledging the situation Lance expanded his answer.

"Last fall Jerry gave the order to close off all worlds. Ian your jump created chaos that The Evil was better able to take advantage of than Akhona's Guardian. The resistance, was forced to close off communications and seal our portals. After a few months we created a scrambler would allow us to communicate between worlds without The Evil tracking it. The device had to be tested and installed on every planet so Jerry left."

This seemed reasonable, but Ian and the rest of the group felt there was more to this tale and how Jerry had come to such an ill fate. With time short Evan pushed the conversation forward.

"Why are Mikey and Michelle so special?"

"Their jump world is World One," Lance answered emotionlessly.

The group was shocked by the information and Rich was the person who pressed Lance.

"What? How-"

"-We know little to nothing about World One and because of this we know very little about The Evil. We know that their world is more a part of The Dimension than any other and has been impossible to find. The Evil use The Dimension to hide in plain sight and with Mikey and Michelle we can locate World One and level the playing fields. Once Mikey and Michelle make that first jump we will know where and how to attack them."

"What about jumping? How do we control it? How do we do it? And if The Evil is so powerful then why do they not jump here and overtake us?" The questions about jumping jumped out of Ian in a single stream of thought.

"Jumping is tied to a recessive gene. People not tied to this world, through themselves or doubles, must use artificial portals to jump between worlds that are not their home or sister planet. We use artificial portals, like the one John, Rich, and Evan came through, to get people between worlds. These are piggy backed off the portals special jumpers create. This technology is great and helpful; however, The Evil can easily detect the artificial portals and if they break down you will be stranded in The Dimension."

"But, how do special jumpers work?" Ian pressed annoyed that Lance had just parroted things Jerry had told him.

"Every jumper has a unique jump action. For you it's a yoga move. If you are ever stranded in The Dimension do cobra while thinking about the world you want to go to and a portal to that world will appear. Once a special jumper reaches level three, levels two and one are nothing more than arbitrary delineation's on how many worlds you can jump to. A level two can jump to about half the worlds. A level one almost all. Special jumpers do not need to use artificial portals if they have been to the world and are harder to detect because they can jump from within The Dimension."

"But you said that Jerry 'shut down worlds before' what does that mean? How are we able to keep The Evil out of here?" Ian clarified his question.

"Jumping used to be tied to the phases of the moon. At the full moon worlds were open to The Dimension and at the new moon it was almost impossible to jump. This was not consistent and, while you can still use the moons to assist your jumps, technology allowed us to reroute the jump portals. The walls of vaults in the main hall are known as jump vaults. They are the only way in or out of this world."

"During my first jump, I did not come through the vaults?" Ian challenged Lance.

Frowning a little bit Lance tried to gather his thoughts, before answering Ian.

"First jumps are always a little tricky, wonky, and, honestly, we do not know why they cause such chaos. For your jump, we are assuming, our best guess," Lance corrected himself. "Our best guess is that Scoot was near a portal we did not know about while you were making your accidental jump."

Lance's eyes showed the truth on how little they knew. And that their best guess was exactly that: a guess.

"Most worlds have hundreds, if not thousands, of jump points. While it is impossible to discover and monitor all of them the resistance has done their best to locate and close or redirect them." Lance finished through the group's gazes.

"But-" Ian started to ask when Lance tried to calm their fears.

"Each world, the resistance controls, has different safeguards guarding their portals. Here, we funnel all of them to the vaults. Other planets have guards at the portals ready to close them. Others have rerouted their portals into a volcano. The resistance force has gone to great lengths to close, control, guard, and monitor the portals on our planets. The Evil like having free access to their planets so they open them up to The Dimension. This allows them easy access in and out."

"Why?" Marissa asked not letting the question hang.

"Because when a world is open you can enter the planet very easily; however, to leave you still must find a portal to exit through."

This exchange did little to answer Ian's question, but he had to move on. Lance had explained things as best he could and time was of the essence.

"Why is Earth so important? Why did Jerry go to such lengths to protect it?" Ian continued.

"Earth? World 256? Your home world?" Lance asked for confirmation.

Ian nodded.

"There are two key reasons: The marble reserves and Earth is the most diverse and violent world in The Dimension."

The second part of Lance's answer caught Ian off guard, but before he could ask for context

314

the question that he had held on to months, the thing that had bothered him, slipped out.

"The marble-"

"-Reserves," Lance finished Ian's question. "As odd as it sounds Marble is the only substance, that we know of, that The Evil's weapons can't penetrate. While weapons from other worlds can, marble is the most resilient. That is why your armor is a composite of kevlar, marble, and other metals. Pure, natural marble or a compound made with it is the only thing that can survive The Dimension. Steel rusts, aluminum crumbles. Once treated marble can become extremely useful and resilient. Earth's seemingly inexhaustible supply is one of the reasons it is so important. On Earth you use it as counter tops, statues, and flooring. It is a decorative substance and even synthetic marble developed on Earth, while not as effective, still works. In essence, Earth makes our armor and our resistance possible."

Pulling out his sword Ian felt pride swell within him. Holding his pure white sword Ian could not help but feel like Earth would be fighting with him whenever he went into battle. He and the rest of the group were getting a new respect for their gear.

"What about the second reason?" Ian asked unable to think of a better way to state his question.

"Most planets in The Dimension have only one

or two climates across the entire planet. They are smaller: population and diversity wise. As you know Ian, it has been speculated that climate spurred different cultural, religious, and technological developments on Earth. Strife caused by its pure size made Earth one of the most violent planets in The Dimension. Your planets history is littered with war and conflict. This conflict spurred developments in tactics and weaponry not seem on other worlds. In this respect Earth is one of our best resources for war strategy and research within The Dimension."

Thinking back to his history class Ian could only nod in agreement. His world was a violent place. It always had been.

"Why were the seven of us separated?" Ian asked acknowledging John's existence for the first time in weeks.

"Your past, histories, and importance. John, Evan, and Rich have all seen the war first hand. They were distanced and trained so they would not spark fear in the school. Marissa, being Jerry's Godchild, was separated for a variety of reasons, a main one being that she will not be safe until her double situation is dealt with. You now understand why Mikey and Michelle were separated out and your connection to these people, Marissa, Earth, and the simple fact that you had successfully made your first jump is why you were singled out Ian."

"But what about the other students my age? Why

were they left out? Why do they not train with us?"

"Ian every student is important; every person and life in The Dimension is. You were separated because we needed you ready for today. The biggest mistake we ever made was being stubborn, rash, and rushing into things. We lost a generation of generals, soldiers, and special jumpers because we were irresponsible. The seven of you needed to be ready. You were the next soldiers so we devoted our time to properly train you."

Lance's explanation made sense and Ian listened as Lance continued.

"Every student here has different circumstances. Some can't make their first jump, like Marissa, and some simply are not ready to train yet. The truth of the matter is that it takes a lot of time and resources to train any soldier, let alone special jumpers like yourselves. We do not want to completely expose people to the war until they are ready and able to put in the necessary time and dedication. Now that you seven are ready we will start to prepare more students for the transition you went through from student to soldier. Ian we knew we could not train everyone simultaneously and refuse to repeat our past. And I'm sorry about this Ian, but we have to cut this session short. It is time for your first mission."

CHAPTER NINETEEN
A New World

Three hours later Ian found himself inside a marble jump vault with Blake and Rich. He and Rich were responsible for operation Virgin E, which was taking place on Evan's home planet.

For the past three hours Evan had fought to be on the mission; however, Lance insisted that Ian and Rich had to undertake this mission without him. Evan repeatedly questioned why? Arguing that he knew the planet, the jump points, and the city better than any map. The mission was search and rescue and Evan thought he would be the perfect for this mission. Lance would not be swayed and refused to let Evan join.

Instead Evan, Laura, and Marissa were going out to examine and explore the area where Ian and Rich found the unidentified tracks many months ago. The same place they found the tent a few days before. Laura had a hunch they could lead to the traitor. Marissa held out hope it was John. Despite differing opinions, the mission was clear. Find the creator of the tracks and neutralize their threat to the camp.

Ian and Rich felt uncomfortable with Lance's decision to hold Evan back. Evan was the perfect fit for the mission. He knew the terrain, people, and place. Lance had to be holding something back from them. There was no other reason why Evan should not be allowed to go.

"I need to make this quick," Blake stated clearly after he removed his helmet. Ian and Rich followed suit as the vault door was locked behind them. "When the time is right I will signal you to open up your watch's jump program, input the world where you are going, and hit enter. It will take about 30 seconds to create the worm hole and when the time is right you will have to use the voice command we showed you to open the portal. Walk through the portal and if all goes well you will be on world 205 momentarily.

"The portal should be safe. Decoy paths will be created as you leave. If things break down Ian drop to the ground and think about this world while you do your jump move. Grab Rich and drag him through the portal that appears. Rich, just try to stay conscious," Blake said as he turned from Ian to Rich.

"Once we arrive, I will be jumping to my home world and then back here. You will be on your own and your mission is not rescue but elimination." The truth hit them hard as their mission's objective was revealed. "Your target's description and general location will show up on your screens once you reach world 205. I do not know who it is, but they must be eliminated."

Ian and Rich now understood why Evan was not coming and why their helmets had been removed. Evan would not hurt one of his own people and while they were on Esmerelda they would still be heard over the helmet's intercom.

Their silence alerted Blake to their discomfort.

"The target is a double for someone on this planet. We have no chance of ever getting that first jump coordinated as long as that double exists. That double risks the safety of this world and once the target is eliminated their double will become a virgin jumper that can choose any planet as their sister planet."

Understanding the mission did not make it sit any better. Rich and Ian felt sick and wondered how they were going to carry this out. They had fought holograms, never a real person.

Short on time Blake replaced his helmet and signaled them to start their jump procedures. Donning helmets Rich and Ian opened the jump app and entered world 205 into the software. A countdown clock appeared.

"Confirm jump location and approval code," the computer whirred back at them as the clock ticked down from 30.

"World 205, 12/27."

The screen went green as the clock ticked past 23 seconds.

"Confirm identity, destination, and approval code," the computer required as the clock went past 11 seconds

"Ian Alcock, world 205 12/27," Ian repeated back as the clock went past 7.

The screen went green again as the computer registered approval.

Looking through the countdown clock Ian saw a swirling black hole forming in the white marble face in front of him.

3...2...1...

"Let's go," Ian heard Blake yell over their channel.

Running headfirst into the passage Ian had no idea what would greet them on the other side.

They hit pavement running and darted into a back ally where Blake gathered Rich and Ian for one last meeting before he departed.

"The world's security force and The Evil will be alerted to the jump momentarily. I suggest you get at least a mile away from here before you start figuring out your mission. Get safe, stay hidden, and I will see you back home."

Not wishing them luck, Blake's last statement seemed to be his way of telling them they were going to have a good mission. This was just another day, nothing had changed, and they were ready for this.

Blake disappeared down another side street before they could respond. Ian and Rich were just starting to regain their bearings when their helmet's visor whirred to life, a not so subtle reminder that they were alone on a hostile planet.

"Please follow the marked trail to this location for regrouping and planning. Authorities will be here within 50 seconds," the computer informed Ian and Rich indicating a trail leading to a local dump.

Zigging and zagging down side streets their black armor blended into the dark alleys of this smog covered city. Behind them, Rich and Ian heard voices and barking dogs following them.

"I'm assuming the computer translates everything so we can understand?" Rich said as they skirted past another dumpster overflowing with trash.

"I would assume," Ian replied. Splashing over a manhole cover that was slick from a recent rain.

Running through the dead side streets, darting in and out of alleys, Ian became concerned at the lack of life and the circuitous route the computer was moving them along. *We can only avoid them for so long.* Ian thought to himself before voicing his concerns to the computer.

"Computer how far are we from the destination?"

"A quarter mile, three minutes at current pace," the computer whirred back, as they took another turn down a different ally.

Running down the alley their map had them making another few turns and jumping a fence before they reached their destination. Ian and Rich made their last turn when red dots erupted on their radar. Jumping behind a dumpster, they did their best to become invisible as they figured out what was going on.

"What the hell are all of these dots?" Rich asked Ian as he reached for one of his smaller knifes.

"No idea?" Ian said as he peeked out from behind the dumpster.

"The dots are local inhabitants. Undetermined if they are police, Evil, or civilians," the computer answered Rich as a red dot came streaking down the alley.

"Here comes one," Rich said as he took a tighter grip on his knife. On this planet red dots were hostiles and he was ready to strike.

Rich readied to silence the intruder forever and as the dot approached them Rich was about to reach out and grab the person when Ian stopped him. Standing in the darkness they watched a child walk by and retrieve the toy that had just rolled by.

The child's skin which was no longer smooth, but had been replaced by a thick, used, leather like skin. The kid passed them twice before finding her toy. Soon Ian and Rich were alone wondering what The Evil had done to that girl.

"Thanks for stopping me," a troubled Rich whispered as he put his knife away. Frustrated that he had almost killed an innocent child no older than six.

"No problem. I saw the toy," Ian tried to reassure his friend that his instincts had been right. "We need to get to a safe place though."

Their visor filled with more red as it surrounded them. Many following the path they had just taken.

Ian looked around for a way to escape wondering if he had made a tactical mistake. They let the girl survive, but had lost valuable time. The dump's fence was across a street full of civilians. The other way out of the alley was covered by hostiles hunting them. There were fire escapes and roofs but the sound something flying overhead took that option away. Lost for what to do Ian racked his brain for a solution when Rich acted.

"Ian, into the dumpster. Now!" Rich said as he

opened the dumpster and pushed Ian in.

Before Ian could respond Rich pulled himself into the dumpster and was closing the rusty lid.

"Rich what is this?" Ian asked as his visor filled with a sea of red.

"It is our way out.l." Rich said. "Now dig."

Following Rich's lead Ian dug deeper and deeper into the stink as the sea of red seemed to close around the group of dumpsters they were in.

"Nothing in here…" Ian heard someone say.

"Check the next one…"

"Same…. Wait you can't take those…"

Before the lid of the dumpster holding them was lifted Ian heard a small commotion break out.

"I've got to take them to make time. So out of the way."

"We are with APDA and-"

"-and unless you show me a permit or a written order you will get out of my way."

Ian still felt vulnerable as the men hunting them fought with some sort of garbage man. He felt that way until he sensed their hiding place being lifted up and saw the sea of red part around a larger dot. Peaking out a small hole Ian saw that their dumpster had been loaded onto the back of a large flatbed truck and was driving away from their pursuers unfollowed and unscathed. Leathery dogs and local security swept the area with a variety of gadgets as their dumpster disappeared into the city.

Five minutes later the truck stopped. The driver had picked up a few more dumpsters and was negotiating with the dump's owner. Hearing the exchange Rich and Ian took this opening to abscond from the dumpster and into the dump. They used the cover of night to jump the fence and crouched between mounds of trash as they made their way deeper into the dump.

"The planet really is a city," Ian stated the obvious as his eyes scanned the planet's map on his head's up display. "The pollution and soot should give us some cover."

"Yeah. Also, it looks like The Evil have done something to the people here. Oh yeah, and did I mention, we have no idea where our target is? How to get there? Or even what time it is?" Rich sarcastically replied. Frustrated to be sitting in someone else's waste.

"Your target's name is E and this is the picture of record we have on her. We are assuming her appearance has changed," the computer started with a prerecorded message from Lance.

An image of the target popped up on their display. Their target was a girl about their age. She was very pretty and, while they could not place her, Rich and Ian both felt as if they knew her.

"Your target is most likely being housed in the city's main tower: *"The Tower Igante."* The tower is the planet's tallest sky scraper and is about 12 miles from your current location. Once you are within four miles of the target, your system will locate and track her. Your jump took place during sunset around 16:00, the planet has a 40 hour light cycle, and the sun will rise at hour zero. Your movement will best be concealed at night. For your own safety finish the mission before sunrise."

Looking at the target, Rich and Ian still could not believe their mission. The girl had red hair and beautiful amber skin. She appeared gentle with soft eyes and an innocent face. She had no distinguishing marks and wore a necklace with plain clothes. Rich and Ian were sent to kill her, but their gut feeling told them they should save her.

"She is the target?" Rich broke the silence as the computer finished, still digesting the picture and mission.

"I guess so," Ian replied trying to figure out how he knew her.

Although Blake had told them about the mission, right before they jumped, it was not real then. It was abstract and as far as Ian and Rich knew they were eliminating one of The Evil's forces. Now that nameless enemy had been replaced by an innocent girl.

"So we have to find and eliminate her?" Rich asked for confirmation. Not wanting to believe the cold truth of what he just said.

"Affirmative ..." Ian responded. Trying to detach himself from the person they were going to execute. "I do not know where we know her from, and we have to kill her," Ian said before Rich could ask.

Sitting in silence they each wanted to formulate a plan, but were too distracted. This was no longer a hologram and there was no way to stop this mission. They had avoided it so far, but Ian and Rich knew that they would, at least, have the blood of one life on their hands.

Can I take a life? Or will it be like the alleyway? Will I freeze...

Ian's thoughts crawled by. He knew another hesitation could cost them their lives. It could cost the resistance so much more.

"What is the local time?" Rich asked the computer.

"18:00 hours," the computer whirred back without a pause.

"Ian, we have about twenty hours of darkness. We should get moving and complete this mission. The sooner we get home the better."

Nodding in agreement Ian knew that any delay would only make the mission harder and that they could not dwell on their mission. If they over thought it they would never carry it out or make it home.

"Computer mark *The Tower Igante* as our destination. If the target comes into range mark her in orange," Ian informed their high tech helper.

Their visors quickly displayed a bird's eye view of their destination. The building was miles away and they had no good way to get there. The surface streets were not safe and rooftops were being searched.

"Computer give me a layout of the sewage system," Ian requested from the computer.

Both of their maps were replaced with city's sewage system.

"Any know dangers?" Ian asked.

"None. However the tower is on a separate sewage network as is the intercity. Once you get within five miles you will meet a wall dividing the inner and outer city. The inner city is heavily guarded and has limited entrances. Estimated time for sewer travel to the wall is two hours," the computer answered with all relevant facts.

"Looks like we have two hours to figure out how to get in," Rich joked as Ian started to rise.

"I guess so. Two hours for us to figure out how to break into Fort Knox," Ian answered trying to keep the tone light. Trying to distract himself

from their mission and the life they would have
to take.

CHAPTER TWENTY

Just Crazy Enough

Two hours later Rich and Ian crouched on a roof-top a half mile outside of the inner city wall. The air was thick with smog and the sounds of the city below. Search crews had dissipated over the past two hours and now that the sun had completely set they were all but invisible. Blending in as shadows in the night sky.

"What now?" Rich vocalized the omnipresent question they had had since their arrival.

"I'm not sure," Ian answered as he scanned the wall teeming with guards and patrols.

"We need a diversion," Rich kept the dialogue flowing. Still wondering if he could actually take a life or if there was another way.

"I agree," Ian responded wondering if they could make it through this mission only taking a single life.

Five minutes passed. Then ten. A half an hour. It was not until hour 26 when Rich had an idea that may actually work.

"We have to climb the wall," Rich started as another patrol drove past on the street below. "There is no way we can get through any of the four gates, so, we have to climb over the wall."

"Fair enough, but if we start climbing we need a distraction to even have a chance."

"I think I have a plan that will give us just enough time to get up and across," Rich said. His tone sounding noticeably more upbeat.

Over the next five minutes Rich outlined his plan in vivid detail, going over everything from set up to execution. The plan was complex, risky, and a little nuts, but after Rich was done explaining it Ian had one thing to say:

"Rich I think it may just work."

It took a half an hour to set up, but after that Ian found himself a few hundred yards away from Rich. They were on rooftops twenty-five yards from the base of the wall. His bow drawn; Ian was waiting for Rich's signal to begin.

Sitting between them six of their guns were set up and aimed towards the center of the wall, with a wire running through the triggers. On Rich's signal, they would both let a few arrows loose while retracting the cable back to them.

With any luck, the arrows and guns would create enough noise and bedlam to shift the focus to the front gate.

If it worked, the guards patrolling the sections of the wall in front of them would abandon their posts to investigate the commotion, leaving it open to climb. Once the diversion started they would run down the fire escapes, across the street, and up the wall, using whatever they could to climb the smooth surface. The plan was a long shot, but they were running out of time and had to try something.

"You ready Ian?" Rich asked through their intercom.

"Let's do this. No playing the hero I need you inside."

"Coming from you that's funny, but sure sounds good," Rich chuckled back. "On my count: Three, two, one…"

Bangs filled the air, as arrows flew towards the wall. A few guards fell from the top of the wall, most likely out of shock, than actually being hit. Guns hitting his foot Ian holstered them and his bow as he rushed to the fire escape. Ian glanced in Rich's direction, did not see him, and realized that he was falling behind. He had to get up the wall. Streaking down the fire escape, searchlights illuminated the roofs they had just occupied.

At street level Ian took stock of the wall and

found exactly what he wanted: Guards were rushing to the central gate to investigate the commotion. Running across the now barren street Ian grabbed two arrows hoping they would allow him to scale the wall. Taking an arrow in his hand Ian swung it at the wall and felt arrowhead crack the cement. Unfortunately, the shaft broke in his hand.

Cursing under his breath Ian reached for a knife and his smaller axe, hoping they would not break as he scaled the wall. With similar ease both blades broke into the wall and, leading with the axe, Ian began pulling himself up. His boots finding holes made by the axe and knife.

Glancing down an army of trucks streaked past leaving Ian with two possibilities. Either the distraction worked or something went horribly wrong. More vehicles streaked past and Ian feared the latter. Ian thought that Rich was probably in danger. Redoubling his efforts Ian continued to scale the wall.

Reaching the top Ian jumped over the final lip and onto the walkway. While putting his knife away Ian looked right and found that the coast clear. Looking left; however, there were three guards: Two running at him, while the third raced towards the guard tower.

Without thinking Ian dropped his axe, drew his bow, and, in one swift movement had drawn, released, and placed an arrow through the back of the guard reaching for the phone at the tower.

The other two froze as Ian shot and the second they took to look back at their friend gave Ian the opening he needed to strike. Putting his bow away Ian picked up his axe, threw it, and hit one of the guards square in the back, splitting his spine.

With his partner falling to the ground the final guard turned around to see Ian running at him with his sword drawn. Quickly slashing through the guard's abdomen Ian had created three corpses.

Falling to his knee Ian stabbed the guard one last time to put the man out of his misery. Using his knife, Ian stopped the other man's pain as he removed the axe. It was gruesome, but Ian remembered his training and what Blake told him: never leave a witness.

Reaching the tower Ian pulled his bow and laced one arrow through the final guard. His first shot had not killed the man, but sent him into the wall. Ian's last shot allowed the man to close his eyes forever.

Pulling both arrows from his victim Ian closed his eyes and apologized to the people he had just killed. The first part of the plan was complete and Ian was sad that he had taken three lives.

At ground level Ian quickly crossed the wide street before scaling the first building he met. The lack of enemies worried Ian as he bounded across rooftops trying to get closer to Rich's dot on his display. Taking cover behind a metallic chimney, a quarter mile inside the wall, Ian tried the intercom to find Rich.

"Where are you Rich?"

No answer came.

"Rich where are you?"

Still no answer.

"Rich where-"

"-I'm running to you... I got a little caught up," Rich erupted through the head set gasping for breath.

Thinking fast Ian used his computer to get Rich's exact location. Before Ian finished the command his heads up display showed Rich's dot on a map about a half mile away.

"I would agree that you got a little caught up," Ian replied. Rich's a green dot was darting in and out of alleys a few steps ahead of a sea of red.

"Ha ha, real funny man. I can only dodge for so long and could really use a distraction," Rich yelled back.

Checking his map Ian thought quickly and moved over a few roofs. From his new spot Ian was staring down the only straight road in the Greenwich Village like area. Ian needed this lane to help Rich, but before he could Rich would need to get out of the alleys and into this street.

"Do you see the road, on your visor, to your immediate left."

An explosion burst through the intercom as Rich responded.

"The one on the other side of the buildings? Yeah I see it."

"Get there and I can help you. If you follow the alleys I have marked it should take you about thirty-seconds."

Looking at the road Ian asked the computer what vehicles were most likely following Rich. Streaming across his visor Ian was looking for something, he was not sure what, but he knew he would know it when he saw it.

"Rich, I need to know what vehicles are following you. Is one of them the A-4350, a trike vehicle with the large canon and a single driver?"

"Really Ian?!?! Really?!?! Your question is what is the biggest vehicle following me? I haven't really taken too much time to look back as I have been running for my life." An agitated Rich responded as another explosion filled the head set. "Well, the A-43 whatever is right behind me in the middle of the group."

"That's good. Rich just get to the street," Ian reassured his friend as he prepared for the shot. Details of the A-4350 running across his visor as he did.

Knocking an arrow Ian drew and was ready for his shot. If Rich was right the A-4350 was going to be the key to their escape. It would take a precise shot, but Ian knew he could make it. Once he did Rich would have the cover he needed to escape.

Out of the corner of his eye Ian watched explosions of red and orange fill the air. Glancing at his map Ian knew that he only had one chance and refocused on his task. Another flash illuminated a single side street as Ian watched a black blur round the corner against the orange flames.

"Okay I'm here..." Rich yelled out. Exhausted from his run.

"There is a side street five hundred yards away on your right. That is your escape route."

"Okay... Fine... But, how do I get there?" Rich responded zigging and zagging his way up the street as his pursuers rounded the corner.

Watching their enemies round the corner and Ian saw exactly what he needed to. The A-4350, its single driver, and large cannon were perfect for his plan. Letting his arrow loose, Ian knew his aim was true and waited to watch his plan unfold when Rich spoke up.

"Ian..."

"Rich, just keep running," Ian implored his

friend.

"What about the army coming towards me?"

Distracted by the people following Rich, Ian had not noticed another militia racing towards Rich, past Ian's perch, down the street. Drawing another arrow Ian took aim at another A-4350. The large war machine was much closer this time and, although Ian could not see the driver, he saw the cable holding the cannons' aim true. Prepared to fire a giant explosion shook the ground. Killing his aim and footing.

Behind Rich, a rouge vehicle was creating mass chaos. The driver inside the A-4350 was slumped over in an eternal slumber and his vehicle was out of control barrel rolling through the street as the cannon shot wildly. A sea of fire flooded the street as the war machine was propelled back into its allies and through buildings after the cannon blasted off the asphalt.

The army coming towards Rich immediately stopped pursuing him and instead tried to dodge the devastation caused by the large tank ricocheting around.

The rogue trike took out soldiers, buildings, and had caused its friends to drive into buildings on their own.

"Shit.... What did I do?" Ian let out an audible thought as he tried to calculate the destruction his one arrow had caused.

"Ian get moving!!!"

"What?" Ian absentmindedly replied.

"Get moving now!!!" Rich yelled a little louder this time.

Rich's tone brought Ian back to reality just in time.

On the street below the trike had been brought to a halt and the small army that had been heading to Rich turned their attention to find the source of the chaos. Streaks of red rushed by Ian's face before he backed off the ledge and disappeared towards their rendezvous point.

...

Crouching on a rooftop Ian and Rich were resting, regrouping, and recuperating from the excitement that had just passed. The local time was 28:00 and with only 12 hours of darkness left they both stared at the *Igante Tower* that stood over two miles away.

"Ian we have no idea where she is and we are exhausted. Let's rest up for six hours and then get back to work," Rich offered.

They had hit a wall and Ian knew Rich was right. They needed rest, but burning half their remaining time did not sit well with Ian. Scattered spotlights searched the city's roofs and streets for them and that did not make Ian feel any better about Rich's idea.

"We can nap in shifts, an hour at a time. Every two hours we move hoping that our computer will find her. After six hours we are awake and moving no matter what," Ian offered Rich a compromise he was too tired to fight.

Two moves and five hours later Ian was about wake Rich for his shift when an orange dot started moving towards them very fast. His screen was filled with life for the first time in hours and Ian shook Rich awake.

"Rich do you see this?" Ian asked as the orange dot passed them. Heading to the city's north western wall.

"Yeah..." Rich confirmed Ian's visor. "Where is she though?"

Following the dot, via rooftops, it took Rich and Ian a few minutes before they found the small convoy of cars on the street below. Dropping back, to stay concealed, they followed the convoy for a few more minutes before the dot finally came to rest. A moment later the dot moved, much slower, before becoming sedentary. After ten minutes of rest Ian and Rich bounded towards their mission target.

"What is this?" Rich asked Ian as they approached a walled compound their target resided in.

Rich and Ian were across the street from some type of military research facility. Its walls were much shorter than the one they had scaled to get into the city. A few guard towers ran along its edges and, considering their height, zip lining over to them would be child's play. The hard part would be getting past the guards.

"Computer, can I see a blueprint?" Ian asked hoping it would spark a plan.

In a moment their computer overlaid the compound with the its blueprints. The computer also identified the guards, researchers, and their target. There were around a hundred and fifty people wandering through the compound. A hundred and fifty people separating them from going home.

"It looks like our target is in the middle-ish..." Rich lamented, locating the orange dot at the heart of the complex. "At least the complex is only one floor."

Spotting the dot Ian looked past the room and saw a giant library housing, what appeared to be, a safe.

"Do you see the safe?" Ian asked Rich with a plan brewing to break their mission wide open.

"What?" Rich scoffed.

"In the next room, according to the blueprints, there is a library with a safe. I have a feeling we need to get in there too," Ian answered while thinking about what treasures the safe held.

"Are you nuts!!! Ian we have to finish our mission and get out of here. We have a little under six hours to get her and find a jump point. We cannot add anything else to this mission. We have to finish it and leave."

Ian knew where Rich was coming from, but he could not deny his gut feeling. If Ian had learned anything these past few months it was to trust your instincts.

"Rich knowledge is the ultimate key to our victory and we have a chance to gain some right now. This is the type of thing Jerry told us to keep our eyes out for. This is our chance and we cannot pass it up," Ian tried to defend his gut feeling.

"Ian the vault could be filled with gold, gems, or birth certificates. You have no idea whats inside."

"I know, but it could be something great."

"Or not."

"But, don't we have to try? Don't we owe it to Jerry and the resistance to try?"

The truth of Ian's statement echoed in Rich's helmet where after a long moment he nodded.

"If we have time. But Virgin E first. Ian, more importantly, how are we getting in?"

"That's easy. Through the front door."

It took a minute for Ian to explain his plan, but

it was pretty simple. Zip line to the closest tower, incapacitate the guards, run to the front door, incapacitate those guards, and enter the compound. All while the patrols were far away.

Rich knew that while the plan was simple and a little too optimistic, it was also sound. The patrols were predictable and if they could take out the tower guards the run between the wall and the doors was so short they could be inside before anyone knew what was hitting them. Taking an extra second to think Rich nodded and agreed verbally: "Okay Ian, let's do it."

Ten minutes later, when the patrols were approaching the apex of their routes, Ian loosed an arrow deep into the guard towers' roof. Securing the rope to their roof Rich checked it once before zipping across the night sky.

All the guards heard was a little hum before they met their fatal end. The guards looked up just in time to see Rich's mace contact their skulls as he entered the tower. They never knew what hit them as Ian rolled into the tower behind Rich.

As soon as they hit the tower's platform Ian and Rich were running down the stair case to the ground below. With muffled steps it only took a few moments before they were at ground level darting towards the front door. They had timed their attack perfectly and could not be seen in the pitch black. By the time any of the patrols got back to the guard tower Ian and Rich would be long gone, hopefully, jumping back to the safety of Esmerelda.

Retrieving his bow Ian knocked an arrow and took aim at one of the two guards forty yards away. They were next to the doors they needed to go through. Taking an extra second to take aim Ian was ready to loose his arrow when a siren broke his concentration. Ian's arrow flew wide. They had been discovered.

"Shit," Ian swore under his breath as he knocked another arrow. Rich swirling his mace next to him as he prepared to throw it at his guard.

Despite the siren and searchlights Ian and Rich had not been spotted. They were fairly certain that someone found a fallen comrade and raised the alarm. With confidence Ian and Rich raced to the door and their goal.

With less than ten yards left to the door Ian and Rich watched two more guards come through the door they were approaching. The guards who had stepped out watched their friends fold life-lessly to the ground. An arrow embedded in one's chest, a mace in the other. Shouldering his bow Ian pulled a battle axe as Rich drew a knife. They bolted towards the doors and the two remaining guards.

Reaching the compounds steps Ian and Rich each had to dodge a red projectile fired from the two remaining guards. Considering their training and the guards fear this was not difficult. It only took a few long strides to dodge and ascend the steps separating them from the door.

Ian's axe sliced through one guard with little resistance. Tearing the guard from hip to shoulder. Next to him, Rich tackled and stabbed his mark. After retrieving his mace Rich smashed the suffering guard's chest putting an end to his agony.

"Let's get inside..." Ian said to Rich as spotlights found them and more guards rushed to the doors.

Entering the compound Rich smashed the keypad lock. Trapping them inside and their aggressors out. After smashing the lock Rich wished he had waited a moment because his choice cost him the seconds he needed to dodge oncoming weapon fire.

"Ahh.... FU....." Rich exclaimed as his torso was sliced open with what appeared to be a red feather.

"What is it Rich?" Ian asked from a crouched position. Loosing an arrow into the guard that had hurt his friend.

"Their weapons can cut through the armor," Rich responded instinctively placing his hand on the bleeding wound as his under suit attempted to mend it. "Ian, I will be fine; the suit is taking care of me. There is nothing we can do about it now. Our mark is close. Let's move and get home," Rich finished through labored breaths.

Rising to their feet the two of them set off again. Rich clutched his side while using his free hand, and mace, to smash anyone who got in the way of their final goal.

Outside of the guard that hit Rich they did not meet much resistance inside. Making one final left Rich broke into a room about halfway down the hall. It was the room that held their target. Hoping to buy them some time Ian, took a page out Rich's book, shot the lock with an arrow.

"Rich is she in here?" Ian asked. Listening to the sounds of their enemy with his ear pressed against the door as he caught his breath.

Rich was silent.

"Rich you okay?" Ian asked again.

Turning around Rich was standing in front of their target, obscuring her from view. Rich no longer held his wound that slowly dripped blood onto the floor and his mace fell limp next to his side. Ian's partner was nothing more than a statue in the middle of the room.

"Rich what is the hold up?" Ian asked as the door began to shake. "Rich you have to complete the mission?" Ian reminded him as he scanned the room for another exit.

"Ian I can't... it's.. Our... mar..." Rich started to answer before stepping aside to the side to show Ian. "Evankila." Rich finished his horrifying statement as an arrow whizzed by him and Evankila slumped over, dead, in the chair.

CHAPTER TWENTY-ONE
Safe Cracking

Time stood still as Ian looked over Evankila, Evan's love. Ian found the necklace he had hoped not to find. It was exactly the same as Evan's, its stone still shining, Ian turned it over to see the initials E.S. on the back.

"Shit…" Ian whispered under his breath, taking stock of what had just happened. Finally understanding why Blake had kept Evan in the dark.

"We killed her… we killed…" Rich mumbled. Unable to understand what they had just done.

Ian was also terrified, but his mind and body were moving on, racing away from what had just happened, and back to the mission. They completed their objective; it was time to leave.

"Rich…"

"We… Killed her….."

"Rich, Come on." Ian tried to break Rich out of the his trance. "Rich come…"

"We killed her. We killed the love of the one I love."

Ian wanted to move, but stopped.

What? Ian thought to himself. *Rich loves Evan?*

It all made sense: why Rich couldn't kill Evankila and what he had meant months ago. There was nothing between Rich and Marissa. Evan was the person Rich loved.

The door shook violently behind them but Ian did not care. It was doing a marvelous job at holding the intruders at bay. Ian could not believe the reality rushing towards him.

What did I just do…Rich loved…. How could I? Oh God… Evan knows, the necklace…

Ian's mind raced away from the mission and back to Evan, whose necklace most certainly had just gone dark. Ian wondered if Evan had put the pieces together and if he was raising hell on Esmerelda. So lost in his own thoughts Ian was only brought back to reality when Rich slumped to the floor.

"Rich … Rich… You okay? Rich," Ian asked dropping into the pool of blood next to his friend. "Rich move your arm I need to see your wound."

In a daze Rich revealed a wound much deeper

than either of them had thought. Reaching around his back Ian located one of his first aid kits and began to bandage his friend.

"You okay man?" Ian tried to keep Rich conscious as he gave him a pill from the pouch. The door still shaking behind them.

"Rich. Come on man. Stay with me." Ian said as he waited for the pill to numb the pain. His patch work compress helping Rich's under suit stop the bleeding.

"I'm not leaving you," Ian said to his friend, still fighting his body that wanted to leave this room before the enemy broke in.

"I don't care..." Ian said to himself. "Screw the training, I'm not letting Rich go."

"Yeah. I'm good," Rich said with a slight moan. Breaking Ian out of his internal struggle.

Ian smiled and knew Rich was far from fine. He also understood that everything would be fine if they could just get home.

"Computer show me where the air vents go," Ian asked letting his training and instincts take over as the sound of door hinges failing greeted his ears.

A blueprint of the building's ventilation system, appeared on his screen. The vent above them led to a junk room with a sewer entrance.

"Is there a jump point inside the city?" Ian asked.

"The city has been shut down from The Dimension."

"So there is no jump point inside the wall?"

"Affirmative."

"Outside the wall is still open?" Ian asked hoping that The Evil had not shut down the whole planet.

"Affirmative. Outside the wall the city is still open to The Dimension."

"Computer does the sewer lead to the city wall?"

"Yes. There is a grate separating the inner and outer city. Estimated time to cut through grate with current weapons is two hours."

Ian scowled under his breath. He knew they did not have two hours, but it was their best option. They had to move or they were dead.

Taking Rich's mace Ian broke the grate above their heads right before kicking over the chair holding Evankila. Ian stood Rich up on its solid steel legs and started to boost him into the grate.

"Rich, come on. Up," Ian encouraged his friend as he boosted him into the vent.

"Rich crawl down the vent. In about thirty feet, you will reach another vent. Kick it in and you will be in a junk room. Get into the sewer and run west to the city's edge."

Rich managed to groan "Okay," as he crawled away.

Watching Rich crawl away Ian knew they needed extra time to escape.

"Computer please show Rich the path to the grate," Ian asked as he retrieved Rich's mace and charged the door hoping to wedge it in place.

Striking the door Ian's plan only half worked. Instead of jamming the door, the mace threw it off its hinges and into the hall. The force knocked over a few troops and sent the rest jumping for cover. Wasting no time Ian ran towards the chair, clipping Rich's mace to his belt, while simultaneously pulling Evankila's necklace off. In a single movement Ian jumped into the vent and out of sight. Red beams criss-crossing the place he had stood moments before.

Doing everything he could to buy Rich more time Ian used his axe to crumple the vent in the direction his friend had escaped. With one way blocked Ian followed the vent to the adjacent room, the library, hoping to find another exit.

Kicking out the vent Ian jumped onto the library's wooden floors. Scanning the room Ian drew his bow and fired at the door's lock knowing he needed more time.

So, I need a better way to cut through the grate and I need to find a new exit. Ian thought to himself before a noise behind him alerted him to his enemy planning their next move. *And I need to do it fast.*

Rows of bookshelves lined the room. A painting was the only other feature in the room and Ian guessed that was where the safe would be. The books would not be of much use and their only chance was that the safe held something that could help them escape.

Around him Ian heard his defenses starting to give way as the vent rumbled with life. The library doors were starting to buckle to an impact just beyond them.

Reaching the opposite wall Ian was greeted by an ancient painting. Created to personify the golden age of a once prosperous and peaceful world Ian unceremoniously slashed it in two with an arrow. Exposing a steel door with no markings or handles.

"Really?" Ian said to himself as the noises around him grew louder.

Exploring the safe Ian looked for anything: a scanner, a dial, a keypad, anything that would let him break in. His search was in vain. Hand falling beside him Ian found the grip of Rich's mace when a thought hit him.

"It's worth a shot," Ian shrugged as he unclipped the mace and took a swing.

The fist strike did nothing but make a resounding clang. Ian reached back and struck again and again. On the fifth strike the clang was more of a creak as the safe started to give a little.

The slight dent exposed the safe's hinges at the top of the safe. Beating the, now exposed, hinges they quickly gave way as the safe door fell to the floor with a thud.

Inside the safe Ian found no weapons and instead grabbed an old leather bound book. It's cover carrying a symbol Ian had never seen. Emptying one of his suits compartments of food rations and supplies Ian placed the book inside his suit. Ignoring valuable jewels Ian grabbed any other document he saw, storing them alongside the book inside his suit.

"This is good," Ian said to himself as he grabbed and stored the last piece of paper. A little relieved Ian was ready to search for an exit when red darts streaked past him.

Ian turned to see enemy forces flooding through the vent he had entered from. Drawing his bow Ian shot an arrow through the head of the first soldier poking out of the vent. The soldier's body fell to the floor as Ian laced another few arrows towards the vent.

The arrows were true and gave Ian enough time to hurl Rich's mace at the vent. With a deafening thud Ian watched the vent crumple in on itself. A few soldier's bodies trapped inside.

One down. Ian thought to himself as the library's doors broke open.

Ian turned towards the door and laced two arrows at incoming attackers. The arrows were true, but the enemy soldiers kept flooding in. Shouldering his bow Ian knew there were too many to take them out one by one. It was time to make his exit.

Weaving in and out of bookcases shots flew all around Ian as he made his way back towards the vent he entered through. The red bolts cut through wooden shelves like a hot knife through softened butter.

Ian picked up Rich's mace as a feather fluttered right past him. Instinctively Ian grabbed one of the fallen guards gun and fired it at the man behind him. His shot went wide, but following its path, Ian watched it cut straight through the metal safe on the opposite wall. A little-astounded Ian clipped the gun to his belt with a plan forming in his head.

"Computer how long will it take me to reach the city wall once I find an exit?"

Red bolts fluttered around him as fifteen soldiers raced towards him. Their shots coming at him with varying degrees of accuracy.

"About a minute-thirty seconds once you are in the vent," the computer whirred back.

"What vent?" Ian asked running between shelves trying to escape his attackers.

"The vent on the West side of the room," the computer responded marking the exit on his map.

"Why didn't you mention this before?" Ian rhetorically asked.

"Question does not compute."

Turning another corner Ian drew his sword ready to knock away the red beams only to find it was not the best solution. His beautiful blade could knock them away, but was also becoming nicked and chipped as he did. Wandering through the shelves Ian finally located the vent and knew he needed a distraction for his plan to work.

"Rich where are you?" Ian yelled into his helmet hoping the com still worked.

"I'm in the sewer about twenty feet from our jump point," He responded through the static. "We need something to cut this grate. Our weapons will take too long," Rich continued as Ian batted away another shot. The tip of his sword getting knocked off in the process.

"I'm on it Rich. Make sure the portal is ready to jump in three minutes."

"Three minutes? That does not give us much time," Rich started to question his friend.

"Three minutes and we'll be heading home."

"Okay. Ian... Three minutes."

Ian knew that Rich would be ready he just had to get some things done before they could escape.

The chase around the library was quickly exposing the guards' conditioning. Out of the fifteen, only one was keeping up. Three had been downed by friendly fire and the rest were either lagging behind or bent over catching their breath. With only one guard following him Ian took a risk, turned, and put a shoulder into a bookshelf he had just passed.

The heavy wooden shelf teetered for a moment and then fell. Like dominos, bookshelves fell as they were struck by their peers. The chaos of crashing shelves echoed through the air and the guards panicked. Not wanting to become trapped they gave up on chasing Ian retreated for safety. The guard closest to Ian tried to call some order before being crushed by a falling shelf.

After the dust settled Ian found himself ten feet away from four guards who stood fifteen feet in the opposite direction of his exit

Ian smiled as he ran towards his enemies. They were unprepared for any of this and Ian knew he had him where he wanted them.

With his sword drawn Ian easily batted away their erratic shots. Ian reached them and slashed through two guards with one swipe. His arching slash cleaving off one of his assailant's arms, the other's leg.

Paralyzed in shock the other guards were dispatched in no time as Ian delivered a final blow to each of them. Sheathing his sword, Ian grabbed a few more of their firearms and ran to his exit grate.

...

"Ian you're here," Rich questioned the footsteps splashing behind him.

"Yeah, I'm here."

"About time."

Racing down the sewer Ian saw an open portal behind one last obstacle blocking their way home.

"How long do we have?" Ian asked Rich.

"About fifteen seconds. You were a little late," Rich hissed worried that they had missed their chance.

"Aim at the edges and fire, " Ian said passing Rich two of the local guns.

Rich did not need to be told twice and together the two of them shot at the grate, the feather like bolts cutting through it without resistance.

"Ian we gotta go..." Rich yelled out in a panicked tone as grate whined on its supports.

Glancing back Ian saw what Rich had: a group

of enemies racing towards them as his computer chirped at him.

"Portal closing in five, four,"

Supporting Rich Ian ran towards the portal. Ian threw their weight at the weakened grate, it gave way, and Rich and Ian disappeared into the fading portal.

CHAPTER TWENTY-TWO
Betrayed

"Where did Ian learn how to shoot archery?" Blake hissed at Ian with a blade pressed against his throat.

Disoriented from the jump, Ian blurted out "Medicine bow…" and the pressure was relieved.

Regaining his bearings Ian opened his eyes to see Blake moving towards Rich. The three of them were inside one of the jumping vaults. Rich and Ian had made it home. They were safe.

"Blake. It is Rich, he's hurt, and I can vouch for him," Ian muttered out trying to think of anything to give Blake the information he needed.

Ian's explanation apparently was enough. Blake put his knife away and offered Ian a hand up, which, Ian gladly took, before speaking again.

"Blake, Rich needs help."

Without waiting for another word, Blake scooped up Rich and took off.

We're safe, Ian thought to himself. After a long day Ian was ready to relax and spread the news about their mission.

Stepping out of the vault Ian froze in shock at the carnage that greeted him.

The once magnificent marble hallway was little more than a battle field. The walls were in pieces, dented and chipped, as large chunks of rubble mixed with bodies on the blood stained floor.

What happened? Ian thought as he surveyed the scene.

Teachers, workers, soldiers, and medics were running in all directions. Some removing bodies, others tending to wounded until the medics could reach them. The smell of blood, flesh, and smoke filled the air. Such concentrated carnage made Ian wonder if this was possibly worse than what he had just left.

Standing like a black statue in a sea of red Sara easily spotted Ian.

"Was it a success?" Sara asked as she tapped him on the shoulder.

Ian nodded mindlessly still trying to understand the scene in front of him. Ian fiddled with the book he had taken out of his armor at some point.

"Looks like you have extras," Sara mentioned spotting the book and documents in his hand. "Follow me Ian. There is nothing more you can do here. Come on follow me."

In a daze Ian followed Sara. As they walked further away from the vaults, the carnage diminished, but Ian's thoughts about what happened didn't. Finally, Sara brought Ian into an office he had never entered.

"A lot happened while you were gone. Take a seat. It will only take me a minute to find Evan. Then we will catch up."

Ian wandered around the blank office alone with his thoughts. A computer sat on a marble desk. A few chairs and a couch were the only other things that populated the large office.

Coming out of his daze Ian placed his new bounty of documents on the desk before sitting down on the couch.

"Computer, if you can, analyze the blood on my sword and show me who it belonged to."

His adrenaline gone, Ian was finally coming down from the high the battle had caused. His morals and fears came back to him as he asked his computer the question that had bothered him all day.

After a few silent moments pictures filled his visor with people from, what looked like, a once vibrant and happy Telvena. Glancing through the pictures Ian could tell that they were a few years old. The people he killed had not looked like this, but they were these people.

Ian felt his stomach drop. He knew his request was a long shot, but these pictures made him realize that in his sea of bodies he had not killed a single evil soldier.

From what he saw it looked like neither he nor The Resistance had killed a single soldier from World One. They only got their pawns.

Am I worse than The Evil? Were the people I killed working for The Evil? Had they been changed, or were they simply defending themselves? Could we have completed our mission peacefully? Did we really have to take all those lives? We never even gave the people a chance to help us....

Taking off his helmet Ian needed to see the world for himself. Not through his visor and some computer program.

Ian's armor was splattered in blood. His boots were leaving a red trail wherever he went. Seeing the carnage with his own eyes made Ian feel sick.

"What have I done…"

Ian's weapons were designed to tear through the most evil things in The Dimension; something his victims certainly were not. The people Ian slayed had not stood a chance. He tore through them without hesitation or a second thought.

His weapons only worked with a wielder and it was his responsibility to distinguish the enemy from the civilians. Ian could not understand or justify what he had done.

"What have I become…"

"Ian you had to kill them," Blake answered Ian's question. He had just entered the office. Sara and Evan were right behind him. "They are not the same people they used to be. They are a part of The Evil now and would have killed you without a second thought."

Blake's words were hollow. No matter what he said neither one of them would ever know the true thoughts or intentions of the people Ian killed. All Ian knew was what Evan had told him about his home world. With that as his evidence Ian knew the people were not killers.

Looking right at Blake Ian could not help but think about the child he and Rich had almost killed. They had almost killed a kid looking for a ball. Ian wondered if everyone on Telvena was innocent like her.

"Ian, I need to know, did the people look normal or were they different?" Sara said as she seated herself behind the desk.

"They looked like a patchwork quilt made out of used leather. It had replaced their skin," Ian answered emotionlessly.

"It is exactly what we feared," Sara nodded to

Blake "They are opening worlds up to The Dimension and the people... The people are changing. This confirms it. It explains why so few World One soldiers attacked us today. Blake you realize if this the case on every planet their army-"

"-Could out number us 10,000 to one." Blake finished her statement.

To Ian's left and tearing up Evan had just taken a seat on the couch. Blake stood by the door as he considered what this could mean for The Resistance. Evan cried for the fate of his world.

"But if the world were opened to The Dimension wouldn't the people die?" Ian asked not wanting to think about what those numbers would mean to the war.

"I'm sure some did. The Dimension has a different atmosphere than most worlds but as time progressed people's bodies adjust to survive. It would not surprise me if these people could survive in The Dimension for a short time. At least long enough to get to a new world for an attack," Sara speculated.

"They were not specially trained or armored," Ian rebutted. "Why would The Evil ever fight with them? Why would they send them into battle? They would do them no good. They did not fight well. They were scared. They were simply scared people caught in the middle of a war."

Ian fought himself as much as Sara with his response. Troubled that The Evil could send thousands to die, while also trying to remind everyone that they he had just killed people, not some faceless enemy.

"Ian, those people are no longer people."

"They are," Ian replied defiantly. "They might have fought against me, they might have looked different, but they are still people. People that at one point we cared about."

"Of course they are," Sara apologized slightly. "But Ian, they are also pawns for The Evil. Ian you have to understand that with the numbers The Evil controls they can sacrifice an entire population to kill a few hundred of us. That is a win. They are not afraid of loss."

"Isn't it our job to free them then? Just because they are with them does not mean it was by choice. Don't we owe these people a chance to escape?"

"Ian we don't," Sara answered bluntly. "As much as it sucks once The Evil has opened a world to The Dimension there is little we can do. The Evil will take control of everything: food, water, medical supplies, the economy, everything. They cultivate the people for their needs. Ian, I cannot understate how much you need to understand that The Evil will sacrifice a thousand people to kill one or two of us."

Tension in the room was thick. Blake stood silent, but agreed with Sara. Evan fought to hold it together. Ian was not sure what to think.

Looking at his friend Ian was surprised. Evan was doing a remarkable job of keeping everything together. From time to time, a tear would run down his cheek, but he would not let his grief out.

"Sara you weren't there. How can you give up on them?"

"Ian, we haven't given up on them. But we have a mission that needs to be completed. We care about every world, every life, but people die during war. Peaceful negotiations would be great, but is not an option. Ian you are a soldier now. You have to understand this or you will die."

Sara was not mincing words. For the first time Ian was not being coddled at all and understood that he was no longer a student. Looking at Sara Ian did not want to think she was right, but deep down he worried she was.

"It's tough Ian but do you think they wanted to talk to you when they shot Rich? Do you have any idea what hit him?"

Reaching down Ian unclipped one of the guns from his belt and placed it on the desk. Sara picked it up and examined it before passing the gun to Evan.

"It is a feather shooter. The bolts are a synthetic compound that look like feathers, dyed red, razor sharp, aerodynamic, and designed to cut through many things," Evan explained in a dead voice. Still battling the grief he felt for his world.

"Is there anything it cannot cut through?" Sara asked him. Trying to understand what they were up against.

"There are a few alloys on my planet that we can re-create to reinforce the armor but the best way to avoid damage is to take them head on or dodge them entirely. The sides of the feathers are sharp. When they hit with the tip, they wilt and fall."

As if to prove his point Evan held the gun in front of his own armor and pulled the trigger. A red feather shot out, hit Evan square, and wilted harmlessly into his lap.

"See."

Understanding Evan's pain Sara passed on any other questions. She did send Blake to the medical ward with this new information as the room went quiet. Heavy with regret and uncertainty.

"Did she suffer?" Evan asked Ian after a few minutes of silence. Evan was staring down at his necklace clutched in his hand. The gem no longer glowed.

Pulling out the necklace's other half, Ian handed it to Evan and softly said, "I'm sorry."

Breaking into tears Evan grabbed the other half and placed it with his own. Evan knew it would fit even though he did not want it to. Breaking down Evan threw the necklace onto the desk and punched the marble wall behind him. Breaking a knuckle in the process.

"I am so sorry about this Evan. I am so sorry you had to do it Ian, but it was necessary," Sara commented as she inspected the necklace.

The two pieces together created a stunningly beautiful piece. Even with one of the stones dormant and black the necklaces were delicate and intricate. Soft silver interwove itself in an ethereal pattern of harmony and chaos to create a magnificent piece. Looking it over once more Sara seemed content that it provided evidence of Rich and Ian's success.

Silence fell again as a million questions swirled in Ian's head:

Why did they have to kill her? Did Jerry know who Evankila was? Whose double was she?

Ian wanted answers but knew that Evan could not handle that right now. If Evan was not ready to ask these questions neither would he.

"What happened here?" Ian asked instead.

"Ian we were betrayed," Sara stated emotionlessly after taking a deep breath.

"By who?"

Sara was silently fighting her answer. Ian could tell they knew who betrayed them. He could tell they knew, but that Sara still did not want to believe it.

"Who?" Ian asked again, wanting to know who had caused so much destruction.

"Laura," Evan answered for Sara. "Laura betrayed us to The Evil…"

Shock overwhelmed Ian as he tried to understand Evan's words. Laura, the person who always told him the truth, the person who had always looked after him, for his best interests, she had betrayed him. She betrayed them all.

Unable to say a word Ian sat as Evan and Sara filled him in on the events that had transpired since his departure.

According to Sara and Evan after Ian and Rich jumped Laura offered to switch roles with Sara. Thinking nothing of it Sara left with Marissa and Evan to investigate the tracks. Laura went to watch and protect Mikey and Michelle.

After locating the river Marissa, Evan, and Sara searched for an hour before finding John.

John was in a shallow ditch. His tent gone and his sleeping bag nothing more than scraps. John was in bad shape, barely breathing, and on the verge of death, but he was still alive. Marissa and Sara began to stabilize John while Evan tried to call for help. The only problem was communications were dead.

Picking John up they moved him back to camp as quickly as possible. Once they reached the field, they located a few other students who helped them get John to the cabin.

Evan, Marissa, and Sara decided to leave John in his bed not wanting to risk anything. Not knowing what to expect they disappeared to the basement to investigate.

Downstairs all hell had broken loose by the time they reached the basement's forbidden hallway. The sound of death and battle greeted their ears as Evan, Marissa, and Sara joined their combatants to battle back The Evil's forces.

After the battle they were informed that an hour earlier Laura locked herself, Mikey, and Michelle inside a jump vault. With the help of a few sabotaged systems Laura had coordinated and executed Mikey and Michelle's first jump, to World One, before The Resistance could open the vault.

When they finally opened the vault Mikey and Michelle were gone, Laura was dead, and a portal was wide open. Mikey and Michelle's doubles had come through that portal ready to fight with the soldiers that had accompanied them.

Despite efforts to contain the chaos The Evil burst through that vault and managed to open portals in four other vaults before The Resistance regained control of the vaults and portals. The Evil's attack overwhelmed them at first, but was never intended to be sustained.

They managed to close the vaults and portals. They gassed the rooms, killing everyone inside. The Evil outside the vault did their best to take as many people with them before they were eliminated.

"Where is Marissa?" Ian asked finally realizing he had not seen her yet.

According to their tale Sara, Evan, and Marissa had arrived about halfway through the battle, right before they regained control of the portals and vaults.

"Ian, you have to stay calm," Sara started.

"Where is she?" Ian asked again slightly agitated with Sara's response.

"Ian, it's okay. We did not mention what happened to her because we had to catch you up on everything," Evan answered Ian. Trying to settle down his panicked friend.

"What happened to her!" Ian demanded now flush with anger.

"Ian, Marissa was injured during the-"

And before Sara could finish Ian bolted out of the office. Ian had no idea where to go and was blindly darting down different hallways until finally finding a gurney that Ian followed to the infirmary.

Ian was in a large room dotted with beds. He quickly scanned the room and spotted Marissa's weapons and armor at the foot of a bed surrounded by doctors.

"Oww... please watch the arm sweetie I think it may be broken." Ian heard Marissa's beautiful voice tell him after he rushed through to the doctors surrounding Marissa.

Pulling away Ian looked over Marissa and outside of a stitch above her left eye she was as beautiful as ever. Her blonde hair falling around her shoulders with her beautiful chestnut eyes and mischievous smile staring back at him. Kissing Marissa Ian apologized to the, now-chuckling, doctors before letting them set Marissa's broken arm.

Feeling silly Ian backed away from Marissa's bed and spotted a ghost waving to him. Walking to John Ian gave his once-imposing friend a big hug as he greeted him.

"You look good," Ian lied to him as he pulled up a seat near his bed.

"I'm sure," John laughed back at him. "I want to help, but, they won't let me up."

John strained against the jumble of needles and tubes poking into him. Barely able to sit up three inches John fell back into the bed with a laugh.

"Lay down man. There is nothing you can do like this. I need you better so you can join me next time."

For the first time that day Ian smiled as he began to catch up with John. Months of harsh winter weather had taken their toll on John who was a shell of himself. Weak, thin, boney. Simply surviving was a testament to John's health and conditioning. Despite his appearance and everything that had happened John was in good spirits. For Ian it was just nice to have him back.

...

In civilian clothes Ian, Evan, Marissa, Sara, John, and Blake all waited outside the operating room for information about two of their friends. Ian held Marissa on a bench near the operating room doors, while John wheeled around in a wheelchair. Evan and Sara sat across from them while Blake stood next to them.

"You think he will be okay?" Evan asked the small group for what seemed like the hundredth time.

"Which one?" John answered while trying to readjust one of the many tubes running out of his arms.

"I'm sure they both will be fine," Sara chimed in again. Her voice becoming slightly less confident as more time passed.

An hour passed, and then another, and then a

few more. It was not until half the group had fallen asleep when a surgeon exited the operating room with a sullen look on his face.

"I'm sorry but they both have passed. Lance had too much brain damage and Rich had lost too much blood to successfully make the jump. In reality, they were both gone before they hit our table. Lance never had a chance and even with a perfect portal Rich was too weak to make a jump."

The surgeon was quick and to the point without being cold. He had continued his explanation after seeing a look of guilt creep into Ian's eyes and before anyone could ask a question. With the news delivered Blake left the group and disappeared from the infirmary.

The rest of the group sat in silence as they absorbed the loss. Without Lance and Jerry the group did not know how The Resistance would move on.

Before they could deal with the war they had to deal with Rich's death. Rich was a little hot-headed, but had a gentle heart. He would have taken a bullet for any of them and now that he was gone Ian felt like he had misjudged Rich and had let him down.

I should have been first through that door. I should have made it to the portal sooner. I should have helped with the wound sooner. I let Rich die.

Ian did not say any of these thoughts and instead cried with his small group on the benches. And after bringing John back to the infirmary they made their way up the secret staircase to their cabin.

Their beds were unmade, John's armor was in its case, and the room was exactly how they left it. It was exactly the same, except for the fact that everything was different now. Three of the seven beds would remain empty and that was a heavy price to pay. Too heavy of a price. Looking at his bed now Ian wished he had slept in just a little longer.

Sara had accompanied the group to the cabin and without hesitation they accepted her into their family as a new sister. Taking Michelle's bed Sara and Marissa quickly drifted off to sleep. Their bodies forcing them to heal their mental and physical wounds.

Instead of climbing into bed Ian and Evan retreated to the living room. They needed to reflect on everything that had happened.

"I'm sorry," Ian said as he watched the fire flicker in front of them. Disturbed by how much grief he caused Evan.

"Don't be. You did what you had to do and Evankila is out of that nightmare. No matter what you did she was already dead. She never would have been able to make that first jump. You ended her suffering and I am grateful for that" Evan responded with tears in his eyes. In his grief, sincerity rang through every word he said.

"I know. But. But, Evan... I'm sorry that I could not save the two people who loved you most in the world today."

Evan did not understand what Ian was saying. He had taken his love, but his parents had died years ago.

"I'm not sure I understand," Evan commented trying to find more.

"Evan your heart was the taken one," Ian revealed Rich's secret. His eyes locked onto the dying flames as he struggled to understand where they went from here.

ACKNOWLEDGE-MENT

I would like to thank my readers. Without you, these are just words that I put together. So if you have made it this far I hope you enjoyed the book and I cannot thank you enough for reading Jumped.

Second, I would like to thank my wife and mother, both of whom have put up with me more than any reasonable person should allow. They have been saints about all of this and I really thank them for putting up with me all of these years as I worked up to pressing publish and sending this out there.

I would like to thank the editors who helped me put this book together. Who read and re-read it with me to get it just right. Thank you... Thank you for all of your help.

Next I would like to thank my father, Papa Bill, Meme, and all the people who supported my dream to write and publish, but who are no longer with us to see this book take its final shape. I thank you for your support and encouragement. And am sorry I did not get it done just a little faster.

Of course I would like to thank my brother, who always pushes me farther than I thought I could go. I would also like to thank my best friend Tyler, who I discussed this book with, while it was in its infancy, in an airport in Dubai. The person who I first told about this story, about my walks to think up dialogue, and everything else. Tyler and Torin, you two are the best and make me want to be better.

Finally, I want to thank anyone I have forgotten. My beta readers, and again anyone who picks up this book. It is for you that this is written. Hopefully it gave you a place to escape and brought a little joy to your day.

Thank you for your time.

D.C. Reed

find more @

dcreed.org
@dc_reed on instagram
@realdcreed on twitter

ABOUT THE AUTHOR

D.c. Reed

As a philosophy (ethics) and music graduate of the University of North Florida D.C. Reed is an aspiring writer and teacher who has written for sports outlets, Religion Nerd and presented papers at university conferences in the south east. Currently liv- 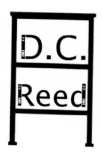 ing with his wife and two dogs in Atlanta Ga. D.C. strives to write stories that present complex ideals through engaging narratives. He believes that Philosophy is one of the most useful and avoided subjects. Limited to those in higher education D.C. Reed strives to bring these issues to life through stories, essays, and other writings so everyone can engage them.

find more @
dcreed.org

Thank you for reading Jumped I hope you enjoyed book one of The Dimension series and eagerly await the release of book two. Please leave a kind review if you enjoyed the book and share with someone else you think will enjoy the story.

You can find more at:

dcreed.org

@dc_reed on instagram
@realdcreed on twitter

Made in United States
North Haven, CT
05 December 2021